NEW YEAR'S EVE
MURDER

Books by Leslie Meier

MISTLETOE MURDER

TIPPY TOE MURDER

TRICK OR TREAT MURDER

BACK TO SCHOOL MURDER

VALENTINE MURDER

CHRISTMAS COOKIE MURDER

TURKEY DAY MURDER

WEDDING DAY MURDER

BIRTHDAY PARTY MURDER

FATHER'S DAY MURDER

STAR SPANGLED MURDER

NEW YEAR'S EVE MURDER

Published by Kensington Publishing Corp.

M

A Lucy Stone Mystery

NEW YEAR'S EVE
MURDER

Leslie Meier

KENSINGTON BOOKS
http://www.kensingtonbooks.com

KENSINGTON BOOKS are published by

Kensington Publishing Corp.
850 Third Avenue
New York, NY 10022

All Kensington titles, imprints, and distributed lines are available at special quantity discounts for bulk purchases for sales promotion, premiums, fund-raising, and educational, or institutional use.

Special book excerpts or customized printings can also be created to fit specific needs. For details, write or phone the office of the Kensington Special Sales Manager: Attn: Special Sales Department. Kensington Publishing Corp., 850 Third Avenue, New York, NY 10022. Phone: 1-800-221-2647.

Kensington and the K logo Reg. U.S. Pat. & TM Off.

Library of Congress Card Catalogue Number: 2004113890
ISBN 0-7582-0699-2

First Printing: November 2005
10 9 8 7 6 5 4 3 2 1

Printed in the United States of America

NOV 0 9 2005

NEW YEAR'S EVE
MURDER

Chapter One

WIN A WINTER MAKEOVER FOR YOU AND YOUR MOM!

A solid month of baking and chasing bargains and wrapping and decorating and secret keeping and it all came down to this: a pile of torn wrapping paper under the Christmas tree, holiday plates scattered with crumbs and half-eaten cookies, punch cups filmed with egg nog, and sitting on one end table, a candy dish holding a pristine and untouched pyramid of ribbon candy. And then there was that awful letter. Why did it have to come on Christmas Eve, just in time to cast a pall over the holiday?

Lucy Stone shook out a plastic trash bag and bent down to scoop up the torn paper, only to discover the family's pet puppy, Libby, had made herself a nest of Christmas wrap and was curled up, sound asleep. No wonder. With all the excitement of opening presents, tantalizing cooking smells, and people coming and going, it had been an exhausting day for her.

Lucy stroked the little Lab's silky head and decided to leave the mess a bit longer. Best to let sleeping dogs lie, especially if the sleeping dog in question happened to be seven months old and increasingly given to bouts of manic activity, which included chewing shoes and furniture. She turned instead to the coffee table and started stacking plates and cups, then sat down on the sofa as a wave of exhaustion overtook her. It had been a long day. Zoe, her youngest at only eight years old, had awoken early and roused the rest of the house. Sara, fourteen, hadn't minded, but their older sister, Elizabeth, protested the early hour. She was home for Christmas break from Chamberlain College in Boston, where she was a sophomore, and had stayed out late on Christmas Eve catching up with her old high school friends.

She had finally given in and gotten out of bed after a half-hour of coaxing, and the Christmas morning orgy of exchanging presents had begun. What had they been thinking, wondered Lucy, dreading the credit card bills that would arrive as certainly as snow in January. She and Bill had really gone overboard this year, buying skis for Elizabeth and high-tech ice skates for Sara and Zoe. When their oldest child, Toby, arrived later in the day with his fiancée, Molly, they had presented him with a snowboard and her with a luxurious cashmere sweater. And those were only the big presents. There had been all the budget-busting books, CDs, video games, sweaters, and pajamas, right on down to the chocolate oranges and lip balm tucked in the toe of each bulging Christmas stocking.

It all must have cost a fortune, guessed Lucy, who had lost track of the actual total sometime around December 18. Oh, sure, it had been great fun for the hour or two it took to open all the presents, but those credit card balances would linger for months. And what was she going to do about the letter? It was from the financial aid office at Chamberlain College advising her that they had reviewed the family's finances and had cut Elizabeth's aid package by ten thousand dollars. That meant they had to come up with the money or Elizabeth would have to leave school.

She guiltily fingered the diamond studs Bill had surprised her with, saying they were a reward for all the Christmases he was only able to give her a handmade coupon book of promises after they finished buying presents for the kids. It was a lovely gesture, but she knew they couldn't really afford it. She wasn't even sure he had work lined up for the winter. The economy was supposed to be recovering, but like many in the little town of Tinker's Cove, Maine, Bill was self-employed. Over the years he had built a solid reputation as a restoration carpenter, renovating rundown older homes for city folks who wanted a vacation home by the shore. Last year, when the stock market was soaring he had made plenty of money, which was probably why the financial aid office had decided they could afford to pay more. But even last year, Bill's best year ever, they had struggled to meet Elizabeth's college expenses. Now that the Dow was hovering well below its former dizzying heights, Bill's earnings had dropped dramatically. The economists called it a "correction" but it had been a disaster for vacation communities like Tinker's Cove, as the big city lawyers and bankers and stockbrokers who were the mainstay of the second home market found themselves without the fat bonus checks they were counting on.

The sensible course would be to return the earrings to the store for a refund, but that was out of the question. She remembered how excited Bill had been when he gave her the little box and how pleased he'd been at her surprised reaction when she opened it and found the sparkling earrings. All she'd hoped for, really, was a new flannel nightgown. But now she had diamond earrings. He'd also written a private note, apologizing for all the years he'd taken her for granted, like one of the kids. But they had surprised her, too, with their presents. Toby and Molly had given her a pair of buttery soft kid gloves, Elizabeth had presented her with a jar of luxurious lavender body lotion from a trendy Newbury Street shop, Sara had put together a tape of her favorite songs to play in the car and Zoe had found a calendar with photos of Labrador puppies—all presents that had delighted her because they showed a lot of thought.

So how was she repaying them for all their love and thoughtfulness? In just a short while she was going off to

New York City with Elizabeth and leaving the rest of the family to fend for themselves. Really abandoning them for most of their Christmas vacation. The bags were packed and standing ready in the hallway; they would leave as soon as Elizabeth returned from saying good-bye to her friends.

She had been thrilled when Elizabeth announced she had entered a *Jolie* magazine contest and won winter makeovers for herself and her mother. Not only was she enormously proud of her clever daughter but at first she was excited at the prospect of the makeover itself. What working mother wouldn't enjoy a few days of luxurious pampering? But now she wished she could convert the prize into cash. Besides, how would Bill manage without her? What would Zoe and Sara do all day? Watch TV? That was no way to spend a week-long holiday from school.

Also, worried Lucy, checking to make sure the earrings were still firmly in place, what if the supposedly "all-expense paid" makeover wasn't quite as "all-expense paid" as promised? Traveling was expensive—there were always those little incidentals, like tips and magazines and mints and even airplane meals now that you had to buy them, that added up. What if it turned out to be like those "free" facials at the make-up counter where the sales associates pressured you to buy a lot of expensive products that you would never use again?

Lucy sighed. To tell the truth, she was a little uneasy about the whole concept of being made over. There was nothing the matter with her. She stood up and looked at her reflection in the mirror that hung over the couch. She looked fine. Not perfect, of course. She was getting a few crow's feet, there were a few gray hairs and that stubborn five pounds she couldn't seem to lose, but she was neat and trim and could still fit in the sparkly Christmas sweatshirt the kids had given her years ago. And since she only wore it a few times a year it still looked as festive as ever.

Now that she was actually giving it a critical eye, she

could understand why her friend Sue always teased her about the sweatshirt. It was boxy and didn't do a thing for her figure. Furthermore, it was the height of kitsch, featuring a bright green Christmas tree decorated with sequins, beads, and bows. Not the least bit sophisticated.

She sighed. She hadn't always been a country mouse; she'd grown up in a suburb of the city and had made frequent forays with her mother, and later with her friends, to shop, see a show, or visit a museum. It would be fun to go back to New York, especially since she hadn't been in years. And she was looking forward to a reunion with her old college buddy, Samantha Blackwell. They had been faithful correspondents through the years, apparently both stuck in the days when people wrote letters, but had never gotten in the habit of telephoning each other. Caught in busy lives with numerous responsibilities, they'd never been able to visit each other, despite numerous attempts. Lucy had married right out of college and moved to Maine, where she started a family and worked as a part-time reporter for the local weekly newspaper. Sam had been one of a handful of pioneering women accepted to study for the ministry at Union Theological Seminary and had promptly fulfilled the reluctant admission officer's misgivings by dropping out when she met her lawyer husband, Brad. She now worked for the International AIDS Foundation, and Lucy couldn't wait to see her and renew their friendship.

Which reminded her, she hadn't had a chance yet today to call her friends to wish them a Merry Christmas. That was one holiday tradition she really enjoyed. She sat back down on the couch and reached for the phone, dialing Sue Finch's number.

"Are you all ready for the trip?" asked Sue, after they'd gotten the formalities out of the way.

"All packed and ready to go."

"I hope you left room in your suitcase so you can take advantage of the after-Christmas sales. Sidra says they're fabulous." Sidra, Sue's daughter, lived in New York with her husband, Geoff Rumford, and was an assistant producer of the *Norah!* TV show.

"No sales for me." Lucy didn't want the whole town to know about the family's finances, so she prevaricated. "I think I'll be too busy."

"They can't keep you busy every minute."

"I think they intend to. We're catching the ten o'clock flight out of Portland tonight so we can make a fashion show breakfast first thing tomorrow morning, then there are numerous expert consultations, a spa afternoon, photo sessions and interviews, I'm worried I won't even have time to see Sam." She paused. "And if I do have some free time, I'm planning to visit some museums like the Met and MOMA. . . ."

Sue, who lived to shop, couldn't believe this heresy. "But what about Bloomingdale's?"

"I've spent quite enough on Christmas as it is," said Lucy. "I've got to economize."

"Sure," acknowledged Sue, "but you have to spend money to save it."

It was exactly this sort of logic that had led her into spending too much on Christmas in the first place, thought Lucy, but she wasn't about to argue. "If you say so," she laughed. "I've got to go. Someone's on call waiting."

It was Rachel Goodman, another member of the group of four that met for breakfast each week at Jake's Donut Shack.

"Did Santa bring you anything special?" asked Rachel.

Something in her tone made Lucy suspicious. "How did you know?"

"Bill asked me to help pick them out. Do you like them?"

"I love them, but he shouldn't have spent so much."

"I told him you'd be happy with pearls," said Rachel, "but he insisted on the diamonds. He was really cute about it. He said he wanted you to wear them in New York."

This was a whole new side of Bill that Lucy wasn't familiar with. She wasn't sure she could get used to this sensitive, considerate Bill. She wondered fleetingly if he was having some sort of midlife crisis.

"Aw, gee, you know I'm really having second thoughts about this trip."

"Of course you are."

Lucy wondered if Rachel knew more than she was letting on. "What do you mean?"

"Haven't you heard? There's this awful flu going around."

"What flu?"

"It's an epidemic. I read about it in the *New York Times*. They're advising everyone to avoid crowds and wash their hands frequently."

"How do you avoid crowds in a city?"

"I don't know, but I think you should try. Flu can be serious. It kills thousands of people every year."

"That was 1918," scoffed Lucy.

"Laugh if you want. I'm only trying to help."

Lucy immediately felt terrible for hurting Rachel's feelings. "I know, and I appreciate it. I really do."

"Promise you'll take precautions?"

"Sure. And thanks for the warning."

She was wondering whether she should buy some disinfectant wipes as she dialed Pam's number. Pam, also a member of the breakfast group, was married to Lucy's boss at the newspaper, Ted Stillings, and was a great believer in natural remedies.

"Disinfectant wipes? Are you crazy? That sort of thing just weakens your immune system."

"Rachel says there's a flu epidemic and I have to watch out for germs."

"How are you supposed to do that? The world is full of

millions, billions, zillions of germs that are invisible to the human eye. If Mother Nature intended us to watch out for them, don't you think she would have made them bigger, like mosquitoes or spiders?"

It was a frightening picture. "I never thought of that."

"Well, trust me, Mother Nature did. She gave you a fabulous immune system to protect the Good Body." That's how Pam pronounced it, with capital letter emphasis. "Your immune system worries about the germs so you don't have to."

"If that's true, how come so many people get sick?"

"People get sick because they abuse their bodies. They pollute their Good Bodies with empty calories and preservatives instead of natural whole foods, they don't get enough sleep, they don't take care of themselves." Pam huffed. "You have to help Mother Nature. She can't do it all, you know."

"Okay. How do I help her?"

"One thing you can do is take vitamin C. It gives the immune system a boost. That's what I'd do if I were you, especially since you're going into a new environment that might stress your organic equilibrium."

Lucy was picturing a dusty brown bottle in the back of the medicine cabinet. "You know, I think I've got some. Now I just have to remember to take it. It looks like we're going to be pretty busy with this makeover."

"Don't let them go crazy with eye shadow and stuff," advised Pam.

"Is it bad for you?"

"It's probably a germ farm, especially if they use it on more than one person, but that isn't what I was thinking about." She paused, choosing her words. "You're beautiful already. You don't need that stuff."

"Why, thanks, Pam," said Lucy, surprised at the compliment.

"I mean it. Beauty comes from inside. It doesn't come from lipstick and stuff."

"That's the way it ought to be," said Lucy, "but lately I've been noticing some wrinkles and gray hairs, and I don't like them. Maybe they'll have some ideas that can help."

"Those things are signs of character. You've earned those wrinkles and gray hairs!"

"And the mommy tummy, too, but I'm not crazy about it."

"Don't even think about liposuction," warned Pam, horrified. "Promise?"

"Believe me, it's not an option," said Lucy, hearing Bill's footsteps in the kitchen. "I've got to go."

When she looked up he was standing in the doorway, dressed in his Christmas red plaid flannel shirt and new corduroy pants. He was holding a small box wrapped with a red bow, and her heart sank. "Not another present!"

"It's something special I picked up for you."

Lucy couldn't hide her dismay. "But we've spent so much already. We'll be lucky to get this year's bills paid off before next Christmas!" She paused, considering. There was no sense in putting it off any longer. "And Elizabeth's tuition bill came yesterday. Chamberlain College wants sixteen thousand dollars by January 6. That's ten thousand more than we were expecting to pay. Ten thousand more than we have."

He sat down next to her on the couch. "It's not the end of the world, Lucy. She can take a year off and work."

"At what? There are no good jobs around here."

"She could work in Boston."

"She'd be lucky to earn enough to cover her rent! She'd never be able to save."

Bill sighed. "I know giving the kids college educations is

important to you, Lucy, but I don't see what it did for us. I'm not convinced it really is a good investment—not at these prices."

Lucy had heard him say the same thing many times, and it always made her angry.

"That's a cop-out, and you know it. It's our responsibility as parents to give our kids every opportunity we can." She sighed. "I admit it doesn't always work out. Toby hated college; it wasn't for him. And that's okay. But Elizabeth's been doing so well. It makes me sick to think she'll have to drop out."

Bill put his arm around her shoulder. "We'll figure something out . . . or we won't. There's nothing we can do about it right now. Open your present."

Lucy's eyes met his, and something inside her began to melt. She reached up and stroked his beard. "You've given me too much already."

"It's all right, really," said Bill, placing the little box in her hand. "Trust me."

"Okay." Lucy prepared herself to accept another lavish gift, promising herself that she would quietly return it for a refund when she got back from New York. What could it be? A diamond pendant to match the earrings? A gold bangle? What had he gone and done? She set the box in her lap and pulled the ends of the red satin bow. She took a deep breath and lifted the top, then pushed the cotton batting aside.

"Oh my goodness," she said, discovering a bright red plastic watch wrapped in cellophane. "It's got lobster hands."

"That's because it's a lobster watch," said Bill. "They gave them out at the hardware store. Do you like it?"

"Like it? I love it," she said. "I think it makes quite a fashion statement."

"And it tells time," said Bill, pulling her close.

Lucy took a second look at the watch. "Was it really free?"

"Absolutely. Positively. Completely."

"I'll wear it the whole time I'm away," said Lucy. "I'll be counting the minutes until I get home."

"That's the idea," said Bill, nuzzling her neck.

The wrapping paper underneath the tree crinkled and rustled as Libby rolled over. Instinctively, just as they had when they'd briefly shared their bedroom with the newest baby, they held their breaths, afraid she would wake up. They waited until she let out a big doggy sigh and her breathing became deep and regular, then they tiptoed out of the living room.

As they joined Sara and Zoe in the family room, where they were watching a "A Christmas Story," Lucy resolved to enjoy the few remaining hours of Christmas. She'd have plenty of time on the plane to break the news to Elizabeth and to try to come up with a solution. A ten-thousand-dollar solution.

Chapter Two

THE ONE BEAUTY AID YOU CAN'T LEAVE HOME WITHOUT!

"Mom, we have to turn back. I forgot something."

Lucy and Elizabeth were driving through the prime-time darkness, approaching the on ramp to the interstate. They were running late because Elizabeth's round of farewells had taken longer than expected. When she'd finally arrived home she decided the clothes she'd packed were all wrong for New York City. The result was a frantic rush to get organized at the last minute.

"What did you forget?" demanded Lucy, slamming on the brakes and pulling to the side of the road. "Your asthma medicine? Your contacts?"

"Water."

Lucy couldn't believe her ears. "Water?"

"Yeah. In the last issue of *Jolie* they said you should take it along whenever you fly. Flying is very dehydrating and you need to drink lots of water." Elizabeth flipped down the visor and checked her reflection in the mirror. "Especially if you're older, Mom."

Lucy signaled and eased the Subaru back onto the road.

"We're not going back for water. You can get some at the airport." She turned onto the ramp.

Elizabeth's eyebrows shot up and her voice became shrill. "But I bought a gigantic bottle of Evian. That's what the models drink, you know. It cost a fortune, and those weasely little worms will drink it."

"Please don't refer to your sisters as worms." Lucy checked her mirrors: not a headlight in sight. The road was clear and she accelerated, speeding down the empty highway as fast as she dared. "And why would they drink your water when there's perfectly good tap water?"

"Just to spite me."

"It would serve you right for wasting money like that. Our water comes from our own well, you know. It's perfectly pure and good."

"It's not Evian."

"It's probably better." Lucy sighed. "Besides, I've heard they won't let you carry liquids onto the plane. There are all these new security rules, you know."

"That's ridiculous! Water's harmless."

"So are nail clippers and tweezers, but you can't have them, either. And how are they supposed to know it's really water? It could be some explosive or poison, cleverly disguised in a water bottle."

Elizabeth yawned. "You're getting paranoid."

Lucy checked the speedometer and slowed to a speed ten miles above the legal limit.

"I'll tell you what I'm paranoid about," she said, lowering her voice. "I've heard they actually have machines that can see through your clothes. And sometimes they do strip searches."

Elizabeth rolled her eyes. "Mom, nobody is going to strip search *you*." Lucy was wondering what exactly she meant by that when Elizabeth chuckled. "But they probably will confiscate that lobster watch. They'll call the fashion police."

"Very funny," said Lucy, flipping on the windshield wipers. "Do you believe it? It's snowing. Again."

*   *   *

When they arrived at the airport they discovered all flights were delayed due to the weather. The snow was accumulating fast, and the runways had to be plowed and the wings de-iced before any planes could take off.

"How long is this going to take?" fumed Elizabeth.

"As long as it takes," said Lucy. "It's never the thing you're worried about, is it? I was worried about getting through security but that was a breeze. I never gave a thought to the weather."

"How come they can send robots to Mars, but they can't get our plane in the air?"

"Dunno," said Lucy, propping her feet on her carry-on suitcase and opening her book. "There's nothing we can do about it so we might as well relax."

For once, Elizabeth was taking her advice. She was already slumped down in the seat beside Lucy, resting her head on her mother's shoulder. Lucy decided it was as good a time as any to break the news about the increased tuition.

"Chamberlain sent a revised financial aid statement along with the tuition bill," she said, getting straight to the point. "It came Christmas Eve."

Elizabeth sat up straight. "What did it say?"

"That we have to pay sixteen thousand dollars for next semester."

"That's crazy!"

"You don't have to tell me," said Lucy, checking the flight status monitor hanging above them. Their flight was still delayed. "I'm going to call the financial aid office and beg for more help, but there's a real possibility we can't afford to send you back. They cut your aid by ten thousand dollars, and we just don't have it. To tell the truth, the six thousand I was expecting to pay will pretty much wipe out our savings."

Elizabeth was frowning, concentrating on her Ugg

boots. "You might as well not bother calling. People always try, but they never get anywhere."

This was heresy to Lucy. "Of course I'll try. A lot of it depends on federal guidelines and stuff. Now that your father's not working we probably qualify for a Pell grant or something."

"Trust me, the most you'll get is a loan application."

"That might be doable," said Lucy, eager to seize the slimmest excuse for hope. In her heart she knew it was unlikely that the family would be able to afford a college loan, and Elizabeth was already saddled with thousands in student loans.

Elizabeth continued studying her boots. "How much do we need?" she asked.

"Ten thousand."

"That's weird." Elizabeth was sitting up straighter. "That's really weird. I didn't tell you before, but this makeover thing is also a contest." The usually sullen Elizabeth was practically bubbling with excitement. "The best mother and daughter makeover team wins ten thousand dollars."

The view through the plate glass windows of the terminal was dark and snowy, but Lucy felt as if it was morning and the sun was shining. "Really? That's fabulous. It's like fate or something."

Elizabeth was actually smiling. "I know. Like it's meant to be."

"All we have to do is be the best makeover?"

"Yeah."

Lucy felt her optimism dim slightly. "How do we do that?"

"I don't know. I think the editors vote or something."

"They're probably looking for the most dramatic change," said Lucy. "We might be at a disadvantage, I mean, we're pretty cute to start with."

Elizabeth turned and gave her mother a withering glance.

"Mom, you're wearing duck boots, a plaid coat and a green fake fur hat—I think we've got a pretty good chance."

Lucy couldn't believe what she was hearing. She'd chosen her outfit carefully and thought she looked fabulous. It was her best coat, after all, and only six years old. The hat had been an impulse purchase and the boots, well, come winter in Maine you didn't leave the house in anything else. "Well then," she finally said, "that's good, isn't it?"

It was well into the wee hours of the morning when the plane landed at New York's La Guardia Airport and Lucy was congratulating herself on her decision not to check their luggage. She was bone tired and didn't want to waste precious sleep time standing around a balky carousel trying to decide which black suitcase was hers. Fortunately, however, they were supposed to be met by a limousine that would, in the words of the official makeover itinerary, "whisk them into the world's most glamorous city for a magical three-days of luxurious pampering and personal consultations with top fashion and beauty experts."

Disembarking from the crowded plane seemed to take forever as passengers wrestled with the maximum number of bags allowable, all of which seemed much larger than the prescribed dimensions. Lucy and Elizabeth finally broke free from the shuffling herd and ran through the jet way, towing their neat little rolling suitcases. There were a handful of people waiting in the arrivals hall, holding placards with names, but none of the names was "Stone."

"The limo must have left without us," said Lucy.

"No wonder. We're late," said Elizabeth. "What do we do now?"

Lucy weighed her options and decided this was no time to pinch pennies by searching for a shuttle bus—if they were even running at this hour. You had to spend money to save it, or in this case, win it. "Taxi," she said.

*   *   *

The ride on the expressway was disorienting, as they sped along in a whirl of red and white automobile lights. The stretches of road that were illuminated by streetlamps gave only depressing views of the filthy slush and ice that lined the roadway, but their spirits brightened when they rounded a curve and there, right in front of them, was the glittering New York skyline.

"Wow," breathed Elizabeth. "It's really like the pictures."

Lucy studied the ranks of tall buildings and looked for the familiar outlines of the Empire State Building and the Chrysler Building, the only two she could identify with certainty. Those and the twin towers of the World Trade Center, but there was only an empty gap where they had stood. The thought made her heart lurch and she was surprised at her reaction; she didn't trust herself to speak about it for fear she would start crying. Instead, she firmly turned her thoughts to the promised "three days of luxury at New York's fabulous Melrose Hotel."

New York must indeed be "the city that never sleeps," thought Lucy, as the taxi pulled up to the hotel and the doorman rushed forward to greet them. "Welcome to the Melrose," he said, opening the door and extending a hand to help them alight from the car.

In no time at all they were checked in and whisked through the marble lobby to the elevators and taken to their room, which Lucy was delighted to discover was decorated in a French-inspired style with wrought iron filigree headboards and wooden shutters at the windows. It was also very tiny and she had to maneuver carefully around Elizabeth before she could collapse on her bed.

"Did you know this used to be the Barbizon?" she asked, quickly leafing through the leather-bound book listing the hotel's amenities.

"Is that supposed to mean something to me?" demanded Elizabeth.

"I guess not," admitted Lucy, reminded yet again of the knowledge gap between generations. "It was a famous hotel for women."

"Like for lesbians or something?"

"No. Girls who were coming to the city for careers would stay here until they got married. It was a safe, respectable address."

Elizabeth was regarding her as if she was speaking in tongues.

"Times were different then," she said, with a sigh. She'd hoped this trip would be an opportunity to spend some quality time with her oldest daughter but now she was beginning to think that three days with Elizabeth might be too much of a good thing.

"We might as well unpack," she said, getting to her feet and lifting her suitcase onto the bed. "Then we can sleep a little later tomorrow morning."

"This morning," corrected Elizabeth, reluctantly dragging herself off the bed and pulling her nightgown out of her suitcase.

They soon discovered, however, that the bank of louvered doors along one wall concealed heating ducts and other paraphernalia, offering only limited closet space that was quickly filled with their coats and boots. A chest of drawers was also a cheat—the drawers weren't drawers at all but a trompe l'oeil door concealing the minibar.

"Where am I supposed to put my stuff?" demanded Elizabeth.

"We'll keep our clothes in the suitcases and slide them under the bed." Lucy's cheery tone belied her displeasure. She hated living out of a suitcase. But when she dropped to her knees to investigate she discovered the bed was too low for the suitcases to fit. She sat back on her heels and sighed. "I'm getting the feeling that *Jolie* must have gotten the cheapest rooms in this joint."

Elizabeth was in bed, reading the breakfast menu conveniently printed on a cardboard tag you could hang on the outside doorknob. "I don't think anything's cheap about this place," she said. "The continental breakfast is twenty bucks."

"Well, I don't think we'll be getting room service," said Lucy, stacking the suitcases in a corner. "There's no place to put the tray."

All too soon they were awakened by the shrill ringing of the phone. Lucy immediately panicked, thinking something terrible must have happened at home, but when she held the receiver to her ear and heard the automated voice realized it was only the wake-up call she'd ordered.

"Up and at 'em," she said, shaking Elizabeth's shoulder, and heading directly for the bathroom. "Today's our first day of beauty."

Lucy's eyes were bleary from sleep, but from what she could see of her reflection in the bathroom mirror she was pretty sure the beauty experts had their work cut out for them. She quickly brushed her teeth, splashed some water on her face, added a dab of moisturizer, and grabbed her hairbrush. There was no time to spare; they were supposed to meet the other makeover winners in the hotel lobby at eight o'clock and it was already a quarter to.

"C'mon, Elizabeth. We've got to hurry."

Elizabeth pulled the pillow over her head and rolled over.

Lucy picked up the pillow, and Elizabeth pulled the sheet over her face. Lucy threw the pillow at her, but she didn't budge.

Lucy sighed and began brushing her hair. A hundred strokes later, Elizabeth's breaths were regular and she'd settled into a deep sleep. Lucy sat down on the bed and dialed room service, ordering a pot of coffee for two at twelve dollars.

The caffeine did the trick and they were on their way by eight-thirty. They'd missed the rest of the group and the limo, but the doorman hailed a taxi for them.

"Better late than never," said Lucy, looking on the bright side as they settled in for the short ride. "You'll love Tavern on the Green. It's beautiful."

And indeed it was, when the taxi turned into Central Park and pulled up at the landmark restaurant. A light snow had started to fall, transforming the park into a magical fairyland, and the trees around the restaurant were outlined in tiny white lights. The inside was warm and welcoming, and they could hear the hum of voices as they checked their bags and coats and hurried off to the ladies' room. Lucy wasn't about to appear before this crowd without checking her hair and lipstick.

"Look," said Elizabeth, pointing to a tray filled with bottles next to the sink. "It's fancy perfume."

Lucy recognized the distinctive bottle of her favorite, Pleasures, and gave herself a generous spritz, then they hurried out to claim their empty places. Lucy squared her shoulders, prepared to do battle for the ten thousand dollars, and followed the hostess to their table. Polite smiles were exchanged as Lucy and Elizabeth sat down and unfolded their cloth napkins, but all attention was on the speaker standing at the podium.

"That's Camilla Keith, the editor," whispered the woman next to Lucy, speaking with a Southern accent. "She's just started speaking."

Even Lucy had heard of Camilla; she was a legend in the magazine business, and her name was always popping up on tabloid-style TV shows, usually in connection with a lawsuit filed by a disgruntled household employee claiming verbal abuse or unpaid wages. Lucy studied her with interest; as editor-in-chief of the magazine her opinion would probably be decisive in choosing who would win the ten thousand dollars. Camilla was a very petite woman with dark hair pulled tightly back from her face, emphasizing her sharply defined cheekbones and chin. She was wearing a white tweed suit that Lucy suspected was a genuine Chanel, and her lips and fingernails were painted bright scarlet. Lucy knew that imitation was the sincerest form of flattery, but she couldn't for the life of her see how she could ever manage to look anything like the sleek and sophisticated Camilla.

"As editor of *Jolie* magazine, it is my pleasure to welcome our twelve winners to our fabulous Mother–Daughter Winter Makeover," she said, giving the group at Lucy's table a nod. "This is a very accomplished group—they had to be to attract the attention of our judges who chose them from more than forty thousand entries."

A collective gasp arose from the crowd assembled in the restaurant, and Lucy wondered who all the people at the other tables were. Her question was answered as Camilla continued speaking.

"I would also like to welcome all of you who got up bright and early to join our winners today at our annual breakfast and fashion show supporting the Jolie Foundation, which you all know is a major contributor to the fight against AIDS and breast cancer."

Lucy checked out the well-dressed ladies and wondered how much they had spent for tickets to the breakfast. These must be the "ladies who lunch" that she'd read about, she realized with surprise. Many of them were much younger than she expected, and she wondered what they did when they weren't eating out at one benefit or another. She suspected their lives must be very different from hers. There was no going out in jeans and sweaters and duck boots for them—they had to keep up with fashion, and that would require lots of shopping. While Lucy could get away with splashing some water on her face and running a comb through her hair, these ladies' polished appearances required hours in the salon, not to mention facials and exercise and waxing sessions. Probably even plastic surgery, she guessed, noticing several extremely tight faces.

Recalled from her reverie by a burst of polite laughter, she turned her attention back to Camilla. "Without further ado," she was saying, "I would like to introduce our winners who have come from all over the country to be with us today."

Lucy smiled at the others at the table, eager to learn more about them. She wondered if they were all as desperate to win the ten thousand dollars as she was.

"I'll begin with our California girls, Ocean Blaustein and her mother, Serena Blaustein, from La Jolla," said Camilla.

There was applause as the two stood. Ocean fulfilled the stereotype Lucy had come to expect from TV, with long blond hair and a tan, dressed in a tummy-baring top and hip-hugging jeans. Serena was a shorter, plumper version of her daughter, with curly red hair and wearing a colorful Mexican-inspired blouse and gathered skirt.

"Moving East, we come to the Great Plains and our winners from Omaha, Nebraska: Amanda McKee and her mother, Ginny McKee."

Lucy smiled and joined in the applause as Amanda and Ginny got to their feet. Amanda was tall and willowy, dressed in a simple turtleneck sweater and skirt. Her mother was also tall and slim, and her red wool suit complemented her dark hair.

"We couldn't ignore a state the size of Texas, so we have Tiffany Montgomery and her stepmom, Cathy Montgomery, from Dallas."

Even if she hadn't been told, Lucy would have guessed Tiffany and Cathy, who was sitting next to her, were from Texas. They were both wearing expensive-looking tweed jackets, they both had big hair, and they were wearing matching coral lipstick on their collagen-boosted lips. They also both appeared to be about the same age.

"The South is famous for its belles, and we have two lovely ladies from Wilmington, North Carolina: Faith Edwards and her mother, Lurleen Edwards."

Lucy guessed that Faith took her religion seriously; she was wearing a gold cross on a chain over her flower-patterned dress. So was her mother, also in a loose-fitting number trimmed with lace. Their faces were devoid of make-up, and their hair was combed back and held by plastic headbands.

"New England is known for its independent, strong-minded women and we have two of those hardy souls with us today: Elizabeth Stone and her mother, Lucy Stone."

Suddenly self-conscious in her best sweater and wool slacks, Lucy discovered there's nothing like a pair of diamond earrings to give a woman confidence. She got to her feet and smiled at everyone, including Elizabeth, who was the very picture of urban sophistication with her shaggy haircut and black turtleneck dress.

"And last but not least we have two uptown girls from New York City: Carmela Rodriguez and her mother, Maria Rodriguez."

The applause was loudest for Carmela and Maria, and Lucy felt a little surge of competitive spirit as she studied the two with their matching heads of thick, curly black hair. Carmela was dressed in a simple black pantsuit, with subtle make-up, but her mother was dressed in a form-fitting orange suit with a very short skirt and matching lipstick and nail polish.

Surveying the assembled group of makeover winners, Lucy wondered if they had really been chosen on the basis of the girls' essays. She doubted that the staff had time to read forty thousand entries, and it seemed suspicious that each of the six mother–daughter pairs came from a different part of the country. As a reporter for the weekly newspaper in Tinker's Cove, the *Pennysaver*, she knew that so-called contests were sometimes shams. Every year Ted, the editor and publisher, asked readers to vote for their favorite businesses in the "Best of Tinker's Cove" contest, but the truth was that few people bothered to fill out the form and mail it in. The last "best pizza" winner received five votes, and the provider of the "best massage" only got one vote, from her mother. Nevertheless, all the winners got official certificates, which they proudly displayed in their places of business.

A sudden burst of laughter drew her attention back to the speaker, who was concluding her talk. "And now, I promise you, no more speeches," said Camilla. "Breakfast will be served, and then we'll show you fabulous fashions from the new spring collections."

Camilla had no sooner left the podium than Lucy found a fruit cup set on her plate. "I hadn't realized I was so hungry," she said, picking up her spoon and surveying the competition.

Ginny McKee was the first to respond, speaking with a midwestern twang. "I noticed you were late—did you have a rough trip?"

"The snow was heavier in Maine," said Lucy. "They had to clear the runway before we could take off."

"You never know what will happen when you fly these days, do you?" offered Lurleen, taking her daughter's hand. "We were praying the whole time we were in the air."

Lurleen and Faith could be trouble, thought Lucy. She was itching to give them some fashion tips herself and she was sure the editors would relish the opportunity to transform these country bumpkins.

"I find a couple of those cute little bottles of scotch quite helpful myself," said Cathy, with a throaty chuckle.

She had a breezy Texan confidence that Lucy found appealing, but she wondered how it would play with the editors. First impressions could be deceiving, but she had a feeling Cathy did exactly what she wanted. The giant diamond on her finger gave Lucy reason to hope she wasn't particularly interested in competing for ten thousand dollars.

"None of that poison for me," said Serena. "I always bring along a vitamin-packed wheat grass smoothie. I can give you the recipe if you want."

"I'll stick to scotch, thanks." Cathy laughed, turning to Maria and Carmela. "You guys didn't have to fly. How did you get here?"

Lucy studied the Rodriguezes with interest, trying to determine how much of a hometown advantage they had. Plenty, she decided, taking in Maria's curves and Carmela's dimples.

"The magazine sent a limo," said Maria. "And I can tell you, it sure beats the subway!"

"The subway!" Lurleen was horrified. "You won't get me down there, that's for sure."

"You're so lucky to live in the city," continued Cathy, ignoring Lurleen. "I come twice a year, but it's not enough."

"Do you come for the shopping or the shows?" asked Ginny, as the waiter refilled her coffee cup.

"Mostly the shopping," offered Tiffany.

Cathy turned to her stepdaughter. "We love it all, don't we, honey?"

"East or west, home is best, that's what I always say," said Lurleen, who was suspiciously poking at her salad with a fork. "What is this red stuff?"

"Pomegranate. It's delicious," said Cathy, rolling her eyes and turning to Maria. "Is it true the really hot new boutiques are all uptown? I've heard Soho's over and Harlem's where the action is these days."

Lurleen began to choke, and Faith offered her a glass of water and patted her back.

"I know a few places," said Maria, smiling broadly. "I could show you."

"Deal," said Cathy.

"Amanda didn't tell me she'd entered this contest," said Ginny. "I didn't know a thing about it until the letter arrived. I almost threw it out; I thought it was a subscription offer."

"Aren't you glad you didn't?" asked Amanda. "This is going to be fun."

"And there's the possibility of winning ten thousand dollars," said Ocean. "If we win, Mom says I can buy a car."

"If we win we're going to donate the ten thousand dollars to our church," said Lurleen. "That's the main reason I came. I mean, if the good Lord presents you with an opportunity you can't turn it down, can you? I just hope they don't change my hair color; that's something I don't approve of. The good Lord knew what he was doing when he gave us our hair, and everything else, too. Like my mama used to tell me, 'Just keep your face clean and your soul pure and your beauty will shine through.'"

Cathy shook her head in disbelief. "You're in the wrong place then, honey. You should've stayed in South Carolina."

"North Carolina."

"Well, wherever you're from, you're in Camilla's hands now. Around here she's the boss, and you better do what she says. Her temper is a legend in the industry, believe me, I know. Back in the days before I met Tiffany's wonderful father, Mr. Montgomery, I was a marketing executive at Neiman Marcus. I dealt with her quite a bit, and I soon learned that there was Camilla's way or the highway. It didn't matter that I was the customer, that I was putting up the money and buying the ads. Being the customer didn't make me right, not with her anyway."

Lurleen looked worried, and Lucy wondered if she'd only consented to the makeover to win the prize money for her church. Lucy understood her anxiety; she hoped the magazine's experts wouldn't make them look ridiculous. Not that she had any complaints so far. The fruit cup had been tasty, and the eggs Benedict was a delicious treat. She realized with a shock that she was enjoying herself, in the heart of New York City. Tinker's Cove seemed very far away.

The waiters were clearing away the last of the dishes when the lights suddenly dimmed and strobe lights began flashing in time to loud techno music. It was the promised fashion show, but Lucy thought the parade of excruciatingly thin models dressed in skimpy outfits was more suited to a Save the Children campaign than daily life. Thigh-high buccaneer boots with pointy toes and stiletto heels, belt-sized miniskirts, and bondage-inspired bustiers were hardly the sort of thing she would wear. Neither were the flowing and fluttering evening dresses constructed of torn bits of fabric and ribbon. None of the moms at her table seemed to know what to make of the molded foam dress with an additional pair of buttocks stitched onto the backside, a detail the announcer described as "humorous whimsy."

"Like I need a second one of those," said Cathy.

"That poor model doesn't even have a first bottom," said Ginny, giggling.

But when the fashion show was over and they were ensconced in a limo with Ginny and Amanda en route to the hotel, Lucy discovered that Elizabeth had a very different reaction.

"I'm too fat, Mom," she said, sighing. "I should never have eaten all those Christmas cookies and stuff."

"Me, too," said Amanda.

"You look great," said Lucy, firmly. "You both look great. You're normal. Those models are freaks, and whether you believe it or not they're putting their health at risk."

"That's not true, Mom. Now they're saying people who stress their systems by skipping meals actually add years to their lives."

"You can't believe everything you read," said Ginny.

"That's for sure," said Lucy. "Besides, they do more than skip lunch to stay that thin. I wouldn't be surprised if they smoke cigarettes and take amphetamines and diet pills."

"Mom, you don't know that. You read it somewhere. So now who's the one who needs to remember you can't believe everything you read."

Lucy was tempted to retort but didn't want to fight in front of Ginny and Amanda. Instead, she held her tongue as they pulled up to the gleaming steel and glass office tower. Looking up, she was suddenly thrilled and excited about the adventure ahead. She could hardly contain herself as she sat waiting for the chauffeur to open the door.

Chapter Three

THE YEAR'S *BEST* AND *WORST* LOOKS

"I don't think the others are as desperate for the money as we are. Take the pair from California, for example. The daughter wants a new car, but the mom is pretty laid back and relaxed. The only others who expressed any serious interest in the money are from North Carolina, and they say they'll give it to their church if they win."

"The others aren't interested?" Bill sounded doubtful.

"I honestly don't think the girls from Texas are. They already seem to have more money than they know what to do with. That leaves the New Yorkers, Maria and Carmela. I don't know much about them yet so I'm keeping an eye on them, and the midwesterners." Lucy paused, thinking about Ginny and Amanda. "They're very polite, and polite doesn't win contests."

Bill chuckled. "I didn't know you were such a cutthroat competitor yourself."

"I'm desperate. I'll do anything to win."

"If you're really serious about this, I've got some advice for you. You know that TV show, *Survivor*? The winners often form alliances with other players to gain an advantage. They help each other wipe out the competition."

"But there's only one prize. Why would you help somebody else win?"

"Because they'll help you in return. Two are better than one."

"And three's a crowd," said Lucy. "That's what my mother used to say." She lowered her voice. "I'm worried about Elizabeth," she whispered. "She hardly ate a bite of breakfast."

"Maybe she wasn't hungry."

"She thinks she's fat."

"That's crazy. She's skin and bones."

"I know, but they had this fashion show today and the models were even skinnier than she is so she's decided she needs to lose weight."

"It's probably just a phase," he said, sounding distracted. In the distance she heard muffled shouts. "Sorry, honey, I've got to go. The girls say the dog knocked over a lamp."

Lucy closed the phone and replaced it in her purse, thinking over Bill's advice. The editors had finally arrived and were shepherding the group through the security checkpoint, where a guard was peering into each woman's purse with a flashlight. Who would make the best accomplice, she wondered, hurrying to join them.

Boarding the elevator, she gave Elizabeth a nudge. "Look, I found this protein bar in my bag. Why don't you have a bite or two, just to keep up your strength."

Elizabeth glared at her. "You're embarrassing me, Mom," she hissed. "It's bad enough you're wearing those duck boots, but now you're fussing at me."

"These boots are practical," muttered Lucy, heading for the revolving door.

"Will you shut up if I take the bar?" asked Elizabeth, when they'd exited onto the eighteenth floor into the magazine's reception area.

"You have to eat half of it," insisted Lucy, trying to hide her disappointment. She'd expected the *Jolie* office to look like something out of the movie "Funny Face" but instead of glamorous chic pink décor there was only utilitarian, understated beige. The receptionist, a mousy little thing who seemed to physically quail under Camilla's gaze, gave them a lukewarm smile as they all filed past.

Camilla stopped suddenly and held up a hand, causing a bit of awkward bumping as the women in back came to a halt.

"Okay." Elizabeth carefully unwrapped the bar and took a bite, chewed slowly and finally swallowed.

Lucy let out the breath she had been holding and turned her attention to Camilla, who was standing in front of a wall decorated with framed cover photos.

"Ladies, ladies!"

The group fell silent.

"Welcome to the world of *Jolie* magazine," she said, waving her arm expansively. "This is where your transformation will take place." She paused dramatically. "Are you ready?"

"You betcha," declared Serena. "Make me into Kate Moss."

"That may not be possi . . ." began Camilla, giving Serena a quick up and down. Then, realizing it was a joke, she trilled, "We'll do our best."

The women all laughed.

"But first on our agenda," she continued, holding up a finger, "is the infamous *before* picture. And for that, I'm putting you in the capable hands of our art director, Nancy Glass." She indicated a tiny woman in oversized tortoise-shell glasses, who was wearing a tight gray pencil skirt, a black blazer, and a shiny pink silk blouse along with high-heeled sandals.

"Follow me, ladies. The photo studio is this way," she said, pointing towards a long, beige carpeted hallway lined with doors.

Once again, they were off and running and Lucy was beginning to understand how city people managed to stay so thin. At home, she drove to the *Pennysaver* office, parked outside the back door, walked twenty feet to her desk, sat down and, often as not, reached for one of the donuts Phyllis had taken to bringing to work every morning.

"Here we are," announced Nancy, dramatically opening the studio door.

Lucy wasn't quite sure what she expected, but it wasn't this large, windowless room with a raised platform at one end. Several contraptions resembling the screens people used to have for showing slides and home movies dangled from the ceiling behind the platform, along with a silvery umbrella. A cluster of tripods was stacked in one corner, a table held a coffee carafe and a stack of cups but no donuts, and a few mismatched chairs were scattered about. There was no sign of the photographer.

"I see Pablo's not here yet," said Nancy, drumming her nails, polished in a shade of pink that matched her blouse, against her pointy hip bone. "I'll have to go find him."

Figuring they might have a bit of a wait, Lucy and Elizabeth joined Ginny and Amanda. Across the room, Maria and Carmela were having an animated conversation with the Blausteins and the Montgomerys, fueled perhaps by the Styrofoam cups of coffee they were sipping. Lurleen and Faith Edwards formed a little island, standing by themselves. It was Ginny who broke the ice. "So what do you think of the competition?" she asked.

Lucy turned to her with interest. "What about you? Are you trying to win the prize?"

"You bet," volunteered Amanda. "Mom and Dad went into business for themselves last year."

"We do upholstery and slipcovers," added Ginny.

"It's been very successful."

"Beyond our wildest dreams," said Ginny. "Unfortunately, we knew a lot more about slipcovers than the tax code.

Our accountant tells us we have to pay the IRS a quarterly payment on January 15 that's almost ten thousand more than we budgeted for."

"We're in a similar bind," confessed Lucy, explaining the financial aid dilemma. "I guess I was kidding myself. I didn't think anybody else was very interested, except for Faith and Lurleen."

"They're definitely motivated," agreed Ginny. "Driven by religious fervor."

"But the gals from Texas certainly don't need the money."

"No, but Cathy had a successful career before she married; she even won a few beauty pageants. She might not be able to resist the challenge."

"I never thought of that," said Lucy, gaining new respect for Ginny. "What about Carmela and Maria?"

"Maria was an abused wife who went to law school after getting her husband sent to jail. She's now one of New York's top divorce attorneys. They call her Merciless Maria."

Lucy didn't say anything but swallowed hard. This was going to be much more challenging than she thought. She was almost ready to give up and go home.

"Serena and Ocean?" asked Elizabeth, her voice practically a squeak.

"Don't be fooled by Serena's California cool. She lets that girl get away with anything—just look at how she goes around with her stomach hanging out in the middle of winter! Trust me, that woman will do anything for that girl, and we already know that Ocean wants a new car." Ginny narrowed her eyes. "The only way we stand a chance is if we team up and help each other."

"That would be great!" exclaimed Lucy, wondering what she could contribute to their partnership. "Tell you what, I'll try to find out the rules for this contest. So far, they've been pretty vague."

"Deal," said Ginny, extending her hand.

Lucy took it and gave a firm shake, just as Nancy returned with Pablo in tow.

"We're good to go," trilled Nancy. "This is our photo editor and I'm sure he's going to get some great photos of you ladies."

Pablo, a muscular man dressed in a black silk T-shirt and pleated-front slacks, gave them a nod. He looked as if he hadn't shaved his chin in a day or two but Lucy decided the look must be intentional since he'd certainly shaved his head that morning: it was perfectly smooth and shiny. He stood silently, arms crossed, and studied them. Then, coming to a decision he snapped his fingers and an assistant magically appeared with a camera. Pablo took it and began snapping photos of the woman, just as they were, scattered around the room in groups.

"What are you doing? This isn't what we talked about," protested Nancy.

"That was no good. This is better. Natural, unstudied. Like Degas backstage at the ballet, no?"

"I see," said Nancy, with a shrug. "That's why he's a genius. Stay as you are, ladies; it seems Pablo's having one of his creative moments."

The camera flashed in Lucy's face, then Pablo was gone, making his way around the room followed by Nancy and the assistant. Nancy kept up a steady stream of chatter while Pablo snapped photos, pausing only to toss his camera to the helper when the film ran out and to snatch a loaded one.

Eventually his energy, or inspiration, seemed to flag and he collapsed into a chair. The assistant vanished with the cameras while another rushed up with a towel and a bottle of water. Pablo wiped his face with a towel, as if he'd just completed the Boston Marathon, and chugged a pint or two of water.

While he rested Nancy gathered the group together on

the platform and began arranging them according to height. Lucy cleared her throat and raised her hand.

"Yes?" asked Nancy. "Is there a problem?"

It was then that Camilla arrived, and stood by the door, watching, her arms folded across her chest. She had changed out of the white Chanel suit and into more practical working clothes, a black jersey dress, black tights and knee-high black boots with stiletto heels and extremely pointed toes. She was a perfect, self-contained package.

"No, not a problem," said Lucy. "But I do have a question. I think we're all interested in the contest for the ten thousand dollars."

This was greeted with a murmur of approval from the others.

"It would be helpful to know on what basis the winning mother and daughter will be chosen."

Camilla's eyes widened, giving her a doll-like appearance. "That decision will be made by the editors," she said.

"Of course," persisted Lucy. "But how will the editors decide? What are the rules?"

Camilla became rigid as a poker, except for one foot, which tapped a rapid beat on the tile floor. "That's for us to know and you to find out," she said, as a tight little smile flitted across her lips and disappeared. "Otherwise it wouldn't be much of a contest, would it?"

"I'd like to get her into my stress-reduction class," whispered Serena. "People really relax after a session or two of genital breathing. Give me a week and I'll have her loose as a goose."

"Genital breathing?" Lucy was intrigued.

"Not in front of the girls," whispered Lurleen, prompting embarrassed giggles from Faith.

"It's just a relaxation technique; there's nothing sexual about it," said Ocean, defending her mother.

"Well, I never," began Lurleen, only to fall silent as

Camilla approached the group for a closer look. The winners shifted uncomfortably under her gaze.

"This is no good," she finally said.

Pablo was on his feet, eyes glaring. "No good? What you mean?"

Nancy was quick to intervene. "If you don't like the group photo we can use individual shots. Pablo took some really nice, creative informals."

"No, that's not the problem," said Camilla, tapping her fingers on her hip. "The problem is . . ."

Nancy leaned forward, as if to catch the words as they fell from her lips. Pablo stood, arms crossed, waiting warily.

"They look too good!"

Pablo threw up his arms and stalked out of the studio.

Nancy was puzzled. "They look too good?"

"This is supposed to be a *before* photo, but they don't look *before* enough."

"Oh," said Nancy. "I understand. Maybe they could take off their make-up. We could change their hair a little bit, give them some ugly clothes. . . ."

Camilla wasn't listening. She rushed forward and pointed a scarlet-tipped finger at Lucy's feet. "What are those?"

Elizabeth looked upward, rolling her eyes in mortification.

"I think they're called duck boots," said Lucy, lifting her slacks to reveal the brown rubber bottoms and tan leather uppers of her footwear. "Everyone wears them at home."

Camilla was examining the rest of Lucy's ensemble with an eagle eye. "What's that?" she asked, pointing at the watch.

"Oh," said Lucy, with a little giggle, "that's my lobster watch. It was a joke present from my husband."

Camilla pulled Lucy out of the group and she blushed,

uncomfortably aware that she was about to be an example. She was pretty sure this was not the way to win the ten thousand dollars.

"Get Deb up here," she told Nancy, who scurried over to the phone on the wall.

Ginny's eyes met Lucy's, and she smiled sympathetically. Serena gazed into the distance, apparently meditating. The others looked down at their feet while Lucy stood awkwardly, waiting for Deb's arrival, whoever she was. Fortunately, they didn't have to wait long.

"Deb Shertzer is our accessories editor," said Nancy, as a woman with short hair burst into the studio. She was dressed in a rosy twin set to which she had added a colorful scarf and small gold hoop earrings, and she was quite breathless. She'd wasted no time in obeying Camilla's order to appear.

"This is interesting," said Camilla, pointing Lucy out. "You can tell this woman isn't from New York just by looking at her boots."

"I brought heels," said Lucy, bristling, "but the streets are slushy and I didn't want to ruin them so I wore my boots. I can get the shoes, if you want."

"No! Don't change," said Camilla, turning to Deb. "Look at her watch."

Lucy obediently held out her arm, and Deb's eyes widened as she took in the red plastic watch.

"The hands are little lobster claws," said Camilla.

"So I see," said Deb.

"I want this for everyone."

"Duck boots? Lobster watches?"

"No." Camilla tapped her foot impatiently. "Regional accessories. Stuff that tells a story. Like the pair from Iowa. . . ."

"Omaha," said Ginny, with a little edge in her voice. "Omaha, Nebraska."

"Whatever." Camilla waved her hand. "She and her kid

can wear overalls and hold a pitchfork, like that paint-ing."

"Grant Wood," said Nancy, nodding enthusiastically.

"Whatever. And the ones from California?"

Serena hesitated a moment before raising her hand. "That's me," she finally said, sounding as if Camilla was taxing even her patience.

"What about a surfboard and swimsuits?" suggested Deb, eager to show her boss that she'd got the idea.

"Cool," said Ocean. "I can show off my tan."

"Hold on a minute," said Cathy, pulling herself up to her almost six-foot height. "I protest. This is tacky. I'm not going to wear a cowboy hat just because I'm from Texas."

"Don't worry, honey," crooned Camilla, "we wouldn't dream of changing a thing." Her voice hardened and her eyes flashed. "With that hair and jewelry you look exactly like the Texas trophy wife you are."

There was a shocked silence, and everyone watched as Camilla turned on her heel and marched out of the studio. When she was gone everyone seemed to let out a big sigh of relief.

"Well now, ladies," said Nancy, stepping forward briskly, "we have work to do."

"You're not kidding," said Deb. "Where am I going to get a surfboard in New York City in December?"

Nancy turned and looked around the studio. "Where's Pablo? Has anyone seen Pablo?"

She rushed out to look for him, and the women, who had been standing shoulder to shoulder on the platform, began to pull apart; Lucy felt suddenly chilly. Her eyes met Ginny's in a mute apology. Ginny shrugged in return, as if to say it didn't matter, but Lucy knew she had handled things badly and hadn't kept her half of the bargain. She had a feeling the alliance had broken down.

Chapter Four

PLUCK OR WAX?
OUR BROW EXPERTS HAVE THE ANSWERS

When the photo session was finally over, the women were divided into three groups and sent to consult with the magazine's experts. Lucy and Elizabeth found themselves paired with Lurleen and Faith Edwards for make-up advice, the Montgomerys and Blausteins were off to a spa, and the McKees and Rodriguezes were sent to the fashion department. As Lucy watched Ginny and Maria walking down the hall with their heads together she wondered if Ginny's offer to team up had simply been a ploy to trick her into making a foolish mistake. If so, it had certainly worked. The editors probably thought she was a troublemaker now, and the other contestants didn't seem to want anything to do with her. Even Lurleen seemed unwilling to "turn the other cheek" and forgive her and was keeping her distance as they followed the directions to the beauty department. It wasn't until they were in the elevator that she broke her silence.

"I'm of half a mind to pack up and go home," said Lurleen, as the doors slid shut. "This isn't at all what I expected. I feel as if I've been put through the wringer."

"Mom was looking forward to some pampering and relaxation," explained Faith.

"You can say that again. Faith here is my oldest, you see. I've got six more at home."

"Seven children?" Lucy's eyebrows shot up as the elevator landed with a thud.

"And another on the way," she sighed, stepping into the hallway. "I'm really looking forward to that massage they promised us, but I don't think there's time today since we're all going to that TV show."

Lucy was consulting the agenda, wondering which TV show they were going to see, but the notation didn't specify. "Maybe it's the *Norah!* show," she said, giving Elizabeth a nudge.

"Doesn't mean a thing to me," said Lurleen. "I can't tell one show from another."

"We don't watch TV except for inspirational videos and Bible stories," said Faith.

Lucy glanced at Elizabeth, who was rolling her eyes as she pushed open the door to the beauty department. Inside they found three desks—small, medium, and large like the chairs and beds in the three bears' house, only Baby Bear was occupying her desk.

"Hi, I'm Fiona. Fiona Gray," she said, jumping up and extending her hand.

Lucy took it, finding it impossible not to smile at this bright young thing. Fiona had short, dark hair in a style similar to Elizabeth's and enormous blue eyes, and she was dressed in a very short teal dress topped with a wide leather belt with oversized chrome grommets and buckle.

"Welcome to the beauty department," she continued, speaking in a crisp British accent. "According to the schedule..."

Lucy was enchanted. Fiona actually pronounced it *shedyule*.

"...you must be the Edwards and the Stones and you're here for make-up. Though I must say, you all look positively brilliant, and I can't imagine what old Nadine, that's Nadine Nelson, our beauty editor, can possibly do to improve you."

"Now, now," clucked an older woman, entering through a door at the rear of the office, "there's always something we can do." She paused. "I'm Phyllis Jackson, the assistant beauty editor. Nadine left instructions for me to get you settled. She'll be in shortly to supervise. Follow me."

As they trooped after her, Lucy noticed that Phyllis had a rather harried and disheveled air about her. Alhough to be honest, thought Lucy, she certainly looked better than the average woman in Tinker's Cove, even with her smudged lipstick and worn shoes. It was only in the rarefied atmosphere of the magazine that you noticed that her olive green blouse didn't perfectly match the acid green flecks in her tweed skirt.

The studio looked like a beauty shop with mirrors, raised chairs, and a counter filled with every imaginable make-up product. Fiona flipped a switch and they were suddenly all bathed in bright light as they seated themselves. Elizabeth was goggle-eyed at the array of cosmetics, but there was no chance for her to get her hands on them as Phyllis tilted the chair back and started sponging her face.

"Fiona, heat up the wax for the brows, and then you can start cleansing Lucy's face," she said.

"Brows?" squeaked Lucy. "Wax?"

"Trust her," advised Fiona, raising one of her own delicately arched brows. "She's a genius at shaping."

"It makes all the difference in the world," said Phyllis. "Really opens up your face and makes your eyes look bigger."

"Does it hurt?" asked Elizabeth.

"Like hell," said Fiona.

When they were through cleansing and waxing and plucking, Lucy had to admit they all looked improved, at least in the brow department. The rest of their faces were a bit like blank slates, however, awaiting the master's touch.

"She's running late this morning," said Fiona, speaking

to Phyllis in a whisper. "I think we should start with the foundation."

"We better wait," replied Phyllis, looking worried. "You know how Nadine is."

"I know," agreed Fiona, "but the next group is due in less than half an hour."

Phyllis pursed her lips anxiously but was spared the agony of making a decision by the arrival of the beauty editor herself. Nadine Nelson thumped into the studio, trailing numerous scarves and carrying an assortment of bags including a purse (Louis Vuitton), brief case (Coach) and crumpled brown paper shopping bags (Bloomingdale's and Schlagel's Bagels).

"I'm exhausted," she said, dropping the bags on the floor and shrugging out of her mink coat. It would have fallen on the floor, too, except for Phyllis who lunged forward and snatched it in the nick of time.

"Still feeling poorly?" inquired Phyllis, draping the coat on a padded satin hanger.

Nadine replied with a burst of coughing, and Phyllis proffered a box of tissues, which she waved away. Instead, she scrabbled around in her enormous purse, finally extracting an eye-catching gold compact lavishly decorated with colorful enamel in a pansy design.

"Ghastly," she said, flipping the compact open and peering into the mirror. She got to work rubbing the puff all over her face, and it wasn't until she'd shut it with a click that she noticed the four makeover winners. "Cripes!" she exclaimed. "That damn makeover. We have them all day, don't we?"

Phyllis's face reddened, embarrassed by her boss's rudeness. "Let me introduce Lucy and Elizabeth Stone and Lurleen and Faith Edwards. We've cleansed their faces and shaped their brows, but we didn't want to go any further without you. . . ."

"I've got to sit down," said Nadine, abruptly interrupting her. "I've got to catch my breath."

Fiona grabbed a nearby chair and shoved it under her, with hardly a moment to spare. The beauty editor sat, knees splayed out, amidst her pile of bags. She looked like an upscale bag lady, despite her expensive designer pants and elaborately beaded sweater. She bore a strong resemblance to the homeless woman Lucy had spotted sheltering in a doorway a few feet from the hotel.

"Shall I start?" asked Phyllis, with a little bob of her head. "I mean, for Lucy here, I was thinking of that Bobbi Brown gloss, some mascara, but I think we should stick with a natural look she can maintain. . . ."

"Did you see the Dior show? They used a lot of color," said Nadine.

"Actually, I didn't. You went but I couldn't get away. It was too close to deadline."

"It was war paint," said Fiona, with a mischievous gleam in her eye. "Big jags of pink and green and yellow, smeared right across the models' noses."

"I certainly don't want that," began Lucy, until she thought of the ten thousand dollars. "But, of course, I trust your judgment."

Lurleen, on the other hand, was determined to stick to her guns. "I'm for the natural look," she said.

"I don't want a green nose, but I wouldn't mind some eye shadow," said Elizabeth.

"Pink's big this season," observed Nadine, opening the compact again.

"As eye shadow?" This was a new one to Lucy.

"It would make you look like you've got conjunctivitis," said Lurleen. "My three-year-old had it last week but, praise the Lord, I got it treated before it spread to the others."

"It was a miracle, that's what Mama said," added Faith, nodding piously.

Lucy thought it would be more miraculous if the child hadn't got conjunctivitis in the first place, but she was determined to be Miss Congeniality and held her tongue.

"Glitter," declared Nadine, patting yet more powder on her nose. "Glitter everywhere." She stopped, powder puff in midair, and sneezed. The compact flew across the room and landed at Elizabeth's feet, releasing a fine dust of powder that settled around it on the floor.

Elizabeth hopped out of the chair and retrieved it, politely returning it to Nadine.

Nadine didn't thank her but instead examined the compact for damage while continuing to throw out extreme suggestions. "Very, very dark lips. Almost black."

"Sounds great," said Elizabeth, brushing a bit of spilled powder off her hands and settling back in her chair. "Bring it on."

"Me, too," said Lucy, determined to play along.

"Trust me," said Fiona, spinning the chair so Lucy's back was to the mirror and reaching for a brush.

When they were finally allowed to see their reflections, Lucy was pleased to discover she still recognized herself. She even looked, she had to admit, improved in a subtle way, and she resolved to take a few minutes every morning to apply a bit of foundation and touch of mascara. She always wore lipstick but she now realized she hadn't been using the right color. The natural brownish gloss Fiona had applied was a lot more flattering than the bright pink she had been wearing.

Fiona and Phyllis had released them from the chairs and were distributing pink and white striped gift bags when they heard the voices of the next group in the outer office. Nadine ignored it, interested only in the contents of the bags.

"What are you giving them?" she asked, pouting.

"A nice assortment of basic cosmetics," said Phyllis,

practically cringing with fear. "It was all donated. Mostly Urban Decay for the girls and Lancôme for the moms."

"How come I didn't know about this?"

"You'd have to ask Camilla. She sent them down."

"Oh, all right then." Nadine dismissed them with a wave of the arm, and they left the studio, but as the door closed behind them they could hear Nadine coughing.

Ginny and Amanda were standing in the office, waiting their turn in the studio along with Maria and Carmela. If Lucy had any doubts that the make-up was a success they were erased when she saw Maria and Ginny's reaction. Both of them looked as if they'd like to kill her.

"You look fabulous, all of you," cooed Carmela. "I hope they do the same for us."

"I was pretty worried for a while there," said Lurleen, who looked years younger now that the dark circles under her eyes were hidden and her cheeks were rosy. "They were talking about giving us war paint."

Both Ginny and Maria seemed more than willing to don war paint, but before they could launch an offensive Lucy offered an olive branch. "They gave us gift bags," she said, holding hers up.

Lurleen also offered her gift bag for inspection, but the newcomers were quickly shooed into the studio.

"Where to now?" wondered Lucy, pulling the schedule out of her bag.

"Photo, again," said Faith. "For *after* photos."

"Lord, give me strength," prayed Lurleen.

"Amen," said Lucy.

Chapter Five

FOODS THAT ACTUALLY TAKE OFF POUNDS!

When Pablo finally finished photographing their newly made-up faces, Lucy was tired and hungry. She never would have guessed that posing was such hard work and had new respect for the models whose pictures filled the fashion magazines every month. She also wondered how they managed to stay so thin since she had worked up quite an appetite.

So far, she decided, the makeover had been surprisingly stressful. Like Lurleen, she had expected to be petted and pampered, but instead she'd spent the morning enduring Pablo's egotism, Camilla's abusive temper, and Nadine's rudeness. Add to that Elizabeth's determination to starve herself and the competitive atmosphere created by the ten-thousand-dollar prize and she was more than ready for a break. Fortunately, she'd arranged to meet Samantha Blackwell for lunch and was looking forward to spending a relaxing hour or two reminiscing about college.

"It's a working lunch," said Elizabeth, reading from the well-worn Xerox schedule. "Deli sandwiches and a motivational speaker in the boardroom."

Lucy stopped in her tracks. "But I have a lunch date with Sam," protested Lucy. The true horror of her situation was slowly dawning. "She promised to make her fabulous brownies for me, the ones with chocolate chunks, pecans, *and* icing."

"No way," said Elizabeth, shaking her head. "It's pastrami on rye with a big helping of team spirit."

"They'll never miss me."

Elizabeth stamped her foot. "Mom! What about the contest? You can't sneak away. You've got to participate to win. That's what you're always telling me. 'Showing up is ninety percent of success.' Right?"

Lucy hated it when her kids quoted her own words back at her, but she knew Elizabeth was right. She pulled out her cell phone and called Sam.

"I'm not surprised," said Sam, when Lucy told her she couldn't make it. "I figured they'd keep you busy. We'll do it another time."

"When?" wailed Lucy. "It's been more than twenty years."

"I know. It's pathetic. But I have an idea."

"Tell me."

"Nope. It's a surprise," said Sam. "Enjoy your lunch."

Nobody enjoyed the lunch. Lucy and Maria were the only ones who actually ate the oversized deli sandwiches which contained at least a pound of salty, highly seasoned meat. Lurleen regarded hers with suspicion, declaring she preferred white bread and mayonnaise to rye and mustard. Cathy followed the Atkins diet, eating all of the meat and none of the bread, and the others ignored the sandwiches entirely and nibbled on the pickles instead. The motivational speaker was a disappointment, too, offering a single message: You can choose to be happy or sad, so why not choose to be happy? She said it various ways, of course, but each rephrasing boiled down to the same idea. Most disappointing to Lucy, however, was the fact that none of the editors had bothered to show up.

"I could have gone to Sam's," she complained, as they boarded the bus that was taking them to the TV studio.

"Shh," cautioned Elizabeth, as the editors began filing onto the bus.

Lucy watched with interest as Phyllis followed Nadine, the beauty editor, carrying her assortment of bags like some sort of native bearer on a safari. She waited until Nadine had taken her place in a window seat and then arranged her bags on the seat beside her before leaving the bus. Phyllis wasn't going to the show, and the other editors Lucy had met were also conspicuously absent. There was no sign of Pablo or the art director, Nancy Glass, or the accessories editor, Deb Shertzer. Instead, Camilla took the front seat, accompanied by a large, almost mannish woman with very short hair wearing a severe gray pantsuit.

Lucy listened to the buzz in the bus. "Who's that?" "Camilla isn't . . . ?" "Oh no, I don't think so." "It would be ironic. . . ." "It would be a hoot!"

Finally, as the bus pulled away from the curb, Camilla stood up and began speaking into a microphone.

"Ladies! Your attention please. As you've probably guessed, we're all going to see the *Norah!* show!" She paused, dramatically holding up her free hand. "As featured guests! You're all going to be on TV and you're all going to meet Norah Hemmings, the fabulous Queen of Daytime TV, in person!"

This was greeted with excitement by the makeover winners, who cheered and applauded. Lucy, however, saw trouble ahead. She hadn't exactly been winning any popularity contests since Camilla noticed her boots and lobster watch at the *before* photo shoot, precipitating the unpopular decision to put them all in absurd regional costumes. To be honest, she certainly wouldn't blame Serena, who didn't share her daughter's enthusiasm for being photographed for a national magazine in a swimsuit, if she never forgave her. Ginny and Amanda had no trouble adopting the glum expressions from the Grant Wood painting; they hadn't appreciated being portrayed as country bumpkins in overalls. Maria and Carmela were enthusiastic sports fans and had enjoyed donning pinstriped New York Yankees uniforms, but Cathy and Tiffany made no attempt to conceal their loathing for the gold-lamé twirler costumes. Lurleen and Faith weren't happy about the Civil War–era hoop skirts they'd had to wear, either.

It wasn't Lucy's fault that Camilla had decided on the demeaning outfits, but she wasn't confident she could convince the others. And now she was pretty sure that the fact that she and Norah were, well, maybe not bosom buddies but definitely more than mere acquaintances, wouldn't sit well with them, either. Norah loved her summer home in Tinker's Cove and made a real effort to get know the locals; she was sure to mention the fact that she and Lucy were neighbors. Even more awkward was the on-again, off-again romance between Elizabeth and Norah's son Lance. The two had been good friends ever since he spent a year in the Tinker's Cove public school while Norah was involved in a nasty divorce.

"You will all be sitting in the front row," continued Camilla, "so put on your smiles, because if you watch the *Norah!* show you know how often the camera pans the audience, especially the lucky ones in the front. Also, our beauty editor Nadine Nelson will select one mother–daughter team to demonstrate the make-up techniques she used this morning."

Nadine, who was slumped in her seat, apparently dozing, didn't respond.

"Also, our fashion editor, let me introduce Elise Frazier. . . ."

The woman who was sitting next to Camilla lumbered to her feet and gave a curt nod. With her lumpish figure and understated business suit she didn't seem at all what Lucy expected a fashion editor to be like, but then, Lucy reminded herself, she didn't really know anything about fashion magazine editors, except for the handful she had met so far. But from the little she knew, Elise seemed to be the exception to the rule that they were obsessed with fashion and diet. Feeling a nudge from Elizabeth, Lucy turned her attention to Camilla, who was continuing to speak.

"Elise is going to choose one mother–daughter team to model outfits she has specially selected from our upcoming issue," she said, bending down so Elise could whisper in her ear.

Lucy imagined she could hear the wheels turning in the makeover winners' heads as they tried to figure out the best way to be chosen for special treatment.

Elise was scanning the group. "Elise tells me the clothes are size four. Confess, now, who wears size four?"

Carmela and Maria were waving their arms and practically jumping out of their seats.

"I guess we have our models, then," said Camilla. "Now, enjoy the ride. We'll be there in a few minutes."

"Sorry, honey," said Lucy, patting Elizabeth's hand. "I don't think I was ever a size four and I'm certainly not one now."

"I don't think Maria is either," said Elizabeth, as the bus pulled to a stop in front of a tall, gray stone building.

A line of women was behind a row of barriers, waiting to be admitted to the studio, and they watched enviously as the *Jolie* group was ushered ahead of them. Lucy wasn't used to such special treatment and found she enjoyed it, but she also felt a bit uncomfortable, as if she didn't really deserve it.

Sidra Rumford, née Finch and the daughter of Lucy's best friend Sue, was waiting to greet them in the hallway.

She was an assistant producer on the show and looked very professional, holding a clipboard and dressed in the New York uniform of a black pantsuit and pink blouse.

"Welcome to the *Norah!* show," she said. "And a special welcome to Lucy and Elizabeth, who are here from my own hometown, Tinker's Cove!"

All eyes were on them as they exchanged hugs and greetings; Lucy could practically feel little darts of jealousy pricking her through her thick plaid coat.

"Back home, we're all so proud of Sidra," she announced to the group in general, as they filed down the hall. "She's a real success story, and so is her husband, Geoff. They've both left our little town and have careers in the big city."

No one replied as they passed through a series of doors and eventually arrived in the studio, where they were seated in the front row, just as Camilla promised. A couple of make-up technicians immediately began touching up their faces with powder while Camilla and Elise consulted with Sidra. Nadine was nowhere to be seen.

After making a few notations on her clipboard, Sidra squared her shoulders and addressed the group. "There's been a change," she said. "Unfortunately, Nadine Nelson, who was going to do a make-up segment for the show, will be unable to appear today because of illness so we're going to have to scratch the beauty and fashion feature to accommodate our substitute guest."

The women groaned, politely, and Sidra held up her hand. "I'm really sorry about this. I know it's disappointing for the moms and daughters who were chosen, but I'm afraid it's unavoidable. You're all still going to be on TV, and Norah herself will introduce you all by name."

This pleased the women, who began patting their hair and checking their reflections in their pocket mirrors. All except for Lurleen and Faith, that is, who apparently didn't carry pocket mirrors and were too disappointed to bother to use them in any case. Maria and Carmela seemed to be taking it better, shrugging and chatting animatedly with each other.

"I wonder what's the matter with Nadine?" asked Cathy, who was seated next to Lucy.

"Probably the flu," said Lucy. "My friend told me there's an outbreak. I've been taking vitamin C."

"That's a good idea," said Cathy. "I'll get some. In fact, I'll get enough for everybody."

"That's a great idea," said Lucy, wishing she'd thought of it. It would have been a good way to rehabilitate her tarnished reputation.

Behind them, the audience members were beginning to file in. Cameramen and other technicians were taking their places and checking their equipment. It was all very casual and seemingly disorganized until suddenly the house lights went down and the familiar theme music came up, and Norah herself appeared, somehow looking larger than life as the audience burst into enthusiastic applause.

"We have a knockout show for you today," began Norah, listing guests including pop singer Beyoncé, sitcom star Trina Hamilton, and "a special segment on kitchen design—I know you're going to be interested in that because we all have to cook, right?"

Norah looked right into the camera and gave her signature moue, and the audience burst into laughter; she had them all in the palm of her hand and she hadn't even announced the free music CDs they'd all be getting.

"But first, I want to introduce our special guests—the winners of the *Jolie* magazine winter makeover for moms and daughters!"

Here we go, thought Lucy, as the hot spotlights hit them. They were so bright that she wanted to squint but reminded herself to smile instead as Norah approached and hugged her.

"I can't believe it!" exclaimed the star, standing between

Lucy and Elizabeth and holding them by the hand. "These are my neighbors from Tinker's Cove, in Maine, where I have a summer home. Lucy and Elizabeth Stone."

To Lucy it sounded as if the audience was applauding madly.

"New York is very different from Tinker's Cove, isn't it?"

"It sure is," said Lucy, suddenly finding herself speechless.

"Are you having a good time?"

"We sure are," said Lucy, nodding and smiling for all she was worth.

Norah turned to Elizabeth, who had suddenly gone pale. "Me, too," she managed to squeak, and Norah gave them each a parting hug before moving on. Lucy heard Norah proclaim that Cathy was from Texas, but the rest was a blur as she concentrated on collecting herself. Who would have thought that a brief moment on the small screen would have such an effect? Lucy's head was swimming, her heart was pounding, her mouth was dry as cotton, and her hands were sweaty. She reached over and took Elizabeth's hand; it was ice cold. "Whew," she whispered, hoping they were out of camera range.

"That was intense," said Elizabeth, also whispering.

The show went to commercials after Norah finished introducing the others—at least that's what Lucy assumed was going on as Norah settled herself in a chair and was immediately surrounded by hair and make-up technicians who made minute adjustments to her appearance. Sidra also appeared, escorting a nattily dressed man in his mid-fifties and seating him in the guest chair.

Then, Norah was sitting up straighter and talking into a camera.

"Have I got something amazing for you," she began, introducing a video clip. "Just you watch, you won't believe this."

The audience was directed to a series of video monitors

that hung from the ceiling where a model was demonstrating a state-of-the-art kitchen. Norah hadn't overstated the case; the kitchen was equipped with an oven that could hold a dish at refrigerator temperature all day until signaled by telephone to begin cooking and a refrigerator with a digital display that warned when milk and other staples were getting low. When the video was over, Norah introduced her guest, real estate developer Arnold Nelson.

"Now, Arnold, is this stuff for real?" asked Norah. "I mean, I want it, we all want it, don't we?" The audience, including Lucy, responded by clapping enthusiastically. Norah continued, "But where can we get it?"

"Well, Norah, these are the kitchens that we want to put in our new City Gate Towers, which we hope to build right here in New York on Governors Island."

Lucy leaned back, half dozing, as Arnold described the luxury condominiums that were going to be located on an island in New York harbor formerly used as a Coast Guard base.

"You're joshing me! You mean I can actually get a kitchen with all this space-age equipment right now?"

"In a year or two," answered Arnold, "if things go according to schedule. As you know, a citizens' committee is currently considering a variety of proposals for the island, and we're awaiting their recommendations. We certainly hope that City Gate Towers will be part of the final plan."

A second video began to run showing architects' drawings of the towers rising from the green and wooded island. The camera appeared to swoop around the towers, showing them in relation to landmarks including the Verrazzano Bridge, the Statue of Liberty, and the skyscrapers of Wall Street.

"That is a magnificent setting," cooed Norah. "Imagine waking up every morning to that view."

"And freshly prepared hot coffee, too, at the push of a remote button."

Norah's eyes bugged out, and the audience burst into applause.

"Our residents will have the whole city at their feet," continued Arnold, "but they'll also have the charm—and the security—of island living. It's absolutely unparalleled. There's nothing like it anywhere in the world."

"Well, sign me up," gushed Norah. "All that—and remote control coffee. It doesn't get better than that, does it?"

The audience jumped to their feet, clapping, and the cameras turned to pan them in preparation for another commercial break. Seated once again, Lucy found herself wondering about Norah's choice of Arnold as a guest. The segment had been little more than an infomercial for his development, but perhaps he was the best they could find as a last-minute substitute for Nadine.

"Do you believe it?" whispered Cathy.

"Some amazing kitchen," said Lucy, keeping her reservations to herself.

'No, I mean about Arnold."

"What about him?"

"He's Nadine's husband."

Lucy considered the implications of this. "At home, everybody knows everybody, but I didn't expect it to be like that in New York City."

"It isn't," said Cathy, lowering her voice as the house lights went down. "Here it's only everybody who's *anybody*."

As the show continued, Lucy wondered how the last-minute switch had been arranged. Had Nadine made a quick call from the bus when she realized she was too sick to go on? Lucy hadn't noticed if she had; she only remembered seeing her sleeping. Maybe she'd given a message to Phyllis, while she was helping her get settled on the bus, and she'd made the arrangements from her office. It all seemed less than entirely square to Lucy, who was used to following Ted's strict rules at the *Pennysaver* about keeping advertisements separate from editorial policy. She shrugged mentally. Maybe TV had different standards from newspapers; she really didn't know.

Then Beyoncé was singing, and then the show was suddenly over; everybody was on their feet, applauding madly. Even Lurleen and Faith had forgotten their earlier disappointment and were smiling and clapping.

The high spirits engendered by the show continued as they all boarded the waiting bus for the ride to the hotel, where they would have an hour to rest and change for dinner and a promised Broadway show. Petty jealousies and rivalries were forgotten as Maria treated everyone to a medley of songs about New York, finally getting them all to join in for a rousing chorus of "New York, New York."

A wave of tiredness overcame Lucy as she disembarked from the bus and crossed the hotel lobby, but she was surprised when Elizabeth's steps dragged, too. She was beginning to wonder if she was coming down with the flu when the desk clerk called her name.

The others, who were gathered by the elevator, watched curiously as he presented her with a couple of square, white envelopes. Lurleen, whose eyes were practically popping out of her head, couldn't restrain herself. "What's that?" she demanded. "How come we didn't all get them?"

Lucy examined the envelopes, which were addressed to her and Elizabeth in calligraphic script. "I don't know," she said, turning them over. Seeing the name and address of the sender, she smiled. "It's nothing to do with the magazine," she said. "It's from my friend who lives in New York."

"They look like invitations," said Cathy. "A wedding, maybe?"

"I don't think so. I haven't heard anything about a wedding." Lucy was wondering what was keeping the elevator. She wanted to open the envelopes in private, in her room.

"Goodness, we're all forgetting our manners," said Ginny. "Lucy doesn't need to share her private mail with us."

"I think it's some sort of joke," said Lucy. "Probably one of those funny greeting cards."

The arrow next to the elevator was alight, signaling it was on its way down.

"I could use a joke," said Cathy.

"Oh, all right," said Lucy, slipping her finger under the envelope flap and pulling out an engraved cardboard square. The others were clustered around, craning their necks and reading over her shoulder.

"Oh my," she said, breaking into a big smile. "It is an invitation. To a ball at the Metropolitan Museum of Art. Tomorrow night."

"The AIDS gala," said Cathy, as the doors slid open.

The women crowded aboard, surging ahead of Lucy and Elizabeth, who found themselves outside, looking in at a full car.

"Sorry, no room," chirped Lurleen, as the doors closed.

Lucy and Elizabeth stood in place, looking at each other, then they burst into giggles. "A ball!" exclaimed Elizabeth, jumping up and down with excitement. "There'll be famous people, fabulous dresses . . ."

"Oh dear," said Lucy, her heart sinking as they stepped into an empty elevator. "We don't have a thing to wear!"

Chapter Six

LUXE LOOKS FOR LESS!

When the clock radio woke Lucy on Tuesday morning, she doubted there was much chance of getting Elizabeth out of bed. She refused to even open her eyes, instead putting a pillow over her head to block the music and burrowing deeper under the covers.

"You'll miss breakfast," warned Lucy, but there was no answer.

Lucy could barely remember the days when she preferred sleep to food and could only dimly remember the days when a day off meant sleeping until noon. Although, she admitted to herself as she stretched and got out of bed, she could use another hour or two of sleep herself. The magazine was certainly keeping them busy—they hadn't got back to the hotel from the theater until well past eleven the night before.

Stopping at the window to check the weather—gray and cold, what did she expect?—Lucy noticed the invitations to the ball that were perched on the sill. She'd tried to call Sam last night, but all she'd gotten was a busy signal. Her cell phone was also on the sill, charging completed, so she took it with her into the bathroom.

"I'm sorry to call so early," she began, when Sam answered in a groggy voice.

"No, no. I'm up, I'm just not awake yet."

"Same here," said Lucy, chuckling. "I got the invitations. . . ."

"Are you coming? Please! I've been working on it for months, and I know you'll have a great time. All sorts of famous people are coming; there'll be music and dancing and fabulous food. It's going to be *the* social event of the season, at least I hope it is."

"Since when did you become a party planner?" asked Lucy, perching on the edge of the tub.

"Don't ask," groaned Sam. "I got stuck when our fundraiser left for another job. This isn't the sort of thing I usually do at all, and I don't really like it. I prefer working with clients, making policy, stuff like that. This has been horrible, which is why I really, really want to see some friendly, supportive faces, like yours."

"Oh, believe me, I'd love to come but Elizabeth and I don't have anything to wear."

"No problem," said Sam. "Do what I did. Go to a consignment shop. You can pick up designer duds cheap, and you can even return them the next day."

Lucy was shocked. She couldn't imagine Sam doing anything so tacky as buying a dress for a special occasion only to return it afterward.

"No, it's okay. They don't mind. That's how these consignment shops work. You won't get back as much as you paid, but it's still a good deal."

"The other problem is the makeover. The schedule's brutal, and I'm trying to win this ten-thousand-dollar prize for the best makeover so Elizabeth can go back to college next semester. I can't go sneaking away to a ball."

"*Au contraire*, Lucy. It just so happens that *Jolie* magazine has a table. Camilla Keith's coming, along with several other editors. This is your chance to wow them."

Lucy's mind was spinning. "If they're at the ball, they're not going to be with the makeover winners on the 'round-the-island dinner cruise. . . ."

"So you'll come?"

"Sure," said Lucy. "So where's this consignment shop?"

When Lucy got downstairs there was only a scattering of people, mostly dressed in business attire, in the dining room, but she spotted two familiar faces. Lucy would have preferred to sit by herself but decided it might be viewed as impolite, so after helping herself to fruit salad and yogurt from the buffet she joined Ginny and Serena at their table.

"Where is everybody?" she asked, as the waiter filled her cup with coffee.

"The girls wanted to get an extra hour of sleep," said Ginny.

"Elizabeth, too." Lucy yawned and took a sip of coffee. "Frankly, I could use a bit more sleep myself."

"I know the feeling," agreed Serena. "My biological clock hasn't adjusted to Eastern time. It's seven-thirty for you but it's more like four-thirty for me. I fell asleep during that massage yesterday."

"How was the spa?"

"Very relaxing," said Ginny. "It was the best part so far."

"I'm really looking forward to it," said Lucy. "I don't know how people keep up this pace. Things are a lot slower in Tinker's Cove."

"I could never live in the city."

"Me either," agreed Serena. "Everybody's in such a hurry here. They don't know how to relax and chill."

"And they're so rude," said Ginny.

"I think it's the weather," said Serena. "It's so cold and there's not enough sunshine. It makes people irritable and depressed."

"Have you seen the subway? I'd sure be depressed if I had to face that every day. It's so dirty and nasty. The streets are dirty, too. We wouldn't tolerate it in Omaha."

"I guess it's just a by-product of city life," said Lucy. "So many people and cars in a small space."

"It doesn't seem healthy to me."

"Well, believe it or not, New Yorkers are supposed to be the healthiest people in the country because they're so fit. They walk miles every day. And they also consume less energy. Big cities are actually good for the environment."

From their expressions it was clear that Ginny and Serena didn't believe her.

"It's true," insisted Lucy. "Look at Maria and Carmela—they look fabulous."

"They sure don't hide their figures," said Serena, smoothing her Juicy Couture tangerine hoodie over her ample bosom.

"You'd get arrested if you dressed like that in Omaha," said Ginny, adjusting her turtleneck. "Yesterday you could actually see Carmela's bra. What was she thinking, wearing a black bra under a sheer white blouse?"

"What was her mother thinking, letting her out of the house like that?" Serena's vehemence shocked Lucy, who had yet to see Ocean with her belly covered.

"Not that Maria is much better. I don't know how she gets in and out of those skirts. They're so tight they look like she sprays them on."

"And those nails! They must be two inches long. How can she do anything?"

"Mine break," said Lucy, with a sigh, opening the morning paper. The headline wasn't encouraging: FLU DEATHS RISE.

"I hate stories like this," said Lucy, showing the others. "What are you supposed to do? Stop breathing?"

"Wash your hands," said Ginny.

"Take vitamin C," offered Serena. "And echinacea."

"That's all well and good, but somebody can still sneeze in your face, like Nadine. She was sneezing and coughing all over the place yesterday."

"Do you think she has the flu?" asked Ginny.

"I wouldn't be surprised," said Lucy, spooning up a big chunk of vitamin-C-rich grapefruit.

When Lucy and Elizabeth arrived at the *Jolie* offices, Lucy was relieved to discover they'd been paired with Cathy and Tiffany for wardrobe consultations. She hadn't much liked listening to Serena and Ginny's complaints about the city and she suspected their comments about Maria and Carmela had more to do with racism than fashion choices. Lurleen and Faith, on the other hand, were sweet and nonjudgmental, but Lucy feared that given half a chance they would try to convert her to their evangelical faith.

Cathy was breezy and cheerful as ever as they made their way to the fashion department, and Lucy suspected her positive attitude was bolstered by the mink coat and five-carat diamond ring she was wearing, not to mention the Hermes Kelly bag she was carrying. Lucy didn't believe you could buy happiness, but she figured a well-padded bank account could smooth a lot of bumps in the rocky road of life.

She was also impressed that Cathy got along so well with her stepdaughter Tiffany, even though the two were close enough in age to be sisters. At least that was the impression she got from their body language and relaxed banter.

"I wonder what they're planning to dress us in?" mused Lucy as they stepped into the elevator that would take them up several floors to the fashion department. "I didn't see anything at the fashion show that I could possibly wear."

"You better be ready for feathers and see-through net dresses, if that make-up session yesterday was any indication," said Cathy. "That Nadine wanted to put a green stripe across my nose."

"And she wanted to give me blue lipstick," added Tiffany, giggling.

"I think she gave me the flu," said Elizabeth, who looked as if she'd like to go back to bed.

"That reminds me," said Cathy, digging through the fabulous purse as if it were just a plastic number from Wal-Mart, "I've got vitamins for everybody." She finally produced two bottles of vitamin C and gave them to Elizabeth and Lucy as the elevator doors slid open.

Fashion editor Elise Frazier was in the hallway, ready to greet them, dressed again today in a mannish pantsuit. "Welcome, welcome to the fashion department," she said in a flat voice as if she were reciting a tired refrain. "Here we believe we can make every woman look fabulous no matter what her shape or figure flaws."

"So much for all those hours at the gym," joked Cathy.

"Oh, you know what I mean," replied Elise, who was shaped rather like an NFL fullback. "We can all use a little help. I wear heels to make my legs look longer, and I always dress in one color from head to toe because it makes me look slimmer."

"At least that's the theory," muttered Elizabeth, getting a giggle from Tiffany and a sharp look from her mother.

"Oh, here's our accessories editor, Deb Shertzer," trilled Elise. "If you ask me, she's got the best job at the magazine. Shoes, scarves, bags—her office is like Aladdin's cave. You should see the jewelry."

Looking at Elise, Lucy thought her enthusiasm for accessories rang a bit hollow, considering she wasn't wearing a single piece of jewelry and her shoes were simple black pumps with sturdy heels.

"As jobs go, it's not too hard to take," replied Deb, with a sparkle in her eye. Unlike most of the women working at the magazine she was wearing flats, and her black slacks and colorful sweater looked both attractive and comfortable. She turned to Lucy and gave her a big smile. "You're the one with the lobster watch, aren't you?"

Elizabeth looked as if she'd like to disappear.

"It was just a joke present from my husband," said Lucy, sliding up her sleeve to give a better view of the red plastic timepiece. "He got it free at the hardware store."

"Well I think it's adorable," said Deb. "A lot of designers are coming out with similar ideas for summer. There's one that has a beach umbrella on the face and a smiley yellow sun on the hour hand. I'm going to feature it in the June accessories roundup."

Lucy gave Elizabeth rather a smug look.

"Well, come along and we'll get started," said Elise, leading them into a large room filled with racks of clothes. A cluster of portable screens were arranged at one end to serve as changing rooms, along with a three-sided mirror. "If you ladies don't mind, it would be a lot easier if you'd strip down to your undies, but we have arranged dressing rooms, if you'd prefer."

"Not a problem for me," said Lucy, shrugging out of her coat. "I put on clean underpants this morning."

"Mom," groaned Elizabeth, sinking into a chair.

"It was just a joke," said Lucy, bending down to unlace her duck boots.

"Well, well, I see we don't have to disguise anything," said Elise, looking her up and down. "You have a very trim shape—not a saddlebag in sight." She narrowed her eyes, and Lucy found herself tucking her bottom in and straightening her back. "I think we can try to give you a bit more height; black is good for that."

She turned to Deb, who was sitting on a folding chair with a notebook in her lap. "And heels, of course."

Deb nodded and wrote it down.

Elise turned to Elizabeth, who was slowly divesting herself of her clothing as if it was a painful task. "Such a sweet face," she crooned. "We can give you a bit more sophistication. Something with couture details, and I think black would really set off your lovely pale skin."

Tiffany was next to Elizabeth, slumping a bit to disguise her height. She didn't fool Elise, however. "You're so tall, you could carry a fuller skirt. I have just the thing in black net. We'll top it with a silky turtleneck over a good padded bra."

Tiffany shot her a murderous look but Elise missed it, moving on to Cathy. "Those hours in the gym have certainly paid off for you!" she exclaimed. "Definitely something to show off those toned arms." She stepped back, her hand on her chin. "Though with those boobs we have to be careful—definitely no turtlenecks; they'll make you look like you've got three chins, and we need something fitted at the waist." She clucked her tongue. "I really do think silicone is a bad idea. Those doctors tend to go overboard."

"Hey!" protested Cathy, pointing to her lacey black bra, "this is all me. I didn't have surgery."

Elise looked doubtful. "Right. I'm so sorry. I certainly didn't mean to insult you."

"I'm beginning to feel like a human pincushion," complained Cathy. "First it was Camilla making that crack about trophy wives and now you're knocking my boobs."

Elise drew herself up to her full height, a sight that reminded Lucy of a dragon in some animated Disney film. "I'll thank you not to criticize Camilla. The woman's a genius—and she happens to be one of my best friends."

Glancing at Deb, who was going through a box of scarves, Lucy thought she detected a smirk.

"She may be your friend," said Cathy, "but you have to admit she can be bitchy. Everyone knows that."

Elise was getting quite red in the face, and Lucy was afraid she'd begin breathing fire. "Friendship is a wonderful thing," she said, hoping to defuse the situation. "I think women especially need friends, for a support system. I don't know what I'd do without my friends."

"I met Camilla in college," said Elise, flipping furiously through a rack of clothes. "We were in the same class at Barnard. Nadine, too, and we've been friends ever since."

"Like the Heathers," said Cathy, with a wicked gleam in her eye.

Lucy wished she'd let it drop, but Elise either didn't hear the comment or decided to let it pass. "Now where is that pinstripe pantsuit?" she muttered, marching over to another rack.

The rest of the morning passed without further fireworks between Elise and Cathy, and the women were soon outfitted and accessorized. Lucy had to admit she looked great in the pantsuit and high-heeled boots Elise chose for her, and she was thrilled to learn they would all be able to keep their outfits, even though she couldn't quite imagine what sort of occasion in Tinker's Cove would require such a dressy ensemble.

Cathy, on the other hand, wasn't impressed. "I always wear designer," she said, with a sniff. "I haven't worn anything off the rack since I can't remember when."

"Oh, I can tell you," snapped Elise, unable to resist getting in another dig. "I'll bet it was when you married Mr. Montgomery."

Lucy expected Cathy to answer with sharp retort but, instead, she smiled at Tiffany. "Mr. Montgomery is a generous husband, and father, isn't he? He always says he's got great-looking girls and he wants us to have pretty clothes."

Hearing this, Elise looked fit to be tied. "If you'll be so kind as to take these things off so I can label them for tomorrow's photo shoot I would appreciate it," she said, speaking to the room in general and avoiding eye contact.

*   *   *

Back in their own clothes, Lucy and Elizabeth made a break for the exit. They had to get dresses for tonight's ball and were planning to use the lunch break to make a quick trip to the designer consignment shop. They were on their way when they encountered Fiona in the elevator.

"Aren't you coming to lunch?' she asked, noticing they were wearing their coats. "They've got a top dermatologist talking about skin care."

"No lunch for us, we're going shopping," said Elizabeth.

"Do you have anyplace particular in mind?"

"Actually, we do," said Lucy. "It's a consignment shop on Sixty-sixth Street."

"Brilliant!" exclaimed Fiona. "Do you mind if I tag along?"

"Please do. We can use your expert advice," said Lucy.

Since time was short Lucy splurged on a cab, and they all piled in together for the ride uptown.

"So how do you like the makeover so far?" asked Fiona.

"It's pretty intense," said Lucy. "Especially with this contest."

"It's exhausting," said Elizabeth.

Lucy quickly added, "But we're loving every minute."

"You don't have to put on a brave face for me," said Fiona. "I'm just the hired help, and if things work out I won't be at *Jolie* much longer."

"Are you looking for another job?" asked Elizabeth.

Fiona was looking out the window. "You could say that."

"I don't blame you," said Lucy. "It must be very stressful working there. It's a very tense atmosphere, at least it seems that way to me. Maybe all fashion magazines are like that."

"Not the ones that are making money," said Fiona.

"Is *Jolie* in trouble?" asked Lucy.

"You bet. And Camilla with it. The publisher gave her

an ultimatum that she has to turn a profit in six months or else."

"Or else what?"

"Heads will roll," said Fiona, drawing a finger across her throat. "But I bet it won't be hers."

"Why not?" asked Elizabeth. "She's the boss, after all."

"She's also a survivor. She's very good at rising above the fray. I think she'll fix it so that people she doesn't like, like Pablo and Nancy, will be blamed. The ones who actually have good ideas and work hard will get the ax and she and her Barnard buddies will probably get raises."

"So much cynicism in one so young," said Lucy

"Listen, I come from the land of Henry VIII and Richard III. Treachery is like mother's milk to me." She looked up as the taxi pulled to a halt in front of the pink and white striped awning of the New to You thrift boutique. "I also love a bargain. Did you ever hear how Henry VIII snagged Hampton Court?"

That night, as she climbed up the steps to the Metropolitan Museum of Art on Fifth Avenue, Lucy could easily imagine that she was attending a royal ball. The museum's classical stone façade was illuminated with floodlights, and strains of music could be heard as they joined the elegantly dressed throng gathered at the door. Once inside, Lucy was overwhelmed by the magnificent great hall, decorated with enormous Christmas trees and floral arrangements; the buzz of voices; and the conflicting scents of perfume.

"Now that we're here, what do we do?" asked Elizabeth. She sounded nervous, despite the fact that she looked lovely in a floaty blue Stella McCartney number.

"Let's cruise around and get something to drink," said Lucy, catching a glimpse of Sam across the room, earnestly engaged in conversation with a photographer. "Maybe we'll run into somebody we know."

"Mom, that's Donald Trump."

"So it is," said Lucy, who had to resist the impulse to gawk.

"And that's Ashton Kutcher."

"Who?" Lucy had spotted a waiter holding a tray of champagne flutes. "Oh my gosh, that's Mikhail Baryshnikov helping himself to champagne."

"Who?"

Lucy was looking for Sam but it was Norah who took them by surprise, engulfing them both in a lavender satin embrace.

"You girls sure clean up nice," she exclaimed. "Isn't this amazing? I bet you've never seen anything like this in Tinker's Cove."

"That's for sure," agreed Lucy.

"If I'm not mistaken, you're wearing Donna Karan. I've got that dress myself."

"It's the first designer dress I've ever worn," confessed Lucy, pleased to have her good taste confirmed. She lowered her voice to a whisper. "I got it at a thrift shop."

"Good for you!"

"Even so, it was awfully expensive. Bill would die if he knew how much I spent."

"Never you mind. You can take it back tomorrow. But tonight, you look like it was made for you."

"Thanks, Norah," said Lucy, stepping aside as Camilla joined their little circle and exchanged air kisses with Norah. She was dressed in a black sheath that emphasized her slimness, with an oversized white ruffle at the neck; Lucy thought it made her look like Cruella De Vil.

"Don't you all look fabulous!" exclaimed Camilla. "I can see my staff has done wonders with, uh, you two girls."

Lucy wasn't about to introduce herself yet again if Camilla couldn't be bothered to remember her name. "What, this?"

she said, indicating her dress. "I just pulled it out of my suitcase."

Norah winked and drifted off to chat with another friend.

Camilla watched her go but could hardly run after her. Left with these nobodies, she fingered Elizabeth's dress. "I do so love Stella McCartney. Such a bright talent. Did you get it here or in London?"

"Here," said Elizabeth. "She's my favorite designer."

"I haven't seen you at one of these affairs before," said Camilla, her eyes darting around the room. "Do you get to the city often?"

"To Boston," said Lucy. "Not New York."

"Boston is such a quaint little town. Who do you know there?"

"Lots of people," said Elizabeth, thinking of her friends at Chamberlain College.

Lucy knew that Camilla was probing purposefully, trying to ascertain Lucy's social status, and she was willing to play the game. "Junior Read is a dear friend," she said, referring to the Pioneer Press publisher who had a summer home in Tinker's Cove. It wasn't such a stretch; she'd helped him out of a tight spot a year or two ago.

"Mom, I see Lance," said Elizabeth, suddenly becoming quite perky.

Lucy followed her gaze and saw Norah's son consulting the seating chart. She tended to still think of him as the gangly middle-schooler who had been Elizabeth's first boyfriend and was shocked to see how elegant he looked dressed in a tux. The garish dyed hair he sported as a kid was gone, replaced with a fashionable close buzz cut, and he looked relaxed and confident.

"Run along," said Lucy. "Have a good time."

Elizabeth departed in a flutter of fashionable blue tatters and was embraced enthusiastically by Lance.

"That's Norah's son, isn't it?" asked Camilla.

"They're old friends," said Lucy.

"From school? I believe Lance went to Exeter," said Camilla, naming the prestigious prep school.

"Right, from school," said Lucy, not finding it necessary to mention that they'd met at Tinker's Cove Middle School.

"So what do you do?" asked Camilla, continuing her investigation.

"I'm active in civic affairs," said Lucy, telling herself it wasn't a lie since she covered town events as a reporter for the local newspaper. "And I lunch with friends," she added, thinking of the numerous peanut butter sandwiches she'd enjoyed with Sue and Pam and Rachel. "You know the sort of thing: mostly fund-raising for local charities." Lucy was a mainstay of the Hat and Mitten Fund committee, which provided warm clothing for the little town's less fortunate children.

"We really ought to do a feature on you country ladies," mused Camilla. "We tend to forget that there's life beyond the city."

"Ah, Camilla! Great to see you."

Lucy's eyes widened as she recognized Arnold Nelson, who she'd seen on the *Norah!* show, and waited for Camilla to introduce her.

"Arnold, this is uh, one of our makeover winners."

Lucy took his hand. "I'm Lucy Stone, from Maine."

"Nice to meet you. I hope you'll do me the honor of dancing with me."

"I'd love to," said Lucy, seizing the opportunity to avoid more of Camilla's probing questions. She was irked that the woman couldn't be bothered to remember her name but could easily recall which prep school Lance Hemmings attended. It just showed her priorities.

Her irritation soon vanished, however, as Arnold spun her around the room in an elegant waltz. He was an excellent dancer, and it was a bit like being in a dream, dancing in the arms of this wealthy man who smelled so good, even if he was a bit thick in the middle and had a jowly chin.

"I saw you yesterday, on the TV show," began Lucy, intending to ask him about the City Gate Towers project he hoped to build on Governors Island.

"You know, you don't look at all like someone who needs a makeover," said Arnold, promptly changing the subject. "You look pretty fine as you are."

"Oh, this is after. You should have seen me before," joked Lucy.

"I'd really like to see you after," said Arnold, his voice deepening. "I've got a bottle of champagne on ice at my penthouse and a fresh delivery of caviar from my Russian friend Ivan. Have you ever tasted caviar?"

"I have and I don't like it," said Lucy, wondering if this was a pass.

"Ah, then you've never had really good caviar," said Arnold. "I'd love to introduce you to it. What do you say? A man can get awfully lonely up on the thirty-seventh floor."

Enough was enough, decided Lucy, determined to put an end to Arnold's propositions as the orchestra played the final chords of the waltz.

"How is Nadine?" she asked. "She seemed so miserable yesterday. I thought she might have this flu that's in the news."

"The doctors are puzzled," he said, turning abruptly to follow a willowy blond model Lucy recognized from the fashion show.

Left to her own devices, Lucy decided to check out the buffet of hors d'oeuvres. She figured it would be a deviled-eggs-free zone, and she was right. She was considering trying a piece of sushi, something she'd never had, when she finally spotted Sam. She would have known her anywhere, she realized with amazement. Even in a fancy evening gown Sam was still Sam, with short red hair, oversized eyeglasses and a huge smile. What was surprising, however, was that she was accompanied by two men, one of whom was Geoff Rumford, Sidra's husband.

After hugs, Sam began the introductions. "Lucy, meet my husband, Brad. . . ."

"It's about time," said Lucy, giving him a hug.

"And I understand you know Geoff from home?"

"I sure do. But how do you know him? It seems incredible to me that two of my friends would meet in a big city like New York."

"New York's big, all right, but it's made up of circles of interest. People who are interested in the same things keep on bumping into each other," said Sam.

"Brad and I met when we were both panelists at a community forum about public education," said Geoff.

"This is the last place I ever expected to see you," said Lucy, remembering Geoff as a suntanned lobsterman in Tinker's Cove.

"He's a tagalong, like me," said Brad, wrapping his arms around his wife's waist. "Sam lassoed me into this. She said if she had to organize it there was no way I wasn't going to come."

"And I'm here because Norah needed to fill her table and drafted Sidra."

"Well, a man's gotta do what a man's gotta do," said Lucy.

"This is weird," said Geoff. "By day I'm a mild-mannered high school science teacher; by night, a man about town."

"I'm sure you fill both roles admirably," said Lucy. "How about you, Brad? Do you get to affairs like this very often?"

"Too often," he said, glumly.

"It's not as bad as all that. The food's good," said Sam, punching his arm.

"And there are plenty of pretty girls to look at," said Lucy.

"So long as he only looks," said Sam.

"You don't need to worry there. I have to save my energy. I'm going to be dragging tomorrow morning, and I've got an early morning meeting."

"Governors Island?" asked Geoff. When Brad nodded, he continued, "How's that going? I heard something about a proposal for a maritime trades high school."

Lucy turned to Sam, hoping to catch up with her news while the men talked shop, but she had spotted trouble across the room. "Sorry, Lucy, I've got to get Lady Warburton away from the bar before she disgraces herself. . . . Call me!"

Lucy gave her a little wave and watched as she steered a tottery old woman with an elaborate hairdo over to the buffet, then turned her attention to Brad.

"Everybody's got proposals," he was saying, "but nobody's got funding, except Arnold Nelson. He could break ground tomorrow while everybody else is scrambling, writing grants, and trying to raise money."

"How does he do it?" asked Geoff.

"Glamour," said Brad, nodding sagely. "He works events like this; he uses his wife's contacts at that fashion magazine. Sam tells me the ladies on the ball committee have all invested in Nelco and can hardly talk about anything else."

Lucy found Nelson in the crowd, dancing with a very tall brunette in a short red dress. She had thrown her head back, and her mouth was open in a laugh as if he'd just said something wonderfully clever. "He just looks sleazy to me," she said with a shrug, "but he sure gets around. He was on Norah's show yesterday, pushing that City Gate project."

"Nelco? Is that his outfit?" asked Geoff.

"Yeah. Have you heard something?" asked Brad.

Geoff considered. "Maybe. If it's the same outfit. Could be Felco or Welco—they all sound the same to me."

"Run it by me and I'll check it out," said Brad.

"Well," began Geoff. The band began playing a loud rock tune, and Lucy and Brad stepped closer to hear. "If it's the same outfit, they're building that new biomedical research lab for NYU. It's a Level 4 infectious diseases facility, and it would be one of only a handful in the country. It's desperately needed but I heard there's been all kinds of problems."

"Shoddy construction? Contract disputes?" asked Brad.

"No. Nothing like that. Vandalism. Sand in the gas tanks, brake lines cut, stuff like that. It's really vicious. There have even been death threats. It's got to the point where suppliers and truckers don't want to have anything to do with it."

"It could be neighbors," said Lucy. "They might be afraid of having a germy old lab in the neighborhood."

"I'd put my money on the unions," said Brad. "There's a lot of frustration out there. Even the cops and firefighters are threatening strikes."

"I know there's some concern that Nelco or whoever it is will pull out, which would delay the project, maybe even kill it." Geoff drained his beer. "That would've been a perfect project for Governors Island, you know, instead of Arnold's pricey condos. What happened to the public–private partnership we heard so much about? I thought the private developers were going to fund some of the public projects in exchange for permission to build."

"They all dropped out when the federal government established the national park and started allowing public access. It was the inaccessibility, the exclusivity that had appeal. Now they're saying nobody's going to pay millions for a ritzy address if the hoi polloi can picnic on the lawn. The only one left is Arnold, and he's playing hardball."

"What's the big deal? Access is still very limited, just Saturdays in the summer."

Brad shrugged. "It doesn't bother Arnold, that's for

sure. He'll wring a sweet deal out of the city and make a bundle. Subsidized housing for millionaires."

Lucy smiled as Sidra joined their group, looking chic in a shimmering satin column of a dress. "If only your mother could see you now," she said, giving her a hug. "She'd be so proud."

"She wouldn't believe it," said Sidra, laughing. "We used to squabble all the time over my fashion choices." She put her hand on her husband's arm. "I'm sorry, but I have to drag Geoff away. He has to get up early tomorrow, and I promised I wouldn't keep him out too late."

They all said their farewells, then Brad asked Lucy to dance, saying he felt quite neglected by his wife, who was too busy making sure the event ran smoothly to pay any attention to him. He wasn't as good a dancer as Arnold, but Lucy enjoyed herself a lot more. When the orchestra played the final song, "I Could Have Danced All Night," Lucy wished the evening would never end.

Chapter Seven

FAB FASHIONS TO DIE FOR!

Unlike Cinderella, Lucy had both her shoes next morning and her Prince Charming was keeping the home fires burning in Tinker's Cove. Today was the final day of the makeover, and she needed to make the most of it if she was going to have any chance of winning the ten thousand dollars, she thought, hurrying over to the one-hour dry cleaners on Third Avenue with the consignment shop dresses.

She wasn't quite sure when she was going to manage to pick them up and get them back to the shop, but she was determined to try despite today's hectic schedule. This morning all the makeover winners were supposed to get their hair done at one of New York's swankiest salons, Rudolf's, in preparation for the afternoon shoot of the "after" photos. That evening the award dinner was planned, followed by the holiday show at Radio City Music Hall, and the makeover would officially be over. Tomorrow she would return home to tackle the sink full of dirty dishes and the mountain of laundry that she was certain awaited her.

The very thought was depressing, and she let out a big sigh as she laid the dresses on the counter in the dry cleaning shop.

"So the party's over," chuckled the clerk, a black woman with a round face and a big smile.

"You can say that again," said Lucy, a bit surprised at how regretful she sounded. After all, she missed Bill and the kids and even the dog, Libby. She couldn't wait to see them. Really. But experience had taught her that even a brief absence could require some painstaking work repairing relationships. The dog, for example, would wag her tail in glee when they returned, but then she'd refuse to come when called or would scatter her food all over the kitchen floor. The same went for the girls. They would greet her enthusiastically when she arrived, but then the tales of woe would begin: "I couldn't find my long underwear" or "Dad wouldn't let me go to the movies with my friends" or even her all-time favorite, "I think I'm getting leprosy." Bill would make her pay, too, in subtle ways. He'd forget to mail the mortgage payment or would flare up angrily over some trifle or would want to know why she never baked apple pie from scratch anymore.

Truth be told, she wouldn't mind spending a few more days in the city. She'd really enjoyed the hustle and bustle of the streets, where the honking horns of the cabs expressed the impatience everybody seemed to share. She'd also enjoyed the chambermaid service at the hotel, where she didn't even have to make her bed. But best of all, she realized, was the attention she'd received from the magazine's experts. Until now, nobody, herself included, had expressed any concern about the shape of her eyebrows or the condition of her skin. Well, except for Sue, who provided a running critique of her appearance. But Sue was always negative, while the people at the magazine had been a lot more positive. It was "this color becomes you," or "try this lipstick," or "let's bring that hem down an inch and see how it looks," which was a lot easier to take than Sue's constant carping. It had been nice to think of herself for a change.

And, of course, there was the ball. The flowers, the music, the food, the dancing, the clothes . . . it had all been wonderful, a once-in-a-lifetime experience, and she'd never forget it.

"Do you want these dresses in an hour or is one o'clock okay?" asked the clerk, bringing Lucy back to reality.

"One is fine," she said, taking the ticket and hurrying back to the hotel, stopping in a coffee shop to get an enormous bagel and a couple of coffees to go. They were due at Rudolf's in less than an hour and, since there hadn't been any earthquakes this morning, she was prepared to bet money that Elizabeth was still asleep.

So sound asleep, in fact, that she didn't stir when Lucy came into the room.

"Come on, honey. We've got a photo shoot today."

"I'm tired."

"Well, what do you expect when you dance all night and drink a gallon of champagne?"

"Didn't."

"Don't try to pretend you weren't drinking," said Lucy, carefully setting the paper cup of coffee on the tiny nightstand. "I saw you with a glass of champagne. I don't know how they get away with serving underage drinkers, but I didn't see any of the servers asking for ID."

"Mom, I think I'm sick. I ache all over."

"Even a glass or two could give you a hangover because you're not used to it."

"I only had a sip or two."

"Really?" Lucy couldn't help thinking of the headline announcing the flu epidemic's rising death toll.

"Yeah. And I've got this bite on my hand that really hurts." She held out her right hand, which was swollen and had a nasty red bump. "There's no bugs in winter, are there?"

"I don't know. Maybe city bugs are different," said Lucy. "Drink some coffee."

"Maybe some water?"

Lucy went into the bathroom to fill a glass for Elizabeth,

and when she returned she discovered the girl had fallen asleep again. She pressed her hand against Elizabeth's forehead and was relieved to find it was cool.

"Come on, honey." Lucy shook her shoulder. "You've got to get up."

The girl's eyes finally opened and she managed to take a sip or two of water. Then, very unsteadily, she made her way to the bathroom.

"Demon rum," muttered Lucy, unaware that she sounded exactly like her great-grandmother, a founding member of the Women's Christian Temperance Union.

Elizabeth seemed to rally when they arrived at Rudolf's exclusive Fifth Avenue salon, where customers were greeted by a constantly flowing wall of water before being ushered into a luxurious waiting area where they were offered a choice of fresh coffee or herbal tea. Not that they had to wait very long; Lucy had only taken a sip of two of coffee before she was whisked into a private treatment room by a white-coat beautician.

Once Lucy was installed in the chair and covered with a smock, the beautician, an Asian girl with flawless tan skin and long, glossy black hair, began examining Lucy's hair.

"Too dry," was her verdict, "and your color is not flattering."

"Really?"

"You need something warmer, a little red perhaps."

Lucy didn't like the sound of this. "Not red."

"Trust me, you'll see," said the beautician, busily squeezing tubes of color into a plastic dish and stirring enthusiastically.

Soon Lucy's head was slathered with a mudlike substance and tightly covered with a plastic cap. Then she was seated under a hair dryer, next to several other makeover winners. They all looked rather nervous.

"Why are we under the dryer?" asked Lucy, raising her voice to be heard above the noise of the machine.

"Beats me," said Ginny.

"I didn't want any color, I insisted," said Lurleen.

"It's a new process," said Cathy, who was flipping through *Town & Country* magazine. "It sets the color faster."

"I don't have color," said Lurleen. "I specifically said I didn't want it."

"Trust me," said Cathy, nodding sagely. "You got color."

Before Lurleen could protest further, the hood of the dryer was flipped back by a remarkably handsome young man wearing a tight white T-shirt that showed his muscles to advantage. "Ready for your shampoo?" he cooed, leading her away. For once, Lurleen was dumbstruck.

"I hope I get him, too," said Cathy.

"Me, too," piped up Ginny, and they all laughed.

When her turn came Lucy didn't get the young man—she got an enthusiastic girl in a smock who she guessed came from Russia.

"First wash, then intense treatment," she said, shoving Lucy back and hosing off the dye. "I give you head massage, no?"

Lucy felt completely powerless as Olga or whoever she was kneaded and pummeled and pounded her head. Then she was rinsed with scalding water, followed by cold, and slathered with some sort of organic substance that smelled like cow manure.

"What is this stuff?" she asked.

"Good for you; good for hair. I be back in ten minutes."

Soothing music was playing, and Lucy decided she might as well relax. These people were experts, they knew what they were doing. She took a deep breath and closed her eyes.

Next thing she knew she was hit with a blast of freezing

water. Reflexively, she jerked to a sitting position and was firmly shoved backward. "Must rinse."

"C-c-cold," sputtered Lucy.

"Good for hair," grunted Olga, apparently ripping Lucy's hair out by the roots. At least that's what it felt like. Only a decade or two later Lucy heard the water stop, a towel was wrapped around her head and screwed tight, and she was propelled upright. "Follow me."

Aware that resistance was futile, Lucy followed the Slavic tyrant down a pink hallway back to her private treatment room. Amazing, she thought, as she seated herself in the chair and studied her reflection in the mirror: there was no trace of the pain she had suffered.

When Lucy's stylist returned and unwrapped the towel, she clucked her tongue appreciatively. "Very good." She proceeded to comb and clip Lucy's hair, working with astonishing speed. Then she was gone and a tall, storklike man wielding a blow dryer appeared. He was completely bald and sported at least twenty silver bangles on each wrist.

"I'm Rudy," he said, whirling her around in the chair so her back was to the mirror.

"Nice to meet you, Rudy," said Lucy, crossing her fingers under the smock. She heard the bracelets jingling as he worked and tried to keep a good thought. It was reassuring to discover Olga hadn't yanked out all her hair; she could feel him brushing and tugging at something. Suddenly the blow dryer's roar was silenced, she was whirled around, and Rudy said, "Voila!"

Lucy was silent, studying her reflection. Her hair was now a subtle auburn, so silky it gleamed. It shimmered and glowed. It looked fantastic. She'd never looked better, and she couldn't understand how a haircut could cause such a dramatic change.

"How did you do that?" she asked.

"Trade secret," he said, and was gone.

When Lucy was escorted back to the waiting area, she discovered all the contest winners were there, congratulating each other on their new hairdos. Everyone except Elizabeth.

Puzzled, and a bit anxious, she turned to her escort. "Where's my daughter?"

"Elizabeth?"

"That's her."

"Don't worry. Just a small delay. She asked if we could stop for a few minutes and let her take a little nap." The girl giggled. "She said she was up late last night, at a ball."

"Can I see her?"

"No. Rudy is finishing her. He doesn't like to be watched when he works."

Lucy seated herself and picked up a magazine.

"Is something wrong?" asked Cathy. "Don't you like your hair? I think it looks fabulous."

"Thanks. Yours, too," said Lucy. "I'm just a little worried about Elizabeth. They say she asked them to let her nap because she was so tired."

Just then Elizabeth appeared and everyone started clapping. The ragged, spiky look had been tamed and her color brightened with buttery blond highlights; she looked radiant, blushing with embarrassment at the group's reaction.

"I hate it," she declared, joking, and everyone laughed.

Fiona was speechless when they arrived at the magazine's beauty department to be made up for the photo.

"Blond! I never would've. . . ."

"Me, either," agreed Elizabeth.

"It looks great."

"Thanks. I wish I'd had it for the ball last night."

"Bummer." Fiona reached for the blush. "Who was there? What were they wearing?"

"Beyoncé is every bit as gorgeous in real life as she is in her videos," gushed Elizabeth. "But Paris Hilton looks even skinnier in real life than she does on TV. Can you imagine?"

"She has great skin, though," said Fiona. "That tan is gorgeous. Fake, sure, but really well done."

"It's actually orange," volunteered Lucy, waiting her turn.

"Elizabeth's a bit peaked today," said Fiona, applying blush liberally with a brush. "Too much champagne?"

"You're starting to sound like my mother," complained Elizabeth.

In the adjacent chair, Lucy suppressed a giggle as Phyllis sponged on foundation.

"Actually, I'm afraid she's coming down with the flu." She paused. "How's Nadine doing?"

"I'm worried," admitted Phyllis. "This isn't like her. She never takes sick days. I can't remember the last time, it was that long ago. She's so devoted to her job."

"Phyllis," said Fiona, leveling her gaze at the assistant beauty editor. "Nadine doesn't even do her job. You do her job."

"Oh, that's not true," protested Phyllis.

"Yes, it is," insisted Fiona. "Think about it. What does she actually do?"

"She's on the phone a lot."

"With her friends."

"She gives assignments."

"So she doesn't have to do them."

"She studies new products."

"Takes them home, you mean. Bags and bags full."

"Well, the manufacturers are developing new products all the time."

"And she scoops them all up. Every single one. When's the last time she offered something to you?"

"It's her prerogative. She's the beauty editor."

"In name only. You do all the work."

"That's nonsense," protested Phyllis, brushing some mascara on Lucy's lashes. "Nadine's the idea person. I just do what she tells me."

"Admit it," snapped Fiona. "If she never came back you couldn't tell the difference, except we'd all get more free stuff."

"You just want the bottle of Penhaligon perfume," said Phyllis.

"Can I take it?"

"Sure." Phyllis giggled. "Just don't tell Nadine."

"Cross my heart," said Fiona, spraying it on liberally.

Lucy was still trying to pin down the fragrance—predominantly floral, but with a hint of something exotic—when they went to the fashion department to try on their new outfits. Lucy had to admit Elise had chosen well: the fitted jacket showed off her figure, and the long, straight pants, with heels underneath, made her legs look longer. Elizabeth's off-the-shoulder top showed off her pale skin beautifully, and the flowing black skirt and boots were a nice change from the jeans she usually wore, yet it still looked fun and casual. They were quite pleased with their made-over selves when they headed for the photo studio.

That satisfaction changed when they saw the other women, all similarly arrayed in varying shades of black. And now that she got a good look at everyone, Lucy realized Rudy had given them all remarkably similar hairdos.

"Oh my gawd," laughed Cathy. "We look like members of the same coven!"

"You shouldn't joke about the devil," said Lurleen.

"That hairdresser was a devil, that's for sure," said Ginny, fingering the shaggy pageboy that was a mirror image of Lucy's and Lurleen's and Serena's styles. "We all have Jennifer Aniston's hairdo."

"But not the rest of her," said Serena, patting her plump bottom, which was now disguised in a black A-line skirt.

A scoop-necked blouse with a fitted waist flattered her ample decolletage while vertical stripes slimmed her middle.

"Well, I like the way I look and once I'm back home, away from you guys, I won't look like I was stamped out with a cookie cutter," said Lucy, as Pablo and Nancy arrived.

They both seemed happy enough with the contest winners' new looks as they wandered from group to group, discussing possible poses.

"Fabulous, fabulous chiaroscuro," murmured Pablo, stroking Elizabeth's shoulder. "I'm thinking Goya, Rembrandt. A play of light and dark, like a classical portrait in a museum. And we'll have a group shot, you know that very big painting of the Spanish royal court?"

"The one with the dwarf?" asked Nancy.

"That's the one," said Pablo, lifting Cathy's face by the chin and turning it from side to side. "But I don't want the dwarf. Maybe a monkey."

"You want a monkey?"

"Yes." Pablo had decided. "I must have a monkey."

"Where am I going to get a monkey? And what if it bites someone. There may be liability issues."

Pablo stamped his foot and tossed his head. "This is what I have to deal with, all the time! How can I be creative when it's always a problem? Just borrow one from the zoo! In Central Park, a few blocks from here, there are plenty of monkeys. I saw them myself."

"Pablo, be reasonable," begged Nancy. "The zoo isn't going to lend us a monkey."

"No?" He hung his head, pouting.

"If you get the pose right you won't need a monkey."

"You're right! Pablo is a genius; I don't need a monkey. The camera is my monkey."

This announcement seemed to satisfy Nancy, but Lucy found it puzzling, as did the others.

"What does that mean? The camera is my monkey?" whispered Lurleen.

"He's an artist," said Lucy, with a shrug.

Before Lurleen could reply, the two women were pulled apart by Pablo's assistant, who was arranging the women according to the photographer's instructions, which he shouted down from his perch on a tall ladder. This familiar routine of being pushed and shoved around and ordered to hold uncomfortable poses for excruciatingly long periods of time was beginning to irritate her. She was also worried about Elizabeth and kept sneaking glances to make sure she was all right, relieved that she was one of the lucky few who'd been posed on a chair. They'd been at it for almost two hours, and Pablo was promising a break when Camilla blew into the studio and planted herself in front of the group, arms akimbo.

"What's going on here?" she demanded.

"This is the after photo," said Nancy, stepping forward. "We're going for a classic look inspired by Goya."

"Goya! Is that why they're all dressed like crows?"

"Actually," said Nancy, "the black looks great."

"It looks like crap."

Nancy shifted uneasily from one foot to another and looked skyward at Pablo, still perched on his ladder. "Pablo says . . ."

"I don't care what Pablo says, I'm the editor here and I say this looks a lot more like *The Stepford Wives* than Goya, despite our little artiste's pretensions, and I DON'T WANT STEPFORD! I want INDIVIDUALITY! I want our readers to think they can buy a new lipstick or get a new dress and it will transform them from ordinary to extraordinary."

Lucy found this exchange fascinating. She had no idea that magazine editors actually uttered the phrases they plastered on the covers. Pablo, however, remained impassive, high above the turmoil below. "Listen," he said, leaning down to speak to her, "this black was not my idea."

"No?" Camilla's back stiffened.

"No! Black is what I got, everyone in black, so I think: What can Pablo do with black? The answer is obvious. Goya. But," he paused and held up a hand, "if it was up to me, I would put each of these lovely ladies in a different color and they would be like a garden of beautiful flowers."

"So who decided to go with black?"

"You know perfectly well," said Nancy, coolly. "Elise chose all the clothes."

Camilla's eyes flashed and there was a collective intake of breath as everyone waited, expecting an explosion. It never came. Instead, Camilla marched over to the intercom and calmly requested that Elise come to the photo studio.

As a reporter, Lucy had learned long ago that bad news travels fast. She figured the photographer's assistant had dropped a word to a friend in advertising department who had run into someone from the fashion department in the ladies' room. That's how it went, whether you were in a little town like Tinker's Cove or a big city like New York. Still, it was disconcerting when Elise arrived in a flood of tears. Somehow Lucy hadn't pictured her as the emotional type.

"Elise, dear," said Camilla, her voice as sweet as sugar, "do you see anything wrong with this picture?"

"Ohmigod," she wailed, wrapping her arms around Camilla and collapsing into her arms. "I can't believe it."

"Now, now." Camilla was staggering under the larger woman's weight. Fortunately, whether her grief made it impossible for her to support herself or because she realized that Camilla's little bird body was about to snap, Elise slid to her knees, still keeping her arms wrapped around Camilla's tiny waist. Camilla looked extremely put out at the situation. "It's not as bad as that," she snapped, trying to squirm out of Elise's constricting grip. "We'll just get them some different outfits."

Elise lifted her tear-filled eyes to meet Camilla's. "Haven't you heard?"

Camilla's eyes flashed, but she managed to retain control of her voice. "Heard what?"

"Nadine's gone." Elise continued her downward slide to the floor, pulling Camilla down with her. "Nadine's dead."

Chapter Eight

BANISH BLEMISHES:
TIPS FROM TOP DERMATOLOGISTS

Apart from Faith and Lurleen, who immediately fell to their knees and began praying, nobody seemed to know how to react to the news. They all stood awkwardly, watching and waiting.

"Nobody dies from the flu," declared Camilla, struggling to get back on her feet but hampered by her four-inch heels. "Who told you she's dead?"

"Arnold's secretary called," blubbered Elise, as her substantial shoulders shook with sobs and she pounded her fists on the floor. "She said there were complications."

Camilla glared at Nancy and Pablo, who were whispering together in a corner. "Help me up, you idiots!" she screamed.

The two rushed over to the entangled pair. Pablo helped Camilla up while Nancy attempted to console Elise, who was now flat on her stomach with her face buried in her hands.

Back on her pointy little Manolos, Camilla straightened her black-and-white tweed suit and ran her hands through her hair, returning it to its previous perfection. She pointed a crimson-tipped finger at Elise. "Get her up!" she barked to Nancy and Pablo.

Pablo and Nancy's eyes met as they each took one of Elise's elbows and gave the old heave-ho, succeeding only in raising her to her knees. With a second enormous effort they managed to get her somewhat upright.

"Bring her along. I'm going to get to the bottom of this," Camilla declared, stomping out of the studio. Pablo and Nancy followed, struggling to support Elise who was now making pathetic mewing sounds and sniffling noisily.

Everyone seemed to expel a sigh of relief when they were gone, except for Faith and Lurleen, who were absorbed in their prayers.

"Well, I for one am glad this makeover is almost over and I can go home to sunny California," said Serena, giving her daughter a supportive hug. "We don't have flu in California, at least I don't think we do."

"Well, we have it in Omaha," said Ginny, "but otherwise healthy people don't die of it. Did she have some sort of condition like asthma? Some sort of immune deficiency?"

"She always seemed pretty healthy to me," said Cathy. "She never missed any promotions at Neiman Marcus, that's for sure. She'd fly two thousand miles for a free meal."

"You ought to be ashamed," declared Maria, eyes blazing. "It's not a joke. The poor woman is dead, just like we all will be one day." She crossed herself, as did Carmela.

"It sure makes you think," said Cathy, shaking her head. "She had everything. She was married to a millionaire, she had a great job on a magazine, she had it all."

"Were there any kids?" asked Tiffany.

"No. No kids," said Cathy. "At least none that she ever mentioned."

Realizing that her own child had been awfully quiet, Lucy anxiously searched the group for her. She wasn't standing with the others in the anxious little knot they had formed but had retreated to the raised platform, where she was slumped over to one side and fast asleep.

Lucy immediately knew something was very wrong.

Elizabeth was a light sleeper and the commotion in the studio would have kept her awake, even if she'd felt tired enough to stretch out on the stage. She also liked her comfort but hadn't even slipped her purse under her head as a pillow. Lucy anxiously remembered how she'd had so much trouble staying awake earlier, and this time, when she felt Elizabeth's forehead, Lucy discovered she was burning with fever. Lucy gave her a shake; her eyelashes fluttered but Lucy couldn't rouse her.

"Is something the matter?" asked Maria. "Should I call an ambulance?"

Lucy shook Elizabeth harder, and her eyes opened.

"Wake up, honey. We need to get you to the doctor. Can you walk?"

"Sure." Elizabeth sat up and Lucy slipped an arm around her waist, pulling her to her feet.

"Thanks, but I think we can manage with a taxi," Lucy told Maria. "Where's the nearest emergency room?"

It didn't matter whether you were at New York Weill Cornell Medical Center or Tinker's Cove Cottage Hospital, all emergency rooms were the same, thought Lucy. She was sitting on one of those standard plastic chairs in the corner of an examining room. Elizabeth was lying on the table, and they were waiting for the doctor. They'd been waiting for what seemed like a long time, and Lucy suspected they'd only been put in the examining room because Elizabeth couldn't sit upright in the waiting room and kept slumping against the other patients. Now she was, once again, sound asleep and the hand with the bite was red and swollen. Lucy didn't like the looks of it one bit.

The door opened and a young man in green hospital scrubs and thick black-rimmed glasses introduced himself as Doctor Altschuler. "What's the problem?" he asked, lifting first one and then the other of Elizabeth's eyelids. Then he slid the stethoscope beneath her sweater and pressed it against her chest, listening intently.

"She's got a fever, she keeps falling asleep, and she's got this nasty bite on her hand," said Lucy. "She's been kind of sluggish for a day or two and I thought she might be coming down with the flu, but we've been very busy, too, and I thought she just might be tired."

"Busy doing what?" asked the doctor, examining Elizabeth's hand.

"We won a magazine contest for a trip to New York and makeovers."

"Where do you live?"

"Tinker's Cove, Maine."

"How long have you been in the city?"

"Since Sunday."

"I assume Tinker's Cove is pretty rural?"

"It's a small town, maybe a couple of thousand people," said Lucy, losing patience. She wanted him to magically make Elizabeth all better. "It's not New York but we have all the modern conveniences."

"Could she have come in contact with a spider?"

"A spider?" Lucy looked at Elizabeth's hand, then at her face. She was a real sleeping beauty.

"In the cellar or something?" prodded the doctor.

"I did have some Christmas presents hidden in the cellar, and she went down to get them," said Lucy, remembering Elizabeth's excited expression as she emerged with the cross-country skis. "I've heard that we do have black widows, but I've never seen one." Lucy grimaced. "I don't know if I'd recognize one, to tell the truth."

"This isn't a black widow bite. I think it's a brown recluse."

Lucy had never heard of such a creature. "Brown recluse?"

"They're called 'recluse' because they're very shy."

Something about the doctor's intensity gave Lucy the idea he had once been a small boy who was very interested in bugs and had probably spent hours at the library learning all he could about them.

"But it's winter," protested Lucy. "Don't they die in winter?"

"They creep into cellars, places like that, where there's enough warmth for them to survive. If they're disturbed, they sometimes bite."

"Is it poisonous?"

"Oh yes."

Lucy's eyes widened. "What's going to happen to Elizabeth? Is there an antidote?"

"No antidote." He shoved his eyeglasses back up his nose and peered reassuringly at her. "Don't worry. They're rarely fatal."

"Rarely! That's not good enough!"

"I'm very confident she'll be fine. She's young and healthy and she'll recover quickly. Of course, we'll keep her here in the hospital and start her on antibiotics as a precaution against secondary infection. We don't have anything to counteract the effects of the bite, but we can treat the symptoms: control the fever, put her on a ventilator if she has trouble breathing, give her medication to control convulsions, that sort of thing."

Lucy was horrified. "Convulsions?"

"Rare, but something we have to watch for."

"Can I stay with her?"

"Absolutely, Mrs. . . ." He paused to check the chart. "Mrs. Stone. But it's not necessary. This is one of the world's premier medical facilities. We have excellent nurses here and . . ." he checked the chart again, "Elizabeth will get the best of care. I suggest you go down to the cafeteria and get yourself something to eat while we transfer Elizabeth to intensive care."

"Intensive care?"

"One of the nurses can give you directions," he said, on his way out the door.

Shattered, Lucy sat back down in the chair and pulled her cell phone out of her purse with shaking hands.

Bill answered on the third ring. Lucy clung to his hearty voice like a lifeline.

"Elizabeth's sick. Really sick. The doctor says it's a brown recluse spider bite."

"What?"

"In the cellar, maybe when she went down on Christmas Day to get the skis."

"She got bit? How come she never said anything? Is it serious?"

"They're putting her in intensive care." Lucy had trouble with those last two words and started to cry.

"Take it easy, Lucy." Bill's voice was strong. "She'll be fine."

"I'm scared."

"Of course you are. Let me talk to her."

Lucy looked at Elizabeth, who was out like a light.

"She's sleeping. That's all she does."

"Oh." Bill paused, absorbing this information. "Well, it's probably for the best."

Lucy was distracted by the arrival of an orderly.

"They're going to move her now. I better go."

"Keep me posted," said Bill.

Lucy couldn't bring herself to leave Elizabeth and accompanied her on the trip to the intensive care unit. Elizabeth was unaware of the move and slept through it, not even flinching when an IV needle was inserted in her arm.

"You look like you need a break," the nurse told Lucy, as she tucked a blanket around Elizabeth. "There's a cafeteria in the basement."

"I'm fine," insisted Lucy.

"Go. Get something to eat. She'll be here when you get back. I promise."

"I couldn't eat."

The nurse looked at her steadily. "This could be a long haul. You need to keep your strength up. And some food will help with that headache."

"I don't have—" began Lucy, realizing that she did indeed have a headache. A real killer. "Okay."

Lucy felt very small in the elevator, as if worry had somehow shrunk her. She also felt fragile and wished Bill were there to take her in his arms and let her rest her head on his broad chest. He wasn't, though, and the nurse was right, she had to keep up her strength. Maybe eating would help with this hollow feeling, as if a strong breeze could blow her over.

She took a tray and shuffled through the line, taking a tuna sandwich, chips, and a cup of tea. She surprised herself by eating it all and went back for a piece of peach pie and more tea. No wonder she was hungry, she realized with a shock. According to the clock on the wall it was long past lunchtime. She'd already been in the hospital for hours, and it promised to be a long day. She was on her way to the lobby to see if there was a gift shop where she could buy something to read, something distracting, when she was surprised to recognize Lance coming toward her in the hallway.

"What are you doing here?" she asked, giving him a hug.

"I'm helping a professor of mine with a research project—this place is affiliated with Columbia, you know. What are you doing here?"

"Elizabeth is sick from a spider bite."

Lance cocked his head, looking doubtful. "That's crazy."

"She's in intensive care."

His attitude suddenly vanished. "That's terrible. Can I see her?"

"I'm not sure what the rules are," said Lucy. "There's no point right now. She's sleeping."

"I'll come back tomorrow." His eyebrows met over his classic Roman nose. "Do you know what kind of spider?"

"The doctor said a brown something or other."

"A brown recluse?"

Lucy suspected Lance may have shared the doctor's interest in bugs. "You've heard of it?"

"Sure, I've heard of it." He looked surprised that she hadn't. "But I'll do some research and brush up on the facts. I'll let you know what I find out."

"That would be great," said Lucy, who felt completely at sea. "I'd really appreciate that."

When she returned to the intensive care unit she found Elizabeth was still asleep, but when she pressed her lips to the girl's forehead she discovered her fever had dropped. Reassured, Lucy settled down in a fake leather recliner and opened the latest edition of *Jolie* magazine, which she'd bought in the gift shop.

It was kind of funny, she thought, as she flipped through the pages of ads. Here she'd had this makeover thanks to *Jolie*, but she'd never actually read the magazine. It was Elizabeth who devoured each month's issue and added it to the growing pile in her room. Lucy had never bothered to read it, assuming it was geared to younger women. She didn't read magazines much, anyway, preferring novels and newspapers, and if this particular issue of *Jolie* was representative of the genre, she figured she'd made the right choice. She could hardly believe what she was reading, beginning with a feature article by Nadine defending the use of animals for testing cosmetics.

Lucy's younger girls had spent the last few summers at Friends of Animals day camp so she knew this was a hot issue. Sara particularly enjoyed horrifying her mother with descriptions of rabbits subjected to eye make-up and piglets forced to eat lipstick ingredients. Trying to joke that at least the test animals would look good went over like a lead balloon. "It's torture, Mom," Sara informed her. "Remember, this is the stuff they're testing. It's not safe, like the stuff you buy."

After reading Nadine's article, Lucy found herself agreeing with Sara. Although she argued her case forcefully, Lucy couldn't agree that testing cosmetics was equally important as testing potentially life-saving drugs, for example. She could rationalize the need for the latter, but not the former. No rabbit needed to suffer for longer, thicker lashes.

Depressed, Lucy turned eagerly to the photo spreads. Having seen Pablo at work she was sure they would be visually interesting. Plus, with her newfound interest in fashion she might get some ideas for a new spring outfit. But when she turned to the spring fashion forecast she was shocked to discover it pictured designer cruisewear modeled in a Caribbean shantytown. Gorgeous models with gleaming skin lounged in scanty outfits on tilting porches amidst piles of garbage and debris. A chicken scratched in the foreground of one picture; a stooped, skinny man in an oversized shirt lurked in the background of another. Reading the commentary offended Lucy's soul: the outfits cost thousands of dollars.

Lucy was fuming about the injustice of a culture that afforded some fortunate people thousand-dollar swimsuits while others couldn't afford the necessities of life when she turned the page and saw the filthy, wrinkled face of a homeless woman sporting a diamond tiara and ropes of pearls. She got the concept, all right. The woman's face expressed human dignity, but the addition of the jewels was demeaning and insulting. Disgusted, Lucy tossed the magazine across the room where it landed with a thud in the wastebasket.

Elizabeth twitched in her bed but didn't wake up, so Lucy reached for the remote to turn on the TV that hung from the ceiling. She was flipping through the channels when the door opened and Nancy Glass appeared, wrapped in a tan Burberry coat. Even Lucy recognized the famous plaid lining.

"How's the patient?" she asked, taking Lucy's hand and squeezing it.

Lucy turned off the TV. "They think she'll be all right."

"I couldn't believe it when they told me she was in intensive care." Nancy's eyes were huge.

"Me, either."

"You poor thing. How are you holding up?"

"I've been better," admitted Lucy. "But at least I know she's getting good care."

"Excellent care. People come here from all over the world. They've developed all kinds of advanced treatments."

"Thanks for telling me that," said Lucy. "I guess they can handle a little spider bite."

"Is that what she has?"

"That's what they say." Lucy was looking around the room for another chair, but there was only the single recliner. "Sit if you want," said Lucy. "I've been sitting for hours."

"No, I'm only here for a minute." Nancy stepped close to the bed and gave Elizabeth's hand a little pat. "You know, maybe we should have her write a first-person account for the magazine. When she gets better, of course. I know Pablo's planning to use some exotic bugs for his next jewelry spread."

"Well, that's a better choice than homeless people." Lucy felt like biting her tongue the minute she said it, but Nancy wasn't offended.

"You didn't like that?" she asked, smiling.

"Not much. I didn't like the shantytown, either."

"I know. Talk about bad taste!" Nancy shrugged.
"That's our Camilla. She thinks controversy sells."

Lucy managed a small smile. "That's what my editor at
home thinks, too."

"Unfortunately, it doesn't seem to be true, in *Jolie*'s
case, anyway." Nancy's eyes had fallen on the crumpled
issue in the wastebasket and she grimaced. "A lot of people agree with you—circulation is dropping, and the magazine is losing money."

"I heard that. Not a good time to lose a key editor.
How's everybody coping?"

"You mean about Nadine?" Nancy was checking her
manicure.

"Everyone must be reeling in shock, no?"

"It could be worse. Nadine was a master at delegating
responsibility. Phyllis knows exactly what needs to be
done and how to do it."

"That's fortunate."

"Yeah. The magazine will be fine." She was looking at
her reflection in the mirror above the sink and tweaking
her hairdo. "The one I feel bad for is her husband."

"Arnold?" Lucy remembered his hand on her bottom at
the AIDS ball.

"He's a lovely man. So sensitive. I'm sure he's devas-
tated."

"You never know how somebody's going to react to a
death in the family," said Lucy, surprised at Nancy's obvious sincerity given her own experience with Arnold.
"Grief takes everyone differently."

"Well, I'm going to do everything I can to help him
through this difficult time," said Nancy, tightening the belt
on her coat.

"Well, thanks for coming by," said Lucy. "I really appreciate it."

"That's me. A regular Miss Goody Two-Shoes," said
Nancy, clicking out the door on her stilettos.

Lucy wasn't sure that was exactly the term she'd use to describe Nancy, but you never knew. Just because a woman was glamorous and fashionable and successful didn't mean she wasn't nice underneath. You couldn't tell a book, or a magazine, by its cover. She retrieved *Jolie* from the wastebasket, flipped through a few pages, and shoved it aside. What she needed was something distracting, something silly. Maybe the Three Stooges. At home you could find the Stooges at any hour on some cable channel or other. Lucy knew; the trio had gotten her through many a sleepless night.

But when she switched on the TV there was no sign of Larry, Curly, and Moe. There was, however, a serious young female newscaster in a navy blue suit reporting that the medical examiner was investigating the death of magazine editor Nadine Nelson, now deemed suspicious.

Chapter Nine

EASY SELF-DEFENSE STRATEGIES ANYONE CAN LEARN

It was supposed to be a vacation but the flight had been terrible. The trouble started at check-in, when the clerk had actually been Moe from the Three Stooges. He was also the pilot, and Larry and Curly were the flight attendants. A couple of passengers got squirted with seltzer water but nobody got drinks, or peanuts, because Larry and Curly were too busy bopping each other on the head and tossing the refreshments around the cabin.

When the plane landed they had to get off by sliding down the emergency chute, and Lucy had to take off her heels, spike heels, before they'd let her slide down. That's why she was running barefoot, trying to catch up with Bill and Elizabeth who were far in the distance on the wide, empty street lined with ramshackle shop fronts. It was eerily quiet, like the set of a cheesy Western movie just before the climactic shoot-out, and people stared at her from the windows and doors but no one spoke.

Suddenly, she was on a beach, a classic Caribbean beach with palm trees, white sand, and turquoise water. She was tired of running so she stretched out in a handy hammock and watched Bill and Elizabeth frolicking in the waves. Then Elizabeth shrieked with delight and plucked something from the water. Waving it, she ran up the beach to show it to Lucy.

It was a shell, a beautiful striated nautilus shell with a pearly lining. But while they were exclaiming over its beauty, something black and evil crawled out of the center. Lucy tried to snatch the shell away from Elizabeth, but before she could grab it the spider hopped onto Elizabeth's hand. Lucy tried to brush it away but paused when she noticed it had a head like a woman. It was a spider with a woman's head, with Camilla's head. She wanted to ask Camilla what had happened, why had she turned into a spider, but before she had a chance, the Camilla spider sank two gleaming white vampire fangs into Elizabeth's hand.

A shriek of protest from the aged recliner chair woke Lucy, and she found herself sitting bolt upright, panting and sweating, in a hospital room. Elizabeth was in the bed, sound asleep.

It was a dream, she realized—only a dream, and there was nothing to be afraid of. She gave her head a shake, clearing her mind of the image of spidery Camilla, and got up to check on Elizabeth. She found the girl was sleeping easily, her forehead was cool, and the bite on her hand was improving: the wound itself was healing and the swelling had gone down.

Reassured that Elizabeth was on the road to recovery, Lucy went out to the nurse's station where she asked for a toothbrush and the nearest ladies' room. When she got back a middle-aged man in pale green scrubs was examining Elizabeth, who was awake and responsive. Lucy gave her a big smile and a thumbs up.

"I'm Dr. Marchetti," he said, shaking Lucy's hand. "I must say I'm quite impressed by your daughter's response to the medication. Antibiotics don't usually have this dramatic an effect on spider bites."

"I'm not convinced it is a spider bite," said Lucy.

The doctor narrowed his eyes. "No? Why not?"

"Well, we live in Maine, for one thing. It's pretty cold

there this time of year and you don't see many bugs. Not any, really. Not even fleas on the dog."

"And I don't remember getting bitten," volunteered Elizabeth. "I hate spiders so I'm sure I would have noticed one on my hand."

"Maybe she got bitten here," suggested the doctor as he consulted Elizabeth's file.

"I haven't seen a single bug here, either, but she was exposed to the flu." Lucy remembered the newscast. "Or what I thought was the flu. Considering the way people zip around on airplanes these days, it could be some bizarre jungle thing like monkey pox or malaria. They're investigating."

"Who's investigating what?"

"Nadine Nelson's death," said Lucy, so eager to inform the doctor of this development that she failed to notice Elizabeth's shocked expression. "It was on the TV. They said the medical examiner was investigating."

"And your daughter had contact with this woman? This Nadine Nelson?"

"Oh, yes, we both did. On Monday, at *Jolie* magazine. It was a contest, you see, for mother–daughter winter makeovers. . . ."

Dr. Marchetti wasn't listening. He was out the door.

Elizabeth was white faced. "She died?"

Lucy wished she'd asked to speak to the doctor privately; she'd forgotten that Nadine's death would be shocking news to Elizabeth. "I'm sorry," she said. "I should have realized you couldn't know. You were really out of things."

"Do I have what she had? Am I going to die?"

Lucy gave her a hug. "Do you feel like you're dying?"

"No," admitted Elizabeth. "I feel much better."

"Trust your body," advised Lucy. "They don't know what it is but the medicine is working and you're much improved. You heard the doctor."

"What if I take turn for the worse?" She flopped her

head over, like a rag doll, then sat up. "Actually, I think I might be dying of starvation."

Lucy opened the door and stuck her head in the hallway to see if there was any sign that dinner was imminent. There wasn't.

"I'm hungry, too," she said. "I think I'll go down to the cafeteria and get some provisions."

Remembering hospital protocol she checked at the nurse's station to make sure Elizabeth could eat and, after getting the okay, headed straight for the cafeteria. She was putting two containers of yogurt on her tray when her cell phone rang. It was Lance.

"How's Elizabeth?" he asked, without even saying hello.

"Much improved. She's sitting up and wants something to eat."

"That's great! But I think I should warn you that brown recluse spider bites are very slow to heal. She could be in the hospital for quite a while."

"That's funny," said Lucy, adding a couple of pieces of fruit. "It's already much smaller."

"What?"

"Yeah. The doctor was amazed. Said antibiotics don't usually work like that on spider bites."

Lance didn't reply and Lucy took the silence to mean he was thinking. She took advantage of it to fill two paper cups with coffee, then got in line to pay the cashier.

"You know, my research also pulled up anthrax," he finally said.

"Anthrax?" Lucy gave the cashier a ten-dollar bill and put the change on her tray, which she carried over to an empty table. "Like those postal workers?"

"Yeah."

Lucy remembered the scare, which had dominated the news for weeks. "Didn't a couple of them die?"

"It can be fatal," admitted Lance.

All of a sudden her heart felt like it was in a vise. "But the doctor says Elizabeth is much better."

"There are two kinds," continued Lance. "Inhalation anthrax; that's when you breathe in the germs. It's very serious. But there's also cutaneous anthrax; you get that if you touch the stuff but don't breathe it. And that's not as serious as the other kind."

"You mean Elizabeth's spider bite could really be an anthrax sore?"

"Yeah. And it would respond to antibiotics."

"What's the other kind like? The inhalation kind?" demanded Lucy.

"Like the flu. Like a really bad case of the flu with respiratory problems."

"Really?" Lucy was thinking of Nadine. "And how do people get it? Is it contagious?"

"It's not contagious. You have to be directly exposed to get it."

"It's a germ?"

"A spore, actually, and it's not usually around in the environment, like most germs. It has to be introduced. The post office workers got sick when the anthrax was shaken out of an envelope by a sorting machine. Some nut was sending it to people in the government."

"Right. They had to shut down congressional offices, didn't they? To decontaminate them."

"And that's the other thing," said Lance. "Most germs have a pretty short life span unless they find a host, but not anthrax. It forms spores that can lie dormant for years until they find the right living conditions. That's why it's such a good biological weapon."

"Biological weapon? I think we're getting a little crazy here. You know, Elizabeth never had chicken pox. The others did but she was away at summer camp and missed it. It could be something like that."

"The doctors will figure it out," said Lance. "You think it's okay if I visit her tonight?"

"I think she'd love it," said Lucy. "Right now she's probably wondering what's taking me so long. I'm supposed to be bringing her something to eat."

As she made her way back to Elizabeth's room Lucy tried to remember everything she could about the anthrax scare a few years earlier. It wasn't much, she realized. She didn't even know if they'd ever figured out who had sent the stuff, or why. The only thing she was sure of was that ever since the attack, the discovery of any unspecified white powder was enough to shut down schools and offices until it was positively identified. Some pranksters had even managed to shut down Tinker's Cove High School for an afternoon last fall by spilling some salt on the assistant principal's desk.

"Is that all you got me? Fruit and yogurt?" demanded Elizabeth, when Lucy delivered the tray.

"It's just to tide you over," said Lucy, amazed at Elizabeth's sudden interest in food. Maybe it was true that every cloud had a silver lining. "They're going to bring you a big dinner, eventually. I saw the meal trolley at the end of the hall."

"I don't know how people survive in the hospital," said Elizabeth, digging into the yogurt with a plastic spoon. "You could starve to death."

"Take mine, too," said Lucy, who was too distracted to eat.

"Aren't you hungry?"

She stood up. "I have to make a phone call. I'll be back in a minute."

Standing in the hallway outside Elizabeth's room, Lucy felt a bit like a cartoon character with an angel perched on one shoulder and a devil on the other. The good little angel was telling her that she really ought to alert somebody at

Jolie magazine about the possibility that the office was contaminated with anthrax, while the bad little devil was telling her it would be a waste of time.

"People's lives are at stake. You must warn them," said the angel.

"How are you going to do that?" scoffed the devil. "Camilla's the one you should call and you can be sure her phone number is unlisted."

"That's just an excuse. You need to find a way," insisted the angel.

"There'll be plenty of time for that later," whispered the devil. "You're exhausted. Frazzled. You deserve some time to take care of yourself."

"You'll never forgive yourself if someone else gets sick because you were too lazy to make a phone call," said the angel.

Lucy checked her watch. It was just after five. That meant the best she could probably do would be to leave a message on Camilla's phone mail. But when she dialed the receptionist answered and put her right through to Camilla.

"I'm so glad I caught you," began Lucy, feeling rather awkward. "There's something I think you should know."

"I heard your daughter's in the hospital. How's she doing?"

"She's going to be fine," said Lucy.

"Well, I'm glad she's recovering. You must excuse me— this is not a good time," she said.

Lucy was suddenly guilt stricken. In her haste to do the right thing she'd completely forgotten that Camilla and Nadine were close friends. The poor woman was probably wracked with grief and completely shattered by her loss.

"I'm afraid there's no good time for what I have to tell you," said Lucy, her voice gentle, "but trust me, the sooner you know, the better."

"Well, go on," said Camilla, impatiently.

"Okay," said Lucy. "I think there's a very real risk the *Jolie* office is contaminated with anthrax."

"What?"

"Anthrax. Nadine's death and my daughter's symptoms are consistent with anthrax, at least that's what I've been told."

Camilla's voice was hard. "That's ridiculous."

"Unfortunately, it's not ridiculous at all," insisted Lucy. "And if the offices are contaminated other people are at risk of getting sick. That would be terrible."

Camilla's words were clipped, precise. "The doctors say Elizabeth has anthrax?"

"Well, no," admitted Lucy. "They're still testing. But I did some research and I'm pretty sure. . . ."

Camilla was practically shrieking. "*You* did some research?"

Lucy felt her face warming. "Well, actually it was Lance, Norah's son. He's a student at Columbia and he does research at the hospital with a professor."

"A college kid has some crackpot idea! And you decide to call me?"

Lucy was flabbergasted. Here she'd gone out of her way to do a good deed and Camilla was practically biting her head off. "I thought the sooner you knew the better."

"Oh you did, did you? Well, I'm going to wait for official notification before I go to the expense and trouble of closing the office and having everyone stay home. Furthermore, I don't know who you think you are, spreading ridiculous rumors like this." Camilla paused for breath. "I'm warning you, if you so much as whisper this preposterous idea to anybody I'll slap you with a lawsuit so fast you won't know what hit you."

"Okay," said Lucy, taking a step backward.

"It's been absolutely lovely getting to know you," said Camilla, her sarcastic tone giving the lie to her words, "but I'm sure you know the makeover is officially over tonight. The magazine will no longer assume the cost of your hotel and I hope you have medical insurance because we are certainly not responsible for your daughter's illness and hospitalization." Camilla paused a moment, as if remembering something. "That's right, you were the one who was so very interested in the ten-thousand-dollar prize, weren't you?"

With all the worry over Elizabeth, Lucy had forgotten all about it. The prize, the makeover, it all seemed part of another life. Elizabeth's illness had changed everything. But now that she was recovering, the money would sure come in handy. "Did we win?" she asked.

"Not in your dreams."

Lucy felt as if she'd been slapped, and leaned against the wall. "Well, thanks for telling me," she said, swallowing hard.

"No problem." Camilla's voice was silky and Lucy knew she wasn't finished. "Have a nice day," she purred.

Chapter Ten

SEXY, SEXY: LINGERIE HE'LL LOVE!

Lucy pressed the "end" button on her cell phone and leaned against the wall. Here she'd tried to help Camilla and all she'd gotten was a stinging rebuke. She felt as if she'd been slapped. So that's what you got for trying to do the right thing, she thought. It was true what people said: "No good deed goes unpunished." Her emotions in turmoil, she called home.

"What's going on?" demanded Bill, picking up on the first ring. "How's Elizabeth?"

"Better," she said, quickly. "Much better. She's sitting up, talking, and the wound is already starting to heal. She even asked for some food."

He let out a big sign of relief. "That's great."

"I know."

"So why don't you sound happy?" he asked. "What's going on?"

"I guess I'm just feeling overwhelmed," said Lucy, hedging. She was terrified by the possibility that Elizabeth might have caught anthrax but she didn't want to alarm Bill unnecessarily. It was a struggle to keep from saying the word. It was right there, on the tip of her tongue, and she had to keep it in while getting other words out. "I don't know how long Elizabeth's going to be in the hospital and

I have to find someplace to stay, there's all these expenses, we didn't win the prize. . . ."

"Hey, hey, hey," said Bill. "Calm down. It'll be okay."

"What about the health insurance?"

"I'll take care of it. You take care of Elizabeth, and yourself."

"I'm okay," said Lucy, biting her lip. "But I don't know what I'm going to do after tonight. The magazine is kicking me out of the hotel."

"What?"

"They say the makeover is over and they won't pay for my room any longer. Like I don't have enough to worry about."

"Calm down, Lucy. Give Sam a call. I bet she'd love to have you stay with her."

"I must be going crazy. I can't believe I didn't think of that."

"It's understandable. You're upset. You're away from home and you have a sick child. It's very stressful. But everything's going to be okay."

"I hope so." Something in the hall caught her eye. It was Dr. Marchetti, heading her way in green surgical scrubs and carrying a chart. "I've got to go. The doctor's coming."

"Keep me posted."

"I will," promised Lucy. She closed the phone and turned to meet the doctor.

"Mrs. Stone, I need to have a word with you," he said.

Lucy's heart gave a little jump in her chest.

"We can talk here," he said, leading her to a small waiting area where the scarred coffee table was covered with well-thumbed magazines. He indicated a bright orange sectional sofa. "Have a seat."

"Is everything all right?" she asked, nervously twisting her purse strap.

"Elizabeth's doing very well and I expect she'll make a

full recovery. In fact, we're going to move her out of ICU tomorrow, if her progress continues." He paused and leaned forward, resting his elbows on his thighs. The move seemed intimate; the scrubs looked like pajamas to Lucy, and she could see his curly black chest hair sprouting at the V-neck.

She slid back in her seat, away from him. "That's good, right?"

"Right. But the bad news is," he paused, giving her time to prepare herself, "she has anthrax."

It wasn't as if she hadn't been half expecting it, but the news was still devastating. She was suddenly cold and she could barely breathe, she felt as if she had to remind her heart to keep pumping.

Dr. Marchetti took her hand. "Are you all right, Mrs. Stone?"

Lucy struggled to put her thoughts into words. "I knew . . . I mean, I thought it might be anthrax . . ." She shook her head. "I still can't believe it. It's crazy." Suddenly, it occurred to her that tests were often wrong. A false positive they called it. She locked eyes with him. "Are you sure, absolutely sure? Maybe it's something else, like chicken pox."

"We're sure. When you told me about the woman at the magazine, Nadine Nelson, I checked with the medical examiner's office and learned the cause of death was anthrax. We then tested Elizabeth for anthrax and got a positive result. But we caught it early and Elizabeth's prognosis is excellent." He looked down at the file in his hand. "Maybe I misunderstood you. Did you say you thought it might be anthrax?"

"A friend mentioned it. He did some Internet research for me."

He slapped the file down on the coffee table. "And what did this friend tell you?"

"It's a spore . . . there's two kinds . . . " Lucy was aware she was babbling, avoiding her fear. "Is this some sort of terror attack?" she asked. "Are we all going to get sick?"

"It doesn't look like it, at least not yet. But of course there are homeland security concerns and there will be an investigation. The FBI is going to want to talk to you and your daughter."

"The FBI? But we haven't done anything!"

"Of course not. I made that very clear to the investigators. But they do need to track down the source of the anthrax. We've been lucky so far, with only two cases. There doesn't seem to be a widespread outbreak. Still, we have to be concerned. There could possibly be more deaths, if the source of the anthrax isn't discovered."

"But Elizabeth's in the clear, right?"

He leveled his eyes at hers and took both her hands in his. "Listen, I learned long ago not to make promises in this business. There are no guarantees in medicine, too much can go wrong. But having said that, and bearing in mind that complications are always possible, I think it's safe to say she's out of the woods."

"So how much longer will she have to stay in the hospital?"

The doctor studied the chart. "I'm afraid I don't really know. We'll just have to see what happens."

"But you said. . . ."

"I said there are no guarantees. We want to keep an eye on her. She's on some serious medication and there could be side effects." He paused. "Anthrax is very rare, you know, and we're not that familiar with the disease itself. And then, there are some curious anomalies in your daughter's case. . . ."

"Anomalies?"

"Some unusual factors we haven't seen before."

Lucy felt like screaming. "Like what?"

"Nothing for you to be concerned about, honestly. Just

variations from the usual course. Frankly, I would have expected her to be sicker."

Relief flooded Lucy. "Oh. That's good then, right?"

"We think so. But we want to be cautious." He got to his feet and handed her a piece of paper. "This is a Cipro prescription for you. You've been exposed so you need to take it as a precautionary measure. Be sure to finish the bottle and take all the pills."

Lucy sat on the couch, staring at the piece of paper in her hand, for a long while after the doctor had left. This was very scary. It wasn't something she was reading about in the newspaper, it wasn't taking place miles away, it wasn't happening to somebody else. It was real life, her life. She folded the prescription and put it in her purse.

When she returned to Elizabeth's room and saw how well she looked, she was reassured. Elizabeth was sitting up in bed eating from her dinner tray. The color had returned to her cheeks and her eyes were sparkling, probably because Lance was perched on the side of the bed. Giddy with relief, Lucy wrapped her arms around her and gave her a big hug.

"Mom! What's the deal?" exclaimed Elizabeth, squirming out her mother's embrace and spearing a chicken nugget.

"You're going to be okay," said Lucy. "I just talked to the doctor. But Lance was right. You have anthrax."

"What's that?" asked Elizabeth, spooning up some applesauce.

"Don't you remember. . . ." began Lance, eager to fill her in.

Lucy stopped him with a glance and a shake of the head. This was no time for a current affairs lesson. "How are you feeling?" she asked Elizabeth.

"Great! When can I leave?"

"I just talked with the doctor and he says you'll probably have to stay for a while."

"Why? I feel much better. Besides, I don't want to spend another minute in this awful johnny!"

Lance laughed. "I think it's kind of cute."

Elizabeth scowled at him. "You would."

Lucy was making a mental note to bring Elizabeth's pajamas when there was a knock on the door and Fiona entered, clutching a bunch of pink and white Oriental lilies.

"I'm not dead," protested Elizabeth, laughing.

"Those are different lilies, I think," said Fiona. "I got these because they smell so nice." She gave them to Elizabeth. "Take a sniff. Heavenly."

"I can smell them from here," said Lucy. "Lovely." She got up. "I'll go see if the nurse has a vase."

When she returned Fiona was also perched on the bed, sitting at the foot, lighting a cigarette.

"You can't smoke in here," said Lucy, horrified. "It's a hospital."

"Really? You Yanks are too much."

"It's not a Yank thing, it's a health thing."

"You know, Americans wouldn't be so fat if they smoked more," said Fiona, putting her cigarettes back in her purse.

"I'll tell the Surgeon General," said Lance.

"It's true," insisted Fiona. "People are much thinner in Europe, much healthier, despite the fact they drink like fish and smoke like chimneys and eat all sorts of fatty foods like fish and chips and foie gras."

"If you like it so much better there, why did you come here?" asked Lance, resentful of the intrusion.

"Oh, I like it here just fine," said Fiona. "And I'd like to stay longer, but I don't think that's going to happen."

"Why not?" asked Lucy, placing the last stem in the vase and setting it on the window sill, where Elizabeth could see them.

"I'm here on a work visa and when the job ends I've got

to go." She drummed her fingers nervously. "Is it true what they say? That Nadine had anthrax?"

Lucy stepped close to the bed and took Elizabeth's hand. "You had a close call but you're going to be fine."

"Elizabeth, too?" asked Fiona, her eyes widening.

"That's what the doctor says."

"Well, I'll be gob smacked," said Fiona. "You mean Nadine didn't have the flu, she had anthrax? And everybody at the magazine was exposed?"

"If a lot of people were exposed, they'd already be sick," said Lance. "Of course, they'll close the offices and bring in the hazmat crews and there'll be a big investigation, but it's really just bureaucrats covering their behinds."

"But who would do such a thing?" asked Fiona, staring out the window. "Who would send anthrax to a fashion magazine? Why would they do it?"

They all fell silent, baffled by a new world order in which ideological and religious beliefs were used to justify violence and atrocities against innocent people going about their daily business. These days taking a train or airplane, sitting in a café, or riding a bus to work had suddenly become dangerous.

Lance finally broke the silence. "You know, I don't think this is terrorism," he said.

Fiona snapped her head around to look at him. "What do you mean?"

"Only two people have gotten sick, right?"

Fiona nodded. "Just Nadine and Elizabeth."

"A lot more people would've gotten sick if it was really a terrorist attack on the magazine. And like you said, why would terrorists attack a fashion magazine, anyway? There's lots of better targets, like the subway."

"But if it's not a terror attack, what could it be?" asked Elizabeth.

"Murder," said Lucy.

"Murder!" Elizabeth's eyes were huge. "Who'd want to murder me?"

"Nobody. But I can think of at least one person who wanted Nadine out of the way," said Lucy, remembering Arnold's pass at the AIDS gala.

"So, just for the sake of argument, let's say somebody sent anthrax to Nadine, how could Elizabeth have come in contact with it?" asked Lance.

"However it was delivered, Nadine must have received a lot more than Elizabeth," said Lucy.

"And she must have inhaled it," said Lance. "The inhalation type is a lot more serious. Elizabeth probably only touched it, which is why she got the cutaneous type."

"But what did she touch that Nadine also handled, but that other people didn't?" asked Lucy.

Elizabeth looked thoughtful, going over her actions at the magazine. "The compact!" she exclaimed.

"That's right! Nadine was powdering her face and she dropped the compact and Elizabeth picked it up," said Lucy.

"That would fit," said Lance. "If the anthrax spores were in the powder, they would have been released when she pressed the puff against her face and she would have inhaled them. When Elizabeth picked up the compact, some of the spores must have gotten on her hand."

"Oh, I remember the compact." Fiona's mouth was a round O. "It came a week or two before she got sick. It was lovely, shaped like a pansy with enamel decoration. It just screamed 'spring' and everybody noticed it."

"Where did it come from?" asked Lucy. "Was it a gift? Was there a tag?"

"I doubt it." Fiona shrugged. "Stuff comes in all the time. New products, samples, gifts—there were boxes and boxes arriving everyday from cosmetics manufacturers hoping for a mention in the magazine."

"It must have been addressed to Nadine," insisted Lucy.

"It would have been too dangerous otherwise. Anybody could have taken it."

"Believe me, anybody who's messing around with anthrax isn't thinking too carefully about the consequences," said Lance.

"That's not necessarily true," said Fiona. "Nadine was known for grabbing everything that came in."

"Wasn't that her job?"

"Up to a point," said Fiona. "As beauty editor she got to decide what products to feature, whether it's something new and exciting that readers will want to know about or a product that fits in with a story idea like fresh new scents for spring, that's her decision. But at most magazines extra products are given to the staff. That way, even if the product doesn't get included in the magazine, it's likely that people will use it and talk about it, give it a little boost."

"But not at *Jolie*?"

"Oh no. Nadine hogged it all and everyone knew it. It was kind of a company joke. An industry joke, really. People used to wonder where she kept it all. Her apartment must have been stuffed with it."

"And the murderer took advantage of it to kill her," said Lucy.

"That's cold," said Elizabeth. "I mean, I can't say I liked her. She was kind of weird and she made it pretty clear that she was only interested in herself, but that's not a reason to kill someone, is it?"

"The only reason a murderer needs is a strong desire to get rid of someone," said Lucy.

"I can think of quite a few people who fit that category," said Fiona. "There'll be a lot of gloating at her funeral tomorrow."

"Tomorrow? Isn't that awfully fast?"

Fiona nodded. "It sure is. Phyllis said Nadine was Jewish and they have some religious rule about burying the corpse within 24 hours."

"I'm surprised the medical examiner went along," mused Lucy.

"I'm not," said Lance, drily. "Arnold raised a ton of money for the mayor's reelection campaign."

"That's politics for you," said Elizabeth. "Money talks."

"There'll be a lot of talk at that funeral, that's for sure," said Fiona. "Everybody at the magazine will be there. We all got a voice mail message from Camilla pretty much ordering us to go. She's actually having the invitations delivered by messenger tonight."

"You need an invitation?" Lucy had never heard of such a thing.

"Oh, yeah. Otherwise homeless people would come in just to get warm and that wouldn't do at Frank Campbell's. It's terribly toney."

"That's too bad," said Lucy. "I'd love to go."

Fiona's eyes widened. "You would? Why?"

"To pay my respects," said Lucy, sounding as if butter wouldn't melt in her mouth.

Elizabeth wasn't fooled. "You mean you want to snoop around." She turned to Fiona. "At home, Mom's the local Miss Marple."

"Are you really?" asked Fiona.

"Not exactly," said Lucy, "but I am a reporter for the local newspaper."

"She's solved quite a few mysteries in Tinker's Cove," said Lance, speaking to Fiona. "Couldn't she go with you?"

Just then there was a knock at the door and two extremely fit and clean cut men in dark gray suits walked in. It was obvious to Lucy that the FBI was wasting no time.

"Excuse us for barging in like this," said the taller agent, a black man. "I'm Special agent Isaac Wood, and this is Special Agent Justin Hall." He indicated his companion, who was shorter and had red hair. "We'd like to ask a few questions."

"We were expecting you," said Lucy. She introduced herself as well as Elizabeth and Lance, but when she turned to Fiona, she discovered that Fiona had slipped away.

"That's all of us," she said, covering the momentary awkwardness with a smile. "Fire away."

"Actually, we're here to interview Elizabeth," said Agent Wood.

"Alone," added Agent Hall, pointedly opening the door and holding it.

Lucy didn't like this one bit. "I don't know," she began.

"It's all right, Mom," said Elizabeth.

Lucy was doubtful. Being interviewed by the FBI was serious business. "I can call Brad," she said. "Remember, he's a lawyer."

"Trust me. That's not necessary."

"Okay," said Lucy. She and Lance left the room reluctantly and the door was shut firmly behind them.

"I hope she knows what she's doing," said Lance, looking worried.

"Me, too," agreed Lucy.

Chapter Eleven

BEST BOUTIQUES: WHERE YOU CAN FIND YOUR OWN LOOK

It was after ten when Lucy left the hospital. She started to hail a cab, then remembered it was only a few short blocks to her hotel. The walk would do her good. But when she reached the corner, she discovered a welcoming coffee shop that was still open and ducked inside, climbing up on one of the stools and ordering the 24-hour special of two eggs any style, toast, home fries and choice of bacon or sausage. She ate it all, even the sausage.

Leaving, she passed one of the newsstands that seemed to sit on every corner, noticing that tomorrow's early edition had already been delivered. The proprietor was busy opening the bundles and arranging them. She paused for a moment to check the headlines, amused by the tabloids' preposterous exaggerations about Jen and Brad, Liza and Martha. She also bought a copy of the *New York Times*, curious as to whether the anthrax attack had been reported.

She flipped through it quickly when she got back to the hotel, but all she saw was an obituary. The funeral, she noted, was scheduled for ten in the morning. It was too late to call Sam, so she took a quick shower and then slipped between the crisp, clean sheets, expecting to fall right to sleep. That didn't happen, though. Her mind was too busy with all that had happened and all the things she needed to do. Her top priority was Elizabeth, of course—making sure she got the care she needed to continue getting well.

Now that she knew for sure it was anthrax, with the possibility that the whole city could be at risk, she found Camilla's reaction to her warning simply unbelievable. Why hadn't she taken immediate action? And, come to think of it, why was she still at the office when Lucy called? You'd think she would have been too upset by Nadine's death to stay at work.

Her reaction seemed awfully weird, thought Lucy, reminding herself that you had to make allowances for the bereaved. Grief took everyone differently; some were immediately blown over, others took a while to acknowledge their loss. Furthermore, doctors prescribed all sorts of drugs to help people manage their emotions nowadays, and those drugs often produced odd behavior, like poor Angie Martinelli who had laughed hysterically at her mother-in-law's funeral last month in Tinker's Cove. Though some people said it wasn't the drugs at all, Lucy was willing to give Angie the benefit of the doubt, figuring that if she really had been thrilled at the old woman's death she would have taken pains to hide it. Then again, she had to admit, a lot of folks in Tinker's Cove actually suspected that Angie had something to do with old Mrs. Martinelli's death.

Of course, the fact that Mrs. Martinelli died after eating a cannolli at Angie's house did seem to cast some suspicion on Angie, even though the cause of death was officially a heart attack. Admittedly, Angie was a nurse and she did have access to all sorts of medications and she could have spiked the fatal cannolli, but how could someone like Camilla get access to anthrax? No, Lucy told herself, apart from the lack of outward grief there was absolutely nothing to indicate that Camilla was a murderer, any more than Angie's hysterical laughter proved she had killed her mother-in-law.

After an hour or so of such unproductive thought, Lucy got up and took a Sominex. She finally fell asleep, listening to the constant hum of city traffic, punctuated by sirens.

The wake-up call came promptly at seven, just as she'd requested. Still groggy from sleep, she panicked when she saw Elizabeth's empty bed. Then it all came back to her and she dialed the hospital, learning that Elizabeth had a comfortable night and was continuing to improve. Reassured on that score, she started on the business of dressing and packing. At eight she figured Sam would be awake and called, immediately receiving an invitation to stay at her apartment. Then, after making a quick call to touch bases with Bill, she went downstairs for breakfast.

Cathy and Maria were sitting together in the restaurant and waved her over, inviting her to join them. "Tell us all about Elizabeth," said Maria. "How is she?"

"She's much better, thanks," she said, taking a seat.

"That's great news," drawled Cathy, her huge diamond ring flashing as she signaled the waiter to bring coffee. "I was awfully worried about her, considering what happened to Nadine."

"And now they say her death is suspicious," said Maria, her big black eyes bigger than ever. "It was on the news."

"I never heard of such a thing," said Cathy, crossing her silky legs and letting an excruciatingly fashionable stiletto shoe dangle from her toes. "How can they investigate the flu?"

Lucy had to bite her tongue, even though she knew it would be irresponsible to break the news; soon enough all the makeover winners would be contacted by public health officials. She certainly didn't want to start a panic so she changed the subject.

"Are you guys going home today?"

"Tiffany and I are staying a few extra days, but I think everybody else is leaving. I figured that if I was going to come all the way from Dallas I wasn't going to leave without taking in the town. Maria's taking us shopping. She knows all the best places."

"Everything from designer boutiques to sidewalk peddlers," said Maria.

"Which is why we're getting an early start. Tiffany wants people to think she's a fashionista and Carmela's upstairs, helping her decide what to wear. It's a lengthy process." Cathy gave the waiter a big smile. "My friend needs a cup of coffee and we'd like a refill."

"Decaf for me. I'm already feeling wired," said Maria.

"So what happened at the magazine after I left?" asked Lucy, as the waiter set a cup down and filled it.

"It was crazy!"

"All the staffers were running around like chickens with no heads," said Cathy. "We weren't sure what to do; we were all standing around like little lost lemon drops, you know, not part of it really and not sure what to do. Nancy finally remembered us and told us we should leave."

"She was very nice. Very apologetic." Maria's hands were everywhere—she was one of those people who spoke with their hands. "But she said they had to cancel the final dinner party and the holiday show at Radio City Music Hall."

"No Rockettes?"

"I guess they felt it wouldn't have been right, under the circumstances." Cathy stirred her coffee.

"But the girls were disappointed," said Maria.

"We all ate here, at the hotel. It was fine." Cathy furrowed her beautifully arched brows and leaned forward. "Camilla stopped by and presented the ten thousand dollars to Lurleen and Faith. No surprise there."

Maria rolled her eyes. "It was 'hallelujahs' all night." She shrugged. "You can't blame them for being excited but everybody else was pretty down. When you and Elizabeth didn't show we were all worried."

"And, of course, people were upset about Nadine."

"So young!" Maria shook her black curls. "And a woman like her! One who could afford the best care, the best doctors."

"Maybe she had a heart condition," speculated Cathy. "Like those athletes who are fine one minute and drop dead the next."

"But your little girl, well, not-so-little girl, will she be all right? We heard she was in intensive care?"

Lucy suddenly felt guilty. What was she doing sitting around gossiping? She needed to get moving if she was going to check out of the hotel and get her bags moved to Sam's apartment before going back to Elizabeth in the hospital.

"She's feeling much better," she said. "Thanks for asking. Now, if you'll excuse me, I've got to get something to eat."

When she returned with a plate loaded with pancakes and sausage, the conversation continued.

"What are they doing for her?" asked Cathy.

"Just fluids and antibiotics." Lucy took a big bite of syrup-drenched pancake.

"Antibiotics?" Maria's brows shot up. "They don't do anything for the flu."

Lucy suddenly wished she hadn't been so open.

"I know about flu," continued Maria. "I had it last year. I begged for an antibiotic but the doctor wouldn't give it to me. He said it wouldn't do any good. He told me to rest and take chicken soup."

"They actually think it's a reaction to a spider bite," said Lucy, spearing a sausage, "but they're not sure. It's probably not the same thing that Nadine had."

"Spider bite?" Cathy was doubtful. "Now if it were me or Tiffany, I'd say that was a possibility, since we live in the South, but you guys come from Maine. Aren't your spiders hibernating?"

"I would have thought so," said Lucy, licking the last

bits of syrup off her fork and placing it carefully on her plate. "I don't really care what caused it, I'm just glad she's on the road to recovery." She stood up. "Now I've really got to go. I don't want to stay away from the hospital too long."

"Have you got a place to stay?" asked Cathy. "I have a suite and we've got plenty of room."

"You could have the couch at my place," added Maria.

Lucy was amazed; she hadn't expected such kindness. "Thanks, that's awfully sweet of you, but an old college friend is letting me stay with her. She's got an apartment on Riverside Drive."

"That's good," said Maria. "In times of trouble, it's good to have a friend."

"Yes, it is," said Lucy, marveling that she'd received three invitations when she'd been worried about finding a place to stay.

Headed uptown in a taxi, Lucy felt lighter, as if sharing her worries with Cathy and Maria had made them less burdensome. Everything was going to be okay. Elizabeth was getting better, she had a place to stay, and she had friends in the city who would help and support her. These were all good things.

She tried to keep that thought as the cab sped through Central Park, but she couldn't quite free herself of the notion that something black and evil had come too close—and it could come back.

The doorman at Sam's building opened the cab door for Lucy and brought the bags inside, but when Lucy explained who she was, he told her no one was home. Sam had left instructions to let her into the apartment but Lucy declined, anxious to get back to Elizabeth in the hospital. She left the bags in his care and, refusing his offer to call a taxi, headed for the subway. It was much cheaper than a cab and faster, too, since the trains didn't have to deal with traffic.

Rush hour was in full swing when she descended the grimy stairs that led to the even grimier station, where the platform was filled with waiting people. Oddly enough, there were free seats on the heavy-duty vandal-proof benches and she sat down, pondering the elements that composed the unique subway aroma. Primarily urine and soot, she decided, with a hint of ozone. She didn't mind the smell; it evoked memories of childhood trips with her mother to see a Broadway show or to shop in now defunct department stores like Altman's and Gimbel's.

Her reverie of days gone by was interrupted when the train rumbled into the station. She got up and joined the mob cramming into the already crowded car, hanging on to a pole for the ride downtown to Times Square, where she took the shuttle over to the East Side and the old Lexington Avenue line. Nowadays the trains had numbers or letters for names but she couldn't be bothered to learn them. The 1 would forever be the Broadway line to her, and the 4, 5, and 6 would be the Lexington Avenue line.

When she exited at Sixty-eighth Street she still had to walk several city blocks to the hospital. No wonder New Yorkers all seemed so trim, she thought, contrasting their way of life with the rural lifestyle in Tinker's Cove. There, everybody drove everywhere. Nobody walked, even if it was only for a few blocks. It was a paradox, really. Somehow you'd think people would be healthier in the country, but in truth they got very little exercise unless they went out specifically looking for it. Taking a walk or going for a bike ride were recreational activities, not everyday means of transportation.

As she walked along the sidewalk, which was lined with tall apartment buildings, she noticed that a lot of people had dogs. Not just little dogs, either, but Labs and standard poodles and even a St. Bernard. That surprised her. It seemed a lot harder to keep a dog in the city, especially considering the requirement that owners pick up their messes. But everyone seemed to be a good sport about it; many carried plastic bags at the ready. The dogs were leashed, of course. They couldn't run free as most dogs did in Tinker's Cove, where people had big backyards and there wasn't much traffic.

Lucy was wondering if dogs were really happy in the city when she arrived at the hospital. A young Lab was waiting outside, tied to a fire hydrant, and she paused to pet it.

"You look like my puppy," she said, thinking of Libby as she stroked the Lab's silky ears.

The puppy wagged her tail and gave Lucy a big doggy smile, and Lucy found herself smiling for the first time that day.

When she got to the ICU, however, she had a scary moment when she found Elizabeth's bed stripped and empty. Then she remembered Dr. Marchetti had told her she would probably be moved to a regular room today and went to the nurse's desk to get directions.

Elizabeth was sleeping when Lucy found her, once again in a single room. Fiona's flowers had been moved along with her, and several new arrangements had also arrived, including a large one from *Jolie* magazine.

Lucy stood for a moment, staring at the card, then checked her watch. It was nine-thirty. If she left now, she could make the funeral. But what about Elizabeth? Lucy checked her forehead and discovered it was cool. Even more encouraging, the sore on her hand was almost entirely healed. She considered her choices: she could either stay at the hospital, watching Elizabeth sleep, or she could go the funeral, and try to figure out who had poisoned Elizabeth and Nadine.

It was no choice at all, really. She checked her cell phone battery and scribbled a note for Elizabeth, leaving it along with some toiletries and fresh pajamas. She wasn't going far and Elizabeth could call if she needed her. She bent down and placed a quick kiss on her forehead, and then she was out the door.

Chapter Twelve

BLACK IS BACK—BUT IT'S ANYTHING BUT BASIC

Lucy had attended plenty of funerals in Tinker's Cove, but they were nothing like this, she thought as she approached the Frank E. Campbell funeral home on Madison Avenue. Temporary barricades had been set up to contain the inevitable celebrity watchers who had gathered to see exactly who was emerging from the line of limousines that was inching its way along the street. There was a smattering of applause when the mayor arrived and, ever the politician, shook a few hands before recalling he was there as a mourner. Assuming a serious expression he stepped under the maroon canopy and entered the gray stone building. Lucy followed, hot on his heels, but was stopped by a stocky young man in a black suit.

"May I see your invitation?"

Lucy opened her purse and began searching for an imaginary invitation.

"Oh, dear, I must have left it home."

"I'm afraid I can't admit anyone without an invitation."

Lucy feigned a panicked expression. "Oh, please let me in. You see, I work at *Jolie* magazine and everyone's been ordered to go and if I don't show up, well, I'm afraid I'll get in big trouble."

The young man seemed doubtful about Lucy's story but

when Fiona trotted up to the door, calling Lucy by name and waving an invitation, he let them both in.

"Thanks," said Lucy. "You arrived in the nick of."

"No problem," said Fiona, as they handed over their coats to the check room attendant. "He was kind of cute, in a 'Six Feet Under' sort of way." She giggled. "Do you think he got to see Nadine naked?"

"Behave yourself," said Lucy, forgetting for a moment that Fiona wasn't her child. "This is a funeral."

"Righto." Fiona adopted a serious expression. "I'll be good."

Together they followed the stream of mourners proceeding down a plush carpeted hall to the memorial chapel. They could hear the soft strains of classical music and when they entered the chapel, which was filled with white-painted pews like a New England church, they found a string quartet was playing.

Nadine's closed coffin was resting in the front of the room. Arnold was sitting in the first pew, in the seat closest to the coffin. He appeared to be weeping and was being consoled by Nancy Glass, who kept him supplied with fresh tissues. She couldn't seem to keep her hands off him and was constantly patting his shoulder or holding his hand.

Hmm. Not so different from Tinker's Cove, thought Lucy, taking a seat beside Fiona. They were in the back of the chapel, appropriate to their lowly status. The front rows, where name cards were affixed to the pews, were filling up fast with family, colleagues and celebrities. Lucy spotted Norah, looking very somber and sitting by herself. Anna Wintour from *Vogue* was there, along with Diane Sawyer and Barbara Walters, plus lots of people Lucy didn't recognize but who seemed important—at least to themselves.

Camilla and Elise were the last to arrive. A role reversal had apparently taken place and today Camilla was the one overcome by grief, leaning heavily on her larger friend as they made their halting way down to their front-row seats. Both were clad in black: Camilla in a couture suit with a fitted jacket and a short skirt and Elise in one of the severe pantsuits she favored. This was a very different Camilla from the woman Lucy had seen at the magazine. She seemed unable to support herself and dabbed constantly at her eyes with a lacy handkerchief. Lucy wondered if the realization of her loss had suddenly overtaken her, which she knew it sometimes did at a funeral, when it became impossible to deny the finality of the situation, or if she was simply putting on a show, which she knew people also did because they thought it was expected. Or, thought Lucy, maybe Camilla had finally realized the gravity of the situation now that the investigation had begun. Health officials would soon be closing the Jolie offices, if they hadn't done so already, and the workers would be told to seek medical advice; police and FBI agents would be questioning everybody.

There was a considerable fuss as Camilla practically collapsed onto her seat and Elise fanned her with a program. A few rows behind them Lucy noticed accessories editor Deb Shertzer and Nadine's assistant Phyllis, whispering together. She nudged Fiona and cast a questioning glance in their direction.

"No tears there," said Fiona. "Phyllis has been promoted to replace Nadine."

"Permanently?"

"That's the word."

Lucy was thinking that the promotion had taken place very quickly indeed when the rabbi, dressed in a black robe with velvet trim and a yarmulka, took the podium. "We are here today," he began, "to celebrate the life of Nadine Nelson. Beloved wife of Arnold, dear friend to many, a tireless worker. . . ."

"He didn't know her very well," whispered Fiona, and Lucy had to stifle a giggle.

The rabbi droned on for almost an hour, recounting one or two anecdotes about Nadine but relying heavily on generalities and religious abstractions for his eulogy. He was the only speaker; there were no heartfelt reminiscences from friends and family; no favorite songs, nothing to signify the loss of a unique and much loved individual. Lucy had trouble keeping her mind from wandering and was wondering if there would be refreshments, compulsory in Tinker's Cove, when the string quartet finally played the final chords of Barber's *Adagio* and the service drew to a close. A few people stood and made their way to the front of the room to pay their respects to Arnold, others lingered in their seats, a few dabbing at their eyes, others no doubt taking a few minutes to meditate on the transitory nature of life, or perhaps to plot the rest of their day.

"I have to speak to Camilla," said Fiona, rising. "I want to make sure she knows I'm here."

Lucy remained seated, watching as Norah paid her respects to Arnold. Others were falling into line, including many of the celebrities. Diane Sawyer was taking his hand when a series of flashes went off. It was Pablo, taking pictures.

"What the hell do you think you're doing?" demanded Elise, confronting him.

"Yesterday Camilla told me she wanted funeral photos for the magazine," said Pablo. "A tasteful round-up, that's what she said."

Elise looked at Camilla, who shook her head weakly.

"Liar!" she growled, grabbing for the camera.

"She's the liar," muttered Pablo, nodding towards Camilla and tightening his hold on the camera.

"How can you? At a time like this."

Everyone was silent. A few high profile guests headed discreetly for the door, others stood awkwardly, watching the scene.

"It wasn't my idea," insisted Pablo, shaking his head.

"She was our best friend," hissed Elise, hurrying back to Camilla, who had slipped on a pair of large sunglasses and was sniffling into a handkerchief. She gently led her out of the chapel, guarding her as ferociously as a pit bull.

"Best friend? I don't think so," muttered Pablo, stalking off.

Lucy was tempted to follow him and ask exactly what he meant, but she hesitated, aware that he was in quite a temper. The last thing she wanted was to create a second scene. So she sat, waiting for the crowd around Arnold to thin, and replayed the confrontation in her mind. She didn't doubt for a minute that Camilla had assigned Pablo to take the photos; the magazine always devoted a page to celebrity appearances. Usually it was balls and fund raisers, but Lucy doubted Camilla would think a funeral was any less worthy of exploitation. After all, the level of taste at *Jolie* was remarkably low, if the issue she read was any indication. Anyone who would have homeless people model jewelry wouldn't hesitate to capitalize on her best friend's death. Lucy could picture it: "Norah Hemmings in Prada, Diane Sawyer in Mark Jacobs and Barbara Walters in Oscar de la Renta console each other at the funeral of *Jolie* beauty editor Nadine Nelson . . . in coffin."

Enough, Lucy told herself. It was time to get moving. Only a few people were standing with Arnold and he was beginning to move towards the door. She'd have a quick word with him and then head for the hospital.

"I'm sorry for your loss," she murmured, approaching him and extending her hand. "My daughter and I enjoyed getting to know Nadine. . . ."

Arnold, however, looked as if he'd seen a ghost. "You!" he snarled, glaring at her. "What are you doing here?"

Lucy's jaw dropped. She certainly hadn't expected this. "I came to express my sympathy," she said, "and I was hoping to have a word with you. Your wife and my daughter are both victims of the same. . . ."

"Not now," he snapped, turning to one of the black-suited attendants. "Get her out of here."

Lucy couldn't believe his reaction. Even worse, two extremely fit young men in black suits were coming her way. "This isn't necessary," she protested. "Please, let me give you my number. I really think we ought to talk."

"We have absolutely nothing to talk about," said Arnold, giving the young men a nod.

Each one grasped her by an elbow and propelled her out of the room, down the hall and through the front door, where they deposited her unceremoniously outside.

"Hey, what about my coat?" she demanded, and one of the young men reappeared in the doorway. Smiling, he tossed it and it landed at her feet, on the gray all-weather carpet tastefully bordered with black.

Chapter Thirteen

CONFUSED BY COLOR? FIND YOUR PERFECT PALETTE

Lucy snatched the coat and brushed it off, trying to ig-nore the curious stares of the handful of gawkers still clustered on the sidewalk. It was horribly embarrassing but she put the best face on that she could as she shrugged into the green plaid coat. She wanted to get away quickly and was walking as fast as she could in her high-heeled makeover boots when she was approached by a woman she didn't know.

Only a few days ago Lucy would have summed her up as a rather pleasant looking thirty-something professional but the makeover had sharpened her eyes. She immedi-ately noticed the cheap haircut, the navy blue pants and trench coat, the imitation leather purse and the sensible, flat-heeled shoes. She also noticed the black vinyl wallet the woman was holding in her unmanicured hand which contained an FBI identification card.

"Do you mind if we talk for a minute," she said, ex-tending her right hand. "I'm FBI Agent Christine Crandall."

Lucy took the proffered hand. It seemed unfair, some-how, that women in official jobs, like cops and firefighters and even plainclothes FBI agents, never looked quite as good as the men. It was almost as if someone, somewhere, was making sure the dress requirements indicated that these really weren't suitable jobs for women. The mannish clothes that signaled authority didn't flatter them, they needed to carry cumbersome purses and no matter how much they exercised they couldn't get rid of those stubborn saddlebags. "Actually, couldn't we do it some other time? I'm on my way to the hospital."

"I'm afraid I really have to insist." Agent Christine wasn't taking no for an answer. "There's a coffee shop a few doors down. Shall we go there?"

"I really can't stay too long," muttered Lucy, regretting her decision to leave Elizabeth alone at the hospital. "Coming to the funeral was a mistake."

"I saw you get the bum's rush," said Christine, pulling open the coffee shop door and holding it for Lucy. "How come?"

"I'm not really sure," said Lucy, taking a seat at an empty booth in the back. "It was by invitation only and I wasn't actually invited, but I can't believe that Arnold had the guest list in his head." If anything, she suspected his reaction had been fueled by a guilty conscience.

"Where I come from you don't need an invitation to attend a funeral. Most everybody in town goes and the family takes pride in attracting a crowd. It's almost like a popularity contest—you don't want to have just a handful of mourners, you want everybody to come."

"That's how it is in my town, too," said Lucy, ignoring the menu which was encased in a sticky plastic sleeve bound with maroon cloth tape. "But I'm beginning to think Tinker's Cove is on a different planet from New York."

Christine laughed. "You could say the same for Chagrin Falls."

Lucy thought it sounded like something from "Rocky and Bullwinkle" but kept that thought to herself. It sure was easy to talk to this FBI agent, though. She hadn't expected her to be so friendly. "And where is Chagrin Falls?"

"Ohio." Christine smiled at the waitress, who was

standing with her order pad at the ready. "I'll just have coffee."

"Same for me," said Lucy.

Once that was out of the way Lucy expected Christine to begin questioning her and she was eager to share her thoughts on the case. She was sure the FBI would want to know all about Nadine's compact and her habit of commandeering all the product samples. She could also offer quite a bit of insight into the rivalries at the magazine, and then there was the fact that Arnold had made a pass at her at the gala which seemed to indicate he was something less than a devoted husband. And, of course, there was Camilla's increasingly strange behavior.

"So how come you and your daughter are in New York?" asked Christine, setting a small tape recorder on the table between them. "You don't mind if I record this, do you?"

The presence of the compact device set off alarm bells in Lucy's head. Maybe all this friendliness was just a trick to get her to let down her guard. "Am I a suspect or something?"

The agent's reply was quick as a whip. "Should you be?"

Lucy felt for a moment as if all the air had been sucked out of the shop. "Oh, no! Not at all."

"Well, then you have nothing to worry about."

"That's what they told Monica Lewinsky," said Lucy. "And Martha Stewart." The waitress set the coffee on the table. "Maybe I should have a lawyer."

Christine ripped a packet of sugar open and poured it into her cup, then peeled open a little plastic bucket of cream and poured it in, stirring smoothly. "That's your right, of course, but I think you're overreacting. Don't you want to help us catch the person who did this to your daughter?"

Lucy lifted her mug and took a sip. "Of course I do.

But, frankly, I don't understand why you're questioning me. Agents Hall and Wood were at the hospital last night and they made it very clear that they were only interested in talking to Elizabeth."

"Really? They were there last night?"

Lucy was puzzled. "Didn't you know? Don't you guys talk to each other?"

Christine took a long, long sip of coffee. "Department policy," she said, finally. "We don't like our left hand to know what our right is doing. It corrupts the investigative process."

It sounded reasonable enough to Lucy. She might even be quoting some FBI manual packed with government gobbledygook. "If you say so."

"Okay, then. What brought you and your daughter to New York?"

"Actually, Elizabeth won a contest for mother and daughter makeovers. *Jolie* magazine flew us to the city and put us up at the Melrose Hotel, all expenses paid."

Agent Christine didn't reply and Lucy found herself babbling to fill the silence.

"It meant leaving my husband and the other kids at home during Christmas school vacation but I thought it would be an opportunity to spend some special time with my oldest daughter. After all, who knows where she might go after graduation? It could be my last chance to have her to myself."

"How many other children?"

"Three others, but my oldest son doesn't live with us anymore so it's really just Sara and Zoe. They're fourteen and eight."

Christine stared at her. "And you really thought it was a good idea to fly to New York?"

Lucy's back stiffened. "Why not? She's not a baby anymore and my husband is perfectly capable. . . ."

"Not that. I meant flying. Haven't you heard about 9/11?"

"Of course I've heard about it." Lucy remembered the beautiful sunny weather that day and how she was unable to pull herself away from the TV set as the horror unfolded. "I was just as upset as everyone else. But, hey, aren't you guys supposed to be making flying safer? Aren't we supposed to go about our lives as normally as possible? Not let the terrorists stop us because that would be a victory for them?"

Christine looked at her as if she were crazy. "All it takes is one extremist with a bomb. And it's not just airplanes. They can hit buildings, subways, commuter trains, buses, you name it. The Statue of Liberty, the Empire State Building." Christine was getting rather agitated and there was a gleam in her eye. "Do you know they have nuclear bombs that can fit in a suitcase? And just imagine what a biological agent could do if it were released in the subway."

Lucy was beginning to feel cornered and she didn't like it. Who did this person think she was to make judgments about her choices? "Well, if something like that happens at least I'll know I looked good when I went," she answered, tossing her head. She knew every hair would fall back into place, thanks to her Rudolf haircut.

As a matter of fact, she was beginning to think Agent Christine should spend a little more time worrying about her appearance and a little bit less worrying about dooms-day scenarios. Of course, that was her job, admitted Lucy, but she could at least try to look her best while pursuing terrorists and criminals. The poor girl had obviously cut her hair herself or had gone to one of those walk-in places that charge eleven dollars. She didn't bother with make-up, her eyebrows needed shaping, and that navy blue pantsuit she was wearing was all wrong with her pinkish complexion and blond hair. The pantsuit was also much too severe, and that red bow she'd tied around her neck went out in the eighties. Where did she buy her clothes anyway? Goodwill?

"You certainly have a great haircut," said Christine. "I've been admiring it. Who did it?"

"Rudolfo. The magazine sent us to his salon."

"Is he expensive?"

Lucy was surprised by the question. Surely everyone in New York knew about Rudolfo and his five hundred dollar haircuts. "Very expensive, but there are plenty of other good stylists. Ask around."

"That's a good idea."

Encouraged by Christine's reaction, Lucy thought she might offer a bit more advice. "You could also have your eyebrows shaped. It really opens up your face, at least that's what they told us. And if you have it done once professionally you can maintain it yourself with tweezers."

"My sister plucked hers and all she's got left are two tiny arches that look ridiculous."

"That's why you need a professional shaping," said Lucy, aware that she was sounding an awful lot like her friend Sue back in Tinker's Cove. What a change a few days could make. She always resented Sue's unbidden advice, but now she couldn't seem to stop herself from doing the same thing. "You could also get your colors done. They told me I'm a winter and I should wear black, white, and jewel tones. I'm no expert but I think you're a spring and you'd look good in soft pastel colors."

"FBI agents don't wear pink."

"Maybe a sage green suit with a pink blouse? Or a little floral-print scarf, tied cowboy style so it wouldn't get in your way? You can be both professional and feminine." Lucy was beginning to wonder if she'd been possessed by some sort of fashion demon. Indeed, Christine didn't seem to be listening. "But we've gotten off track here," she admitted, swallowing the last of her coffee. "I have some ideas about how the anthrax was delivered. As beauty editor, Nadine got a lot of product samples, including a rather fancy powder compact. She dropped it during our consultation and Elizabeth picked it up, which is probably how she got exposed."

The agent looked at her sharply. "How did you get this information?"

"It's just a theory," said Lucy. "One of Elizabeth's friends did some Internet research and that's what we came up with. It seems to fit the circumstances of the case. Nadine was always powdering her nose. I guess she was known for being vain. And it was also widely known that she didn't like to share the samples and kept them for herself. Putting the anthrax in a fancy compact was a clever touch, though. Whoever sent it to her must have known her well and been confident that she would want to keep such a beautiful trinket for herself. The fact that Elizabeth was exposed was simply bad luck; the anthrax wasn't meant for her. Nadine was the real target, and Elizabeth just happened to be in the wrong place at the wrong time." Lucy tapped her upper lip with her finger. "The big questions, of course, are who sent the anthrax and why did they do it? That's what I'd like to know."

"And is that why you went to the funeral today, even though you weren't invited?"

Lucy's jaw dropped. She was beginning to think she'd underestimated Agent Christine. Just when she was beginning to wonder what her FBI superiors would think if they listened to the tape of their conversation and if she'd get in trouble for discussing hairstyles and fashion tips, it occurred to Lucy that all that small talk might have been a ploy to get her to say more than she otherwise would. If it was, she had certainly fallen for it and right now she felt pretty stupid.

"I simply wanted to pay my respects to a woman who

taught me the value of daily moisturizing," said Lucy. She thought about dabbing her eyes with a tissue but decided that would be overdoing it.

"You're an investigative reporter. You want to break this case."

Lucy was stunned. "How do you know what I do? And anyway, that's not important. This is my daughter, you know. Of course I want to find out who poisoned her, but not because I'm going to break a big story. It's because I love her and I want to make sure whoever made her sick doesn't do it to somebody else."

"Which is why you're going to start cooperating and telling the truth," said Christine. "You say Nadine dropped the compact and your daughter picked it up. Why?"

"It practically fell at her feet. It was the polite thing to do."

"Did Nadine throw it at her? Did somebody knock it out of her hand?"

"Nope. She just dropped it."

"How did the others react when she dropped it?"

At this rate, thought Lucy, Agent Christine would be retired before the case was solved. "I don't think anybody noticed. It was all over in a second or two."

"Did anyone else reach for the compact?"

"Not that I noticed. Frankly, I was mostly watching Nadine."

"Why?"

"She was the queen bee, if you know what I mean. Ordering people around, coming up with crazy ideas, and all the time looking at herself in the compact mirror. She was completely narcissistic. I don't think I ever met anyone like her before. Nobody else mattered to her."

"Yeah, I know what you mean." Christine nodded, then seemed to remember her role. "I mean, you picked all this up in less than half an hour?"

"Well, I've had a lot of time to think about it." Lucy's

eyes met the agent's. "Sitting in a hospital room with a sick child does tend to concentrate the mind. I've been over that session in my mind a million times, dredging up every detail."

"Hindsight isn't always accurate," warned Christine. "Your emotions can color your memories."

"I know," admitted Lucy. "But you've probably been talking with lots of people. You're trained to filter out the personal reactions to get to the truth."

"Absolutely."

"So what have you learned so far?"

Christine's unkempt eyebrows shot up and she pursed her mouth. "Any information relevant to this case is strictly confidential and I am not at liberty to divulge it," she said.

There it was again, that darn FBI manual. "Just thought I'd try." Lucy shrugged.

"I don't think I need to keep you any longer," said Christine, crumpling her napkin and tossing it on the table. "But I do think I ought to warn you that obstructing a federal investigation constitutes a felony."

"Felony? That seems kind of harsh. Are you sure it's not a misdemeanor?"

For a brief second Christine seemed confused. "A felony," she snapped, dropping a couple of dollar bills on the table. "Let me make this very clear," she said. "Mind your own business and leave the investigating to the professionals. We don't want you to get hurt."

Having delivered a warning, Agent Christine turned on her heels and sped out of the coffee shop.

Darn, thought Lucy, she hadn't even gotten a chance to share her theory about Arnold or her questions about Camilla.

Chapter Fourteen

ACCESSORIES FORECAST:
BRING ON THE BLING!

Lucy remained at the table after Agent Christine left and pulled her cellphone out of her purse, eager to check on Elizabeth.

"How are you?" she asked.

"Okay."

"Did you find the things I left you?"

"Yeah, thanks, Mom."

"Is there anything else you need? I'm on my way over."

"Right now?" Elizabeth didn't sound eager to see her.

"Yeah," said Lucy. "Is there a problem?"

"Uh, well, Lance is coming. He's bringing me lunch."

"Okay." Lucy sighed. "I'll catch you later."

"No rush, Mom. I'm fine. Really. Come tonight, okay?"

Well, that certainly didn't take long, thought Lucy, ending the call. Already she was a third wheel. She wasn't needed, she was superfluous. That's how it was with college-age kids. One minute you were bailing them out of a crisis and the next you were getting in their hair. She might as well have another cup of coffee. So when the waitress came over with the coffee pot and offered to refill her cup, she accepted and sat, staring into the black liquid, thinking over her conversation with Agent Christine.

The FBI agent was right about one thing. It was ridiculous to think she could identify Nadine's killer. For one thing, she was a fish out of water in the city. Back home in Tinker's Cove she knew her way around, she knew the people. But that certainly wasn't the case here; she'd only been in the city for a few days and hardly knew anyone. And then there was the matter of the murder weapon: anthrax. She hardly knew what it was and didn't have a clue where the killer could have obtained it. It seemed the very last thing that people in Nadine's world of society and fashion could access.

Nevertheless, leaving it to the FBI was like staring at the slick, oily surface of the coffee hoping that a face would magically appear or the steam rising from the cup would take the shape of letters spelling out a name. It was no good. There was no way she could sit around waiting for the official investigation to produce the sicko who had killed Nadine and poisoned Elizabeth. After all, government officials hadn't succeeded in solving the original anthrax attack, and that was years ago. She might not have any better luck, but she had to try.

Investigating was the only thing she knew how to do. She couldn't administer drugs or conduct lab tests to make Elizabeth better; she had to leave that to the doctors and nurses. But as a mother she still wanted, no, *needed*, to help. Even if she only turned up one tiny clue, it would be better than doing nothing.

Besides, if Agent Christine was the best the FBI had to offer, Lucy didn't have a lot of confidence the agency would ever solve the case. She didn't know much about the FBI, but she was aware that its reputation for infallibility had suffered after Oklahoma City and 9/11. Even so, the conversation with Agent Christine had seemed a bit odd. Lucy chewed on her lip. Maybe Agent Christine was new to the job.

Lucy took a sip of coffee and pulled a pen out of her purse. She plucked a paper napkin from the chrome holder on the table and started making a list of names, all possible suspects.

Nadine's husband, Arnold, topped the list. It was a sad but indisputable fact that the husband was always the prime suspect when a wife was murdered, and from what she knew of Arnold he certainly deserved that dubious honor. She clucked her tongue, remembering the pass he made at her at the gala, even while his wife was dying. What a slimeball. She underlined his name and added an exclamation point.

Of course, the fact that he had a roving eye didn't necessarily make him a murderer. Plenty of men felt they had to make a pass at every attractive woman they encountered; it was almost expected, like all men were supposed to love sports. Those who didn't, the guys who'd rather spend Sunday afternoon at the ballet than in front of the TV watching football, were judged as less than manly. Maybe she was placing too much emphasis on one little pass. It had been a clumsy attempt, almost cartoonish, with his talk of champagne and caviar. Maybe he had only been joking and she was such a rube that she didn't get it. Maybe it was some sort of New York compliment.

But that didn't explain his reaction to her at the funeral. You would have thought he suspected *her* of poisoning Nadine, which was patently absurd since Nadine was already sick when they met. Lucy scratched her chin thoughtfully. It could be a smart ploy, however, if he wanted to turn suspicion away from himself. She supposed it could be argued that Elizabeth got sick administering the anthrax to Nadine. It wouldn't hold up for long, of course, but it might give him time to hide evidence or flee to the Bahamas or whatever he might be planning.

And what about Camilla? Lucy wasn't at all convinced that her show of grief at the funeral was genuine. In truth, from what she'd seen of Camilla, it seemed the woman had ice water in her veins. She was essentially interested in only one person—herself. And what had Pablo meant when he'd said Nadine wasn't as good a friend to her as she thought? Had Nadine been angling to get Camilla's job? It was possible; she certainly seemed to have plenty of ideas about how to run the magazine. Everybody knew the magazine was in trouble—did that mean Camilla was in trouble? Camilla was an ambitious woman, and Lucy had no doubt that if she found herself pressured by the publisher on one hand and her old friend on the other, the old friend would have to go. But why not fire her? Did Nadine have some hold on her, some information, that made that option impossible? You didn't need to be a psychiatrist to know that Camilla was driven to succeed. Lucy had no doubt she would do whatever it took, even murder, to maintain her status as New York's most influential magazine editor.

After Arnold and Camilla, the name that came to mind was Pablo, the photographer. He must certainly have resented Nadine's influence at the magazine, where Camilla ignored his ideas in favor of her half-cracked notions. Lucy knew from her own experience how frustrating it was to see her byline on a story she didn't believe in. An example that came to mind was a puff piece Ted had insisted she write about the visit of an aspiring pop star to the outlet mall last summer, even though she had argued that her time would be better spent on a story about the school budget. He'd overruled her, insisting that the story would appeal to younger readers. She'd been embarrassed when it appeared, and she couldn't imagine that Pablo had been very happy about attaching his name to a photo spread of homeless people modeling priceless gems. If he had any artistic integrity at all he must have been mortified to have his talent employed to mock those unfortunate souls.

Pablo's buddy Nancy was no fan of Nadine's either,

thought Lucy, adding her name to the list. Nancy certainly seemed eager to comfort Arnold; she'd been all over the man at the funeral. Perhaps she saw herself as the next Mrs. Arnold Nelson and decided the road to matrimony would be a lot smoother if she got rid of the first? From her point of view it would be a win–win situation: even if she failed to snag Arnold, she would have the benefit of getting Nadine out of the way at work.

Phyllis was another *Jolie* employee who benefited from Nadine's demise: she got her job. Was that reason enough to kill the woman? After all, Phyllis had seemed devoted to Nadine. If the woman told her to jump, Phyllis jumped. That was how it appeared anyway, but Lucy knew that appearances could be deceptive. Maybe Phyllis resented Nadine every bit as much as Pablo did but had been better at masking her emotions. Lucy decided she'd love to know Phyllis's true feelings.

And then there was Elise, the fashion editor who didn't seem all that interested in fashion. She seemed to be working at the magazine only because her old college friends Camilla and Nadine were there. It reminded Lucy of a favorite saying of her mother's: "Three's a crowd." To her mother's way of thinking, people naturally tended to pair off, and not just matrimonially. Two could walk abreast comfortably on a sidewalk, but if there were three someone had to walk alone. Two could sit together at a theater and chat while waiting for the show to start, but not three. Two could ride together in the front seat of a car, but the third had to take the backseat. What if Elise had gotten tired of sitting in the backseat? Would she kill to ride shotgun? Lucy remembered how she had supported Camilla at the funeral, and she added her name to the list, which was growing rather long without even considering the makeover winners.

Most of them could be dismissed, she decided, because they'd had no contact with Nadine before they arrived in

New York. There were a couple of exceptions, though. Cathy, for example, had a history of sorts with Camilla and Nadine, having encountered them through her work at Neiman Marcus. And Maria lived in New York. Maybe she'd had some sort of run-in with her. But where would Cathy or Maria, or any of the other people on her list for that matter, get anthrax? And how could they handle it without getting sick themselves?

Lucy reached for her coffee cup and took a sip, but the coffee was cold. She'd been so absorbed in her list of suspects that she'd forgotten to drink it. Coffee had a way of cooling off, and so did investigations, if you let them sit too long. Lucy knew that time was not on her side if she was going to catch the anthrax poisoner, but she didn't know how to begin. Back home she'd simply grab her reporter's notebook and start asking questions, but it wasn't that simple here in New York, especially since she'd been officially warned off by the FBI. She needed to find a way to investigate that wouldn't rouse suspicion: she needed to fly below the radar. But how she was going to do that was anybody's guess. She got up and shrugged into her coat.

Outside, on the sidewalk, it occurred to her that emotion was clouding the issue. As a reporter she'd conducted plenty of investigations in Tinker's Cove and she'd always been more or less personally involved, but not like this. This time it was her daughter who'd been attacked, and she was determined to do everything in her power to bring the poisoner to justice. The hell with justice, she thought, striding along the sidewalk; she'd like to strangle whoever did this to Elizabeth, or even better, she'd like to give this heartless villain a taste of his own medicine. Or hers. She'd like to inject a big fat horse syringe of deadly microbes into his bloodstream and see how he'd feel then.

Walking along the sidewalk in the direction of the hospital, Lucy passed a newsstand and stopped to read the headlines: "Martha Stewart's Jail Décor," "Rosie's New Weight Loss Plan," "What I Saw in Michael's Bedroom" and "Scott Peterson's Girlfriend Talks." Taking a *New York Tattler* off the pile and paying for it, Lucy looked for the story about Nadine's death, but didn't find anything. Tucking it in her bag she came to a decision. There was one surefire way she knew to ignite an investigation, and she was going to do it. She hailed a cab and gave the address of the *Tattler*. After all, what she had to tell them was a lot more sensational than Rosie's latest diet.

The *Tattler* encouraged tips from readers and once Lucy had cleared the metal scanner and her bag had been checked for guns and explosive devices, she was sent straight up to the newsroom to talk to the news editor, Ed Riedel. Her spirits climbed as the elevator chugged upwards; it was such a relief to be doing something positive. She could hardly wait to tell this Ed Riedel the inside story of Nadine Nelson's death.

But when the elevator stopped and the doors ground open, she found she was not the only person in New York who wanted to spill their guts to Ed. She would have to take a number. There wasn't even room on the long bench in the hallway; she would have to stand.

Just as well, decided Lucy, waiting would give her a chance to organize her thoughts. So she unbuttoned her trusty plaid coat and leaned against the wall, alternately shifting her weight from one foot to the other and wishing she'd worn her duck boots. It wasn't long, however, before a seat opened up. The line was moving along briskly. She hoped that was a good sign. Probably none of the others had a story that was as important as hers.

"Seventy-six," called the receptionist, and Lucy hopped to her feet.

"That's me."

The receptionist cocked her head toward a door, and Lucy trotted in to tell Ed Riedel all about it.

He was sitting at a worn, gray steel desk, leaning on one elbow. His chin was resting in one hand; the other hand was busy doodling on a big pad of foolscap. He looked like an old, tired bloodhound, and no wonder, thought Lucy. The things he must have heard.

"Whatcha got?" he asked, getting right to the point.

"Anthrax poison at *Jolie* magazine. Nadine Nelson died of it and my daughter also has it, but she's getting better," said Lucy, making it snappy.

Riedel's bleary eyes suddenly became sharply focused. She felt as if they were lasers, burning right through her.

"Anthrax?"

"That's what the doctors say."

"And Nadine Nelson is . . . ?"

"The beauty editor, wife of real estate developer Arnold Nelson. Her funeral was this morning at Frank Campbell's."

"Rich broad, huh?"

Lucy nodded. "Somebody sent her a powder compact loaded with anthrax. My daughter got some on her skin. She's in the hospital." Ed seemed to be losing his focus so Lucy added, "The FBI is investigating."

"Your daughter works at the magazine?"

"No. We won a mother–daughter makeover."

Ed gave her an appraising once-over but didn't say anything. Lucy didn't much like it and pulled herself up a little straighter. "Listen, this is a big story. I'm a reporter myself, in Maine, and I know news when I see it. I can give you the inside scoop. I saw Nadine when she was sick, I was there when Camilla Keith learned about her death, I've been sitting at my daughter's bedside in the hospital. Just ask me what you want to know."

Ed's gaze had shifted. He was staring off in the distance, drumming his fat fingers against his chin.

"Nope," he said, shaking his head. "I'm not gonna touch this with a ten foot pole."

"Why not?"

"The FBI's involved, and if it really is anthrax like you say, you gotta figure Homeland Security is all over it." He leveled his eyes at her. "You heard of the Patriot Act?"

Lucy suddenly understood why even the *Times* hadn't printed the story. The realization made her sick.

"So nobody's going to print this?"

He scowled and shook his head, then slowly cocked one eyebrow. "Not unless you can tell me who sent the anthrax. Now that would be worth big bucks."

Lucy was definitely interested. "Big bucks?"

"We pay for stories. Why do you think all those people are out there? A story like this could be in the six figures, if you get it right."

"But how am I . . . ?"

He shrugged. "You say you're a reporter."

"But the government couldn't figure out . . ."

He cut her off. "That's why it's worth six figures. Now get out of here."

Lucy got to her feet, feeling slightly woozy. Six figures. "Did you say six figures?"

Ed nodded. "Take my card. Ya never know."

The elevator creaked and groaned ominously as the car descended with Lucy inside. She felt like groaning herself. Maybe even wailing. What was going on? She had a terrific story, she knew it, but even the *New York Tattler* was afraid to print it because of the government. What was the world coming to?

Lucy wanted to give Ed Riedel a piece of her mind. What sort of journalist was he? Wasn't the truth more important than anything? How was a democracy supposed to operate if newspapers were afraid to print the truth? Somebody had poisoned her daughter, somebody had killed

Nadine and who knows how many other people, maybe this whole flu epidemic was actually an anthrax attack, and they were going to get away with it.

The little sign on the door said PUSH but Lucy slammed her hand against it, making the door fly open. She wanted to shake some sense into Ed Riedel, into those smug FBI agents, into the whole stupid world.

She marched along the sidewalk, building up a head of steam, when somebody grabbed her arm, saving her from an oncoming car. She hadn't noticed the flashing DON'T WALK sign and she'd almost walked right into traffic. Looking around, she couldn't even tell who had saved her, who she ought to thank. It was time to calm down, she told herself as she waited for the WALK signal. She needed to cool off—she needed a little space, a little distraction. Back home she'd go for a walk on the beach, to get some sea air and clear out the cobwebs, but here she'd have to take a ride on the Staten Island Ferry. She headed for the nearest subway.

When the train pulled into the South Ferry stop, Lucy waited for the doors to slide open so she could get off, but they remained stubbornly closed. In fact, she realized, her car was barely in the station. Belatedly, she noticed a sign warning South Ferry passengers that they must be in the first five cars of the train. Furthermore, passage inside the train to the first five cars was not possible when the train was in the South Ferry station.

So she sat and waited as the train snaked its way around the subterranean loop of track at the bottom of Manhattan Island and exited at Rector Street, the next stop. She was surprised, when she surfaced onto the sidewalk, to find herself in front of a quaint little church, clearly a survivor from colonial times. She paused, peering through the wrought iron bars of the fence, and stared at a stone obelisk marking the grave of Alexander Hamilton. It was a shock to realize he wasn't just a name in the history books but a real flesh-and-blood man who had walked these streets and prayed in this church. Tall office buildings now loomed over it; the lower tip of Manhattan was now home to the stock exchange and brokerage houses. Just beyond the church was Ground Zero, where the Twin Towers had stood before the terrorist attack. Lucy paused at the fence enclosing the enormous empty space, now cleaned up and resembling any other construction site.

On the one hand, she thought, life had to go on. Rebuilding was a way of defying the terrorists. But on the other, it was hard to forget the suffering that had taken place that day. Maybe the site should be left empty as a memorial.

She felt terribly sad leaving the site, but many of the people walking briskly along the sidewalk didn't seem to notice it. Of course, she realized, these people worked nearby and they passed it every day. It was in their consciousness, sure, but they couldn't afford to dwell on the past, or the possibility of a future attack. If they did, they'd go crazy. They certainly wouldn't be able to get on the subway or ride the elevator up to the top of one of the adjacent office towers.

She strolled past the famous statue of the bull, that most American symbol of optimism, and noted that it stood on Bowling Green, now a little park filled with homeless people but once the place where seventeenth-century Dutch settlers had once spent their leisure hours bowling.

George Washington had come here, to nearby Fraunces Tavern, to say farewell to his troops. Walt Whitman had written about New York, and so had Herman Melville. He'd written about the Battery in *Moby Dick*, the same Battery Park she was walking in now, on her way to the ferry terminal. And in much the same way as he'd described, people were still drawn there daily to gaze at the Narrows of New York Harbor, now spanned by the Verrazzano Bridge, and to think of the vast ocean beyond.

The ferry terminal itself was under construction, but

renovations to the waiting area were completed, and a small crowd of people had gathered in front of a set of steel and glass doors through which the ferry could be seen approaching. They grew restless as it docked, and they had to wait for the New York–bound passengers to disembark before the doors opened and they could surge forward, down the ramp to the boat. There were plenty of benches to sit on but they were largely ignored by these restless New Yorkers who couldn't imagine sitting down comfortably until the ferry was clear and then strolling aboard in a leisurely fashion. Finally, the crowd thinned, the doors slid open, and the crowd surged forward.

Lucy marched along with the rest down a wide ramp, wondering who all these people were and why they were taking the ferry in the middle of the day. They couldn't be commuters at this hour; maybe they were tourists like her? She glanced about, looking for telltale clues like cameras and shopping bags, and spotted Deb Shertzer walking a few feet from her, wearing her funeral black.

"Hi," said Lucy, with a smile. She was pleasantly surprised to see a familiar face, having grown used to passing hundreds of strangers every day.

"Well, hi yourself," said Deb, falling into step alongside her. "What are you doing down here?"

"I'm just taking a ferry ride to clear my head," said Lucy. "This has all been pretty overwhelming and I need a break."

"No wonder," sympathized Deb, tucking an unruly strand of her short hair behind one ear. "You certainly got more than you bargained for. How's Elizabeth doing?"

Lucy felt that Deb really cared; she wasn't just going through the motions and saying the expected thing. Unlike most of the women at the magazine who took great pains to look smart and fashionable, Deb wouldn't have looked out of place in Tinker's Cove with her boyish haircut, sensible walking shoes, and flower-print cloth tote bag.

"She's much better. Thanks for asking."

A cold blast of air hit them as they stepped aboard the ferry, and Lucy inhaled the familiar scent of gasoline mingled with ozone and salt water and for a moment imagined she was at the fish pier in Tinker's Cove.

"People forget New York is a port city," said Deb, apparently reading her mind. "With all the tall buildings it's easy to forget Manhattan's an island."

"It's not like any island in Maine, that's for sure," said Lucy, peering through the windows in hopes of glimpsing the ranks of skyscrapers clustered around Wall Street. That view was blocked, but she could see a huge tanker passing on the port side, and across the water she could see docks and warehouses lined up on the Brooklyn shore. "I'd like to stand outside on the deck but I think it's too cold."

"Probably nobody out there today but cuddling couples," said Deb, taking a seat on one of the long benches that filled the ferry's belly. "Believe it or not, a ride on the ferry is a popular cheap date."

Lucy had a sudden panic attack. "I forgot to pay!"

"It's free," said Deb.

"That is a cheap date," said Lucy, taking the seat beside her. "Do you make this commute every day?"

"No. I live in Queens and take the subway to work. My mother lives in Staten Island so I'm taking advantage of a free afternoon to visit her." She looked out the window as the ferry started to pull away from its berth. "The offices are still closed."

"What did you think of the funeral?"

Deb looked at her curiously. "That's right, you were there, weren't you? You saw Elise freak out at Pablo." She shook her head. "That's just like her, you know. I have no doubt Camilla told Pablo to take the photos, then got Elise to take it out on him when she changed her mind."

"Camilla was probably upset," said Lucy. "She and Nadine were friends since college, right?"

"Barnard girls. Elise, too." Her lips curved into a small smile. "Believe me, if I had a daughter, I'd send her anywhere but Barnard."

"I'm sure it's a fine institution," said Lucy. "Has anyone else gotten sick?"

"No . . . but we're all keeping our fingers crossed and taking our Cipro. The offices are closed, of course, so the hazmat crew can do their stuff." Deb sighed. "I'm not looking forward to going back."

"They won't let you in unless it's safe."

"It's still creepy."

"Yeah," agreed Lucy, gazing across the water at a fanciful Victorian structure like a wedding cake sitting on an island. "What's that?"

"Ellis Island. Gateway to America for millions of immigrants."

Lucy hadn't realized it was so close to Manhattan. The immigrants would have been able to see the city as they waited to be admitted. "Can you imagine how heartbreaking it would be to finally get here, after a horrendous sea voyage, with your whole family and everything you owned, only to learn you had tuberculosis or something and they wouldn't let you in?"

"They had quarantine wards; they nursed the sick ones and most of them eventually got in."

"I'd like to think so," said Lucy, gazing at the Statue of Liberty and thinking about those World War II movies that ended with a boatful of refugees, or returning soldiers, gazing at the symbol of freedom. She found herself blinking back a tear. "I bet you're used to seeing her."

"Not really. It's always a bit of a thrill. She's fabulous, even if her accessories are rather unusual and that shade of green doesn't look good on anybody."

Lucy was grateful for the joke. "I agree about the book and torch, but I think those foam crowns would make a good gift for my girls at home."

"A good choice, and affordable, too. Personally, I'd go for something a bit more subdued—I don't really have occasion to wear a tiara."

"I'm glad you approve." Lucy couldn't take her eyes off Lady Liberty and fell silent as the ferry glided by. "Where's Governors Island?" she asked.

"I'm not really sure but it might be that one on the other side." Deb pointed towards a sizeable island with numerous buildings. "It used to be some sort of military base but now it's empty and they're trying to figure out what to do with it."

"Right. Actually, I have a friend who's on that committee." Lucy hadn't realized how close the island was to Wall Street, or how magnificent the views would be. It was also much more built up than she expected, covered with neat brick buildings that could easily be converted to luxury housing. It would be most attractive to the well-heeled investment bankers and lawyers and brokers who worked in the financial district; the island would offer unparalleled security only a short boat ride from their offices. Plus, there was even docking space for their yachts. "I heard Nadine's husband is trying to develop it."

"Could be. I never paid much attention to her private life."

"You got enough of her at work?" asked Lucy.

"You said it, not me." Deb's eyes glittered mischievously.

"I get the sense she wasn't very popular at the magazine," said Lucy, putting out a feeler, "but it's hard to believe that one of her fellow workers would actually poison her."

"Are you kidding? I wouldn't put anything past that crowd," said Deb. "They're all self-centered, shallow, ambitious, and ruthless—it's the fashion industry, after all. The most vital question on all their minds right now is whether purple is really going to be the hot new color this spring. There's a lot riding on it, you know." She looked up as the ferry groaned and slowed in preparation for docking. "This crowd is more likely to skewer you with sarcasm. Where would a fashionista get anthrax? It's not like they sell it at Bloomie's."

"I was wondering the same thing," said Lucy. "I suppose it could have been some sort of terror attack, like before, but it seems funny that only my daughter and Nadine were affected."

"I don't know." Deb shook her head as the ferry shuddered to a halt. "After the World Trade Center attacks, I guess anything is possible." She paused. "If you want to ride back you have to get off and walk through the terminal and get back on. You used to be able to stay on the boat but that's changed."

They walked together until their paths diverged in the terminal; Deb headed for the exit while Lucy followed a shuffling homeless man making his way back to the ferry. She wondered if he actually lived on the boat. It was possible, she guessed; the ride took longer than she remembered. This time she buttoned up her coat and pulled on her gloves, stepping onto the outside deck that wrapped around the boat. The windows were closed, but it was still chillier than the inside sitting area. The wind had died down so she leaned her elbows on the railing and looked across the water at the twinkling outline of the illuminated bridge.

Daylight was fading, Lucy realized, checking her watch. It was nearly four o'clock. She ducked inside and crossed the seating area, coming out on the other outside deck facing the city. The boat began to move, gliding across silky water toward the gleaming skyscrapers, now reflecting the last rays of the winter sun. She sat down on the long bench that wrapped around the outside of the cabin, alone except for one or two other hardy souls, and plunged her hands into her pockets. She heard the thrum of the engine and a boat horn or two, but otherwise it was quiet as the ferry picked up speed. The cloudless indigo sky was deepening, growing darker, though not yet dark enough for stars to appear. In the distance, growing closer, were the illuminated towers of Manhattan, creating their own sparkling constellations in the night sky.

Chapter Fifteen

TAKE OUR TEST AND FIND YOUR PERSONALITY QUOTIENT

The city was most magical when viewed from a distance. It didn't have nearly the same appeal when you were deep in its bowels, hanging onto a slippery pole in a packed subway car, decided Lucy. The train was empty when she boarded at South Ferry and she'd gotten a seat, but it had filled up rapidly with homeward bound workers. At 59th Street she gave up her seat to a pregnant woman, and by the time she reached 116th Street people were so tightly jammed together that it was difficult to breathe, and she had to battle her way through the crowd to exit. When she finally managed to extricate herself, she stood on the platform and shook herself like a dog, straightening her clothes and catching her breath.

Once outside she found herself in the dark of late afternoon and she savored the experience, strange to her, of walking down a city sidewalk at night. She wasn't the least bit afraid. The stores were still open and plenty of people were about on Broadway, mostly college and high school students with backpacks and businesspeople with briefcases, many pausing to pick up dry cleaning or a quart of milk or a bunch of flowers on their way home.

It occurred to her that it would be nice to bring Sam some flowers, or maybe a cake from a bakery, and she was trying to decide which would be the better choice when she realized she was walking past Barnard College. The realization energized her, making her wonder if fate was taking a hand and pointing the way. This was her chance to see the institution that had earned Deb's disapproval by nurturing Nadine, Camilla, and Elise. Curious, she peered through the bars of the decorative iron fence into an illuminated, treed courtyard. Noting that the gate was open she wandered in, not quite sure what she was looking for. She passed groups of girls walking in twos and threes, bundled up against the cold and clutching piles of books to their chests; some twenty years ago Camilla, Nadine, and Elise would have made a similar group, hurrying back to their dorm after a busy day of classes. She could picture them: Camilla would be the alpha member of the little pack, flanked on either side by her two less self-assured buddies.

Feeling the cold, Lucy stepped into the inviting student center to warm up. She picked up a copy of the student newspaper and sat down on one of the colorful upholstered chairs clustered in the large room, which seemed to be a combination waiting room and hallway. A bookshelf next to her chair held a collection of yearbooks, and she pulled out one from 1982. Leafing through it she discovered that Camilla had been a member of the class of 1984.

Opening that edition she found photos of Camilla Keith and Elise Frazier on adjacent pages. Oddly enough, considering their friendship, she discovered they had virtually nothing in common during their college years. They lived in different dorms, they belonged to different clubs, and they even looked different. Back then Camilla had a certain sophistication that Elise, with very big hair and a pair of oversized eyeglasses, definitely lacked.

Lucy didn't know Nadine's maiden name so she leafed through the pages searching for her first name. There was only one Nadine, Nadine Smoot. Lucy stifled a giggle as she studied the much younger but still recognizable face of the late Nadine. Lucy guessed she might have been strongly influenced by the militant feminism rampant on campuses at the time; there seemed no other explanation for her extremely short, mannish haircut and the plain T-shirt that strained across her braless chest, proclaiming "Sisterhood is Powerful." Checking the list of undergraduate activities in which Nadine had participated, Lucy learned she had been a founding member of the school's NOW chapter and was also active in the Take Back The Night movement and the women's health initiative.

Weird, though Lucy, replacing the book. What had brought these three very different women together? What had a campus fashionista, a militant feminist, and an ugly duckling (she mentally apologized to Elise) all had in common? They seemed an extremely unlikely group, especially considering the tendency of college students to clump themselves with similar friends. When she was in college she remembered the wide gulf between the jocks, the sorority girls, the theater kids, and the political activists. Once labeled a member of one of those groups it was practically impossible to breach the gap and make new friends.

Looking down at the newspaper in her lap, Lucy had an idea. She got up and went over to the information desk and asked where she could find old copies.

"How old?" inquired the girl, a perky little brunette with stylish black-rimmed eyeglasses.

"From the eighties."

"You'd need the archives," she said.

Lucy suddenly felt very old. "Where would they be?" she asked.

"Wollman Library." The girl pulled out a map, circled the library, and plotted her route. "Ask for the Lehman Archives."

At the library, the student staff member apologized for the fact that the university newspaper wasn't available online. "You'll have to use the microfiche machine," she said, handing Lucy several spools of film.

"No problem," said Lucy, settling herself in front of the big viewing machine. She didn't mind; she liked the whirring sound the film made as she scanned the pages, she enjoyed viewing the old issues as they actually appeared when printed. She got a kick out of the grainy photos from an earlier era, replete with shoulder pads and Farrah Fawcett hairdos. Did people really go around looking like that? It seemed incredible until she spotted one coed in the same platform shoes she had once worn and groaned out loud.

The student who had given her the films hurried over. "Everything okay?"

Lucy chuckled and pointed at the screen. "I used to have a pair of shoes like that."

"Wow, retro," said the girl, obviously impressed. "They get fifty bucks for those in the vintage clothing stores."

Lucy's jaw dropped. "Really?"

"Yeah. Do you still have them? I'd be interested, if you're a size eight."

"No, I'm a seven and they went to the Salvation Army a long, long time ago."

"Too bad!"

Skimming through the pages, Lucy noticed that Camilla's name and face popped up frequently. She was pictured selling used textbooks at a student council fund-raiser. She was presenting a cash gift to a Head Start program. She had won a *Glamour* magazine contest. And then came the stunning headline: Student Leader Attempts Suicide.

Lucy let out a long breath and leaned closer to read the story.

The usual quiet of a weekday evening during midterms, when most students are preparing for exams, was shattered last Tuesday by a scream.

"She's going to jump!" shrieked Nadine Smoot, '84, pointing to a small figure clothed in a dia-phanous white gown perched on the edge of the

Brooks Hall residence roof. She was later identified as Camilla Keith, '84, president of the sophomore class and a member of the student governing council.

A crowd immediately gathered in the Arthur Ross Courtyard, but no one seemed to know what to do. Uncertainty reigned as students discussed an appropriate course of action. Some wanted to call campus police and health officials; others maintained such action would be a violation of personal freedom and individual rights. As the controversy raged, Smoot and Elise Frazier, '84, took action, racing up the stairs and joining Keith on the roof.

The two remonstrated with Keith as students gathered below watched with bated breath. When the sound of approaching sirens was heard, Keith became agitated, stepping closer to the edge. It was then that Smoot lunged at her and brought her safely to the ground in a rugby style lunge, assisted by Frazier.

All three were subsequently transported by ambulance to Columbia Presbyterian Medical Center. Smoot and Frazier were treated for minor abrasions and released. Keith was admitted to the psychiatric unit for evaluation but has since been released. She had no comment, except to thank Smoot and Frazier, whom she said "prevented me from making a very big mistake."

Frazier attributed the happy outcome to Smoot's quick thinking and willingness to take action. "I was terrified." she said, "but Nadine knew what to do."

Smoot said she only did "what any sister would do for another" and went on to point out that women are much more likely to commit suicide

*than men. "We need to establish suicide-
prevention programs here on campus. The ad-
ministration doesn't want to admit there's a
problem but this time they couldn't sweep it under
the rug. Camilla was out there in public, showing her pain, and that was very brave."*

*Personally, Smoot said the incident was an op-
portunity for her to get to know someone she
wouldn't have thought she had much in common
with. "Camilla and I are very different; she's more
establishment and I consider myself a feminist
and a women's rights activist but now I see we're
the same under the skin. There's an old Native
American saying that if you save someone's life
you become responsible for them forever," she
said.*

Lucy felt chills run up her spine as she finished reading
the story. What a creepy thing for Nadine to say. Did she
really feel responsible for Camilla's future welfare? Or was
she taking advantage of an emotionally vulnerable young
woman? And what about Nadine's feminist views? She apparently hadn't hesitated to jettison them when she had an
opportunity to join the "establishment" fashion media.

The friendship had certainly benefited Nadine and Elise,
who had ridden on Camilla's coattails to assume top posi-
tions at *Jolie* magazine. But what about Camilla? Had she
grown tired of this everlasting debt? Had Nadine become
a serious liability? The magazine was in trouble and her
job was in jeopardy, largely because of Nadine's hare-
brained schemes.

It occurred to Lucy that Camilla might have come to believe there was only one way to rid herself of Nadine. But
how would she get her hands on anthrax, wondered Lucy.
Designer clothes, sure, she had an unlimited supply. But

anthrax? Not usually found in the environs of Seventh Avenue.

Idly, Lucy scrolled the microfilm through a few more issues of the paper, stopping when she came to a photo of Elise, pictured with two beaming professors. She was the 1983 winner of the Jackson-Selfridge prize in biochemistry, awarded for "innovative research with potential agricultural applications."

Ohmigod, thought Lucy. Elise studied biochemistry; she might even have worked as a biochemist before coming to *Jolie*. She might have worked with anthrax herself, or she could have connections, friends who worked with it. As Lucy continued scrolling through the microfilm she thought again of a favorite phrase of her mother's. "Three's a crowd," Mom had always advised, whenever Lucy planned to go shopping or to a movie with a couple of friends. "Two can walk together, two can chat in a theater. If there are four, you can make two couples. But three's a crowd. Someone's always left out."

Lucy didn't usually agree, but this time it seemed that Mom may have been right. Maybe three was a crowd and Nadine was the odd one out.

The idea came to mind again when she and Sam were eating microwave dinners in the kitchen, only this time Lucy was worried she might be the third wheel.

"I hope you don't mind," said Sam apologizing for not providing a home-cooked meal, "but this is what I usually do when Brad's not home for supper."

"Fine with me," said Lucy. "I really appreciate your hospitality. I hope it's not a nuisance having me here."

"A nuisance? Whatever gave you that idea?"

"Well, you and Brad are finally empty-nesters, and now you've got me cluttering up your life."

"Honey, I love the chance to visit with you," said Sam, removing the dinners from the microwave and setting the plastic containers on plates. "Besides, my nights have been pretty lonely these past few months. That Governors Island committee is taking an awful lot of Brad's time."

"What's that all about?" asked Lucy, spearing one of the four small pieces of chicken included with the dinner. "I saw it from the ferry. It seems such a waste. All those buildings and nobody there."

"It's a fabulous piece of real estate but nobody's quite sure what to do with it, so that's why they set up the committee. There's been a fort there since the 1700s, the Army had a base there for years and then the Coast Guard had it for a while. Now about half the island has been preserved as a National Historic District and a national monument but there's plenty of acreage left, most of it old military housing."

"It must have spectacular views," said Lucy. "Arnold Nelson wants to build that City Gate development there, doesn't he?"

"Oh yes he does. But Brad and some of the committee members don't want to see it become a private preserve for the very wealthy. They see it as a resource that should benefit all New Yorkers. Right now it's only open to the public one day a week during the summer, but they'd like to expand so people could enjoy it year round. That demand hasn't been very popular with the developers."

Lucy remembered Brad talking about that at the AIDS ball. "It sounds like he's got quite a fight on his hands," she said, scraping up the last bits of broccoli.

"That he does," agreed Sam, clearing the table. "Brownies for dessert?"

"I thought you'd never ask."

After enjoying coffee and brownies and watching the evening news with Sam, Lucy headed back out to visit Elizabeth in the hospital. She had checked in by phone several times but hadn't had a chance to visit all day and was feeling guilty about neglecting her daughter. She needn't have worried. When she arrived she found Elizabeth and Fiona watching newlyweds Jessica and Nick and giggling together.

"I can't believe she actually complimented the Secretary of the Interior on the way she decorated the White House," said Elizabeth.

"I heard one that was better than that," said Fiona. "She read that she was pregnant in a tabloid newspaper so she got one of those tests at the drugstore to see if it was true."

Elizabeth couldn't stand it. She was clutching her stomach and pounding her heels against the bed.

"Well, I guess you're feeling better," said Lucy.

"Oh, Mom. Hi."

"I can tell you missed me," said Lucy. "What did you do all day?"

"They kept me busy with tests and food and medicine. Lance was here most of the day and then Fiona came."

"What's new at the magazine?" asked Lucy. "Any developments?"

"Fantastic news, actually," said Fiona. Lucy loved her British accent. "Nobody else has gotten sick, and they've finished testing the office and it came up clean except for a tiny, tiny trace of anthrax, which they've eradicated."

"That's great."

"It has its downside." Fiona was examining her fingernails. "It means I have to go back to work tomorrow."

Lucy was smiling sympathetically when Sidra gave a little tap on the door and came into the room holding a huge bunch of flowers that was almost as big as she was.

"How's the patient?" she asked, bending down to hug Elizabeth. "I wanted to visit right away, but this is the soonest I could manage."

"I feel great. Thanks for coming," said Elizabeth, taking the bouquet and sniffing it appreciatively. "I've never seen such gorgeous flowers."

"I stole them from the set," she said, looking rather guilty. "Believe me, it doesn't matter. They change them every day anyway."

"I'll see about a vase," said Lucy, heading for the door.

"And I guess I'll get moving," said Fiona, with a big yawn. "Got to get up early tomorrow."

"Who was that?" asked Fiona, as they walked down the hall.

"Oh, I can't believe I didn't introduce you. That's Sidra Rumford; she's my best friend's daughter. She lives in the city and works on the *Norah!* TV show."

Fiona's eyes lit up. "Really? TV!"

"Don't tell me you're starstruck," said Lucy. They had reached the elevator and were standing together.

"Sure, a little bit. Who isn't?" Fiona was blushing. "But the truth is, I'm pretty sick of the magazine and I bet they could use a bright young thing like me on the show."

"I'll ask Sidra . . ." began Lucy.

"Oh, you don't have to do that," said Fiona. "Maybe you could just give me her phone number, and her name again. I think I've already forgotten it."

To Lucy's surprise, Fiona had already produced a memo book and a pencil and was waiting expectantly, so she pulled her cell phone from her pocket and gave her the number.

"Thanks," said Fiona, just as the elevator doors slid open. "Cheerio!"

Lucy continued on to the nurse's station where she was given a vase and returned to Elizabeth's room. She found Sidra and Elizabeth deep in conversation.

"What's going on?" she asked, setting the vase in the sink and filling it with water. Lucy wasn't one for arranging flowers so she picked up the bouquet and plunked it into the vase.

"We were just talking," said Sidra, taking the vase and rearranging the flowers. "I was telling Elizabeth about what happened on the show today."

"I missed it. What was it about?"

Sidra's hands, which had been flying about the arrangement, suddenly stopped. "It was about healthy food choices at holiday parties, and Rachael Ray was making a low-fat veggie dip when these two women in the audience got up and started screaming and throwing tomatoes at her and Norah. Rachael took one right in the face, and Norah's cashmere sweater was ruined."

"How terrible!"

"That's awful," chimed Elizabeth.

"Who were they? I thought everybody loved Norah."

"Not these two, that's for sure."

"What were they so mad about?"

"That's the weird thing. You'd think that the reason they disrupted the show was to get publicity for their cause, wouldn't you? I mean, it goes out live on national TV so you'd think they'd at least have a sign or something. But they didn't. Nothing."

"Maybe it was personal," suggested Lucy.

"Norah says she didn't know them. She was really puzzled. Usually there are at least a couple of lawsuits against her, but right now there isn't anything." Sidra carefully added the last flowers to the arrangement and stepped back to study it. "She's furious at the security people. They not only let them get in with their rotten tomatoes, but they didn't hold them for questioning afterward. They just escorted them out."

"How come they didn't call the police?"

"That's what Norah wants to know. Somebody messed up big-time. This time it was only tomatoes, but next time . . . ?" Sidra left the sentence unfinished and carried the arrangement over to the window where she set it on the sill. "There. Now I've got to go."

Sidra was as good as her word, departing in a flurry of air kisses. But after she left, Lucy had a sense of déjà vu. She felt as if she'd been through this before: another close call, another lucky escape. It was the same thing all over again and she didn't like it. After all, no matter how lucky you were, luck eventually ran out.

Chapter Sixteen

WHAT FRENCH GIRLS HAVE THAT YOU DON'T

Even though Lucy knew the *Jolie* offices had been thoroughly tested for anthrax, scrubbed and decontaminated by hazmat experts, she still hesitated when the elevator doors slid open on Friday morning and it took an act of faith to inhale when she stepped onto the freshly cleaned carpet. It smelled clean, sure, but deadly microbes could lurk in tiny crevices and it only took one to make you sick.

The receptionist at the desk opposite the elevator bank didn't seem concerned about her health, however. She seemed happy to be back at work and greeted Lucy cheerily.

"I heard your daughter is doing much better," she said. "That must be a big relief."

"It is," said Lucy, "thanks for asking about her." She launched into the story she'd concocted to explain her visit to the office. "Actually, that's why I'm here. I'm worried about the hospital bill and need to talk to somebody. . . ."

"Of course, all that time in intensive care, the bill must be enormous." The receptionist pursed her lips and furrowed her brow in sympathy. "Don't you have health insurance?"

"We do, but you know how it is. One big claim and

they drop you. And I really do think the magazine bears some responsibility."

The receptionist chewed her lip and consulted a staff directory. "Actually, this is the editorial side. I don't know much about the business end of things; they're not even in this building. I guess Camilla would be the logical person to talk to."

She was reaching for the phone when Lucy spoke. "She's got so much on her plate right now, I don't want to bother her." She paused before suggesting the true object of her visit. "What about Elise?"

"I think you're right. Elise would be better." After a quick phone conversation she sent Lucy down the hallway to Elise's office.

The fashion editor met her at the door, and Lucy couldn't help thinking how different she looked now from the photo in the yearbook. The nerdy biochemistry student had transformed herself into a sophisticated businesswoman. The glasses were gone, the frizzy hair had been straightened and highlighted, her tweed suit was beautifully tailored, and her make-up was impeccable. She had also made a remarkable recovery from yesterday's funeral. If she was still grieving for her old college friend Nadine, there was no sign of it. Today she was all business.

"Lucy, this is an unexpected pleasure," she said. "Come right on in." When Lucy had seated herself and declined coffee, Elise took her place on the other side of the desk and tented her hands, displaying a flawless manicure and a gorgeous gold ring with a large blue stone. "What can I do for you?"

Knees together, hands in lap, Lucy took a deep breath and studied the large photograph on the wall behind Elise. It pictured a sculpture of a bare-breasted woman on a chariot accompanied by two smaller women, also bare breasted, on either side of her.

Noticing her interest, Elise enlightened her. "Boadicea,"

she said. "As queen of the Britons she led a rebellion against the Romans."

"She must have been quite a girl," said Lucy, taking in the spear Boadicea was holding aloft and the scythed wheels of her chariot.

"Oh, she was," said Elise. "But I don't think you've come here to discuss ancient British history."

"No," said Lucy. "This is a tad awkward, you see, but I've been in contact with my health insurance company, and the legal department there seems to think the magazine bears some responsibility for Elizabeth's situation."

Elise raised her eyebrows skeptically. "I've never heard of such a thing."

"Well, me either," said Lucy. "But they seem to feel that since the illness was the result of an intentional poisoning rather than something contagious like the measles that there was a certain degree of negligence. . . ." She was relieved when Elise interrupted her.

"Enough," she said, rolling her eyes. "I have no head for business. You'll have to talk to our legal department."

"And where would that be?"

"Over on Forty-ninth Street." She was writing the information on a slip of paper and handed to Lucy. "I'll call and tell them to expect you."

"Thanks so much," said Lucy, standing. "I hate to be a bother, especially at such a difficult time." She looked down at the floor for a moment, then raised her eyes. "I know you and Nadine were old friends. From college, right?"

"That's right." Elise checked her watch.

"And Camilla, too. Amazing. It's a new world, isn't it, where women have their own old-girl networks?" She managed a chuckle, which she hoped would signal female solidarity to Elise. "And men always say that women are too catty to maintain long-term friendships. You three are, well, *were*, the exception."

"I'm sorry but I have a meeting. . . ." Elise wasn't about

to be drawn into a discussion of feminine ethics and was on her feet, heading for the door.

Lucy ignored the cue that it was time to leave and sat in her chair, turning to face Elise. "What's the secret?" she asked quickly. "How did you manage it? To stay friends all these years, I mean? Especially when you all have such different personalities. And Nadine had a husband; that must have changed the dynamics a bit, no?"

"We didn't ask awkward questions," said Elise, opening the door and tapping her foot. "I think that was it."

Lucy slid to the edge of her chair and picked up her bag, but rattled on. "You know, I just have one quick question I'm dying to ask you. I hope you don't mind."

Elise definitely looked as if she did mind, but Lucy didn't give her a chance to object.

"I am so grateful that this makeover gave my daughter the opportunity to come into contact with a successful woman like you. I think you have so much to offer, with your example and your wisdom. . . ."

Elise interrupted. "Would you mind getting to the point?"

"Oh, sorry. I do tend to go on," said Lucy, standing up. "Well, the question is this. You see, Elizabeth's been majoring in chemistry, biochemistry in fact, terrific grades, she's a natural. But she's heard that there's a lot of discrimination against women in graduate programs, and she's not sure if she should continue with it or switch to another field that's more hospitable to women, like communications, for example. I mean, she doesn't want to keep banging her head against that glass ceiling, if you know what I mean."

"I'm afraid I don't have any experience with that."

"Really? I thought I heard somewhere that you were a biochemistry major, that's why I thought you'd be the right person to advise Elizabeth. How did you end up

working at a fashion magazine? Do you miss biochemistry?"

Elise was way ahead of her. "No. Mrs. Stone, I haven't
been mixing up anthrax in my home lab, if that's what
you're getting at. Now I really must ask you to go."

"Oh, I never meant to imply anything of the kind," said
Lucy, making her way as slowly as she could manage to
the open door, where Elise was standing. "The thought
never crossed my mind. I just wondered why you left your
field for fashion."

"I think you could say I just fell into it." Elise stepped
forward and raised her arm against the door, effectively
forcing Lucy toward the hallway.

Lucy countered by leaning closer and whispering in her
ear. "I understand. You're probably too good a friend to
say anything, but it was because of Camilla, wasn't it? She
had some serious emotional problems back then, didn't
she? Didn't I hear somewhere that she attempted suicide in
college?"

Elise's face was stony. "Where did you hear that?"

"Oh, I don't know. People talk. Maybe I read it somewhere." Lucy lowered her voice. "Of course I don't believe
half of what I read. It isn't true, is it?"

"I'm not in the habit of gossiping," snapped Elise, giving the door a push. "You'd have to ask Camilla about
that."

"Oh, I wouldn't want to bother her. She certainly
seemed awfully fragile at the funeral," said Lucy, blocking
the door with her foot. They were now standing toe-to-
toe, and Lucy looked Elise straight in the eye. "It was very
obvious how much she relies on you, now that Nadine is
gone."

Elise stared back, and Lucy realized that even brown
eyes could look very cold indeed. "Good day, Mrs. Stone,"
she said.

Lucy had to step smartly to avoid being hit in the face by the door.

Well, well, well, she muttered to herself, heading down the hallway in the direction of the beauty department. Elise hadn't exactly confessed, but she had been extremely defensive about her relationships with Camilla and Nadine and she'd been awfully quick to deny having anything to do with the anthrax. Lucy felt sure she'd hit a nerve and she intended to keep up the pressure.

Meanwhile, she wanted to get on with phase two of her plan, which was to search Nadine's office. She was pretty sure she could count on Fiona to cooperate, considering the way she and Elizabeth had become such good friends. But when she got to the beauty department it was Phyllis who greeted her.

"Hi, Mrs. Stone. How's our little patient? Would she like some cologne or body lotion? This just came in yesterday—a new scent from Stella McCartney."

Lucy took the box, which was beautifully tied with a purple bow. "Thank you. That's very sweet. I know she'll love it."

Phyllis held up her hands in a gesture of innocence. "No anthrax, I promise. The package is sealed."

"It never crossed my mind. Elizabeth was just in the wrong place at the wrong time." Lucy paused a moment, thinking. She hadn't expected Phyllis to be so friendly, especially after her confrontations with Elise and Camilla. She decided to press her advantage. "Any new developments in the anthrax investigation?"

"Not that I'm aware of," said Phyllis.

"What's the gossip here? What are people saying when they stand around the water cooler?"

The question seemed to fluster Phyllis. "I'd love to talk it over with you but I've got to run. I'm already late for an editorial meeting."

"Oh, I shouldn't keep you. Is Fiona here?"

"No, she's in photo."

"I don't mind waiting here," said Lucy, seeing an opportunity to get into Nadine's office. "I have a message for
her from Elizabeth."

Phyllis was fiddling with the doorknob. "Do you believe
it? Now we have to lock our offices whenever we leave
them. It's a new security directive. It's ridiculous but I can't
let you stay here alone."

"Better safe than sorry," said Lucy, who was in reality
feeling extremely sorry. Now she wouldn't be able to get a
look at Nadine's office unless Fiona was willing to risk her
job by violating the new security policy. She decided there
was no harm in asking, but there was no sign of Fiona
when she arrived at the photo department.

"Fiona? I sent her to get rose petals for the shoot," said
Pablo. He was squinting through the camera at an
arrangement of beauty products spread on a white drop.
"The little one continues to recover, yes?"

"Yes, yes she does."

He clucked his tongue. "Such a shame. Nadine, I won't
miss her and her meddling. But for a sweet young girl to
suffer, that is very bad."

"Nadine wasn't very popular here, was she?"

Pablo stood up, one hand still on the camera. He was
dressed in tight black pants and a striped knit shirt; Lucy
couldn't imagine one of the guys in Tinker's Cove wearing
an outfit like that, but it sure looked good on him.

"What is the phrase, you can say that again?"

"That's the phrase." Lucy chuckled. "How come?"

"She was stupid, but she had Camilla's ear." He exhaled
sharply. "That is no way to run a magazine."

"Do you think Camilla might have figured that out?
That she might have wanted to get rid of Nadine?"

Pablo looked at her sideways. "You know what they're
saying? Nadine's husband, the billionaire rich guy, when
he heard the magazine was in trouble with the publisher,

he offered to buy it." He paused. "Only one condition: Camilla would go."

"Who'd be the editor then?"

"Who d'you think? Nadine."

"Nadine?" Lucy was incredulous. "That sounds like a really bad business move."

"He doesn't care. He has lotsa money." Pablo smirked. "He wanted to keep Nadine busy, busy, busy."

Lucy found her heart warming to Pablo. What a guy! He looked good and he loved to gossip. It was almost like talking to one of her girlfriends at home, but better.

"At the funeral, I thought Nancy Glass seemed awfully concerned about Arnold. Do you think he's interested in her?"

Pablo shrugged. "Sure. He's a ladies' man."

This was no surprise to Lucy. "Right. So what does a smart, beautiful woman like Nancy see in him?"

Pablo rubbed his fingers together. "Money."

"Oh."

"You're shocked."

"I guess I think there are easier ways to make a buck than to try to wheedle it out of a fat, ugly rich guy."

Pablo laughed, revealing a mouth full of very white teeth.

"Usually, the husband is the prime suspect when the wife dies, but I guess not in this case," continued Lucy. "Not if he was going to buy a magazine for Nadine."

"It's just a rumor." Pablo's eyes gleamed wickedly. "Maybe he did kill her, but I don't think so. He had a good thing going with her. She liked being the public Mrs. Arnold Nelson, she liked getting good tables in restaurants and getting her picture in the society pages, but I don't think she liked having sex with him." He licked his lips. "I don't think she liked sex at all."

Lucy thought he might be right. Underneath the fashionable clothes and make-up, there was a kind of slovenliness about Nadine. Her clothes didn't fit well, as if she'd recently put on some weight. Her hair color had needed touching up, remembered Lucy, and her nails looked as if she'd just applied polish without bothering to file or shape them. She reminded Lucy of some women she knew in Tinker's Cove who gave up trying to be alluring when they reached a certain age. They cut their hair short and donned elastic-waist pants and devoted themselves to golf or genealogy or anything except their husbands. "But she didn't mind if he had it, as long as he got it from somebody else?"

Pablo nodded approvingly. "In that way, she had a very European attitude."

Lucy was fascinated, but before she could continue the conversation the door flew open and Camilla marched in. Like Elise, she seemed to have recovered remarkably well since the funeral. There was no sign of the grief-stricken woman who had been clinging so pathetically to Elise for support. Today she was clearly in charge.

"Do I have to remind you that we're on deadline?" she snapped at Pablo. Turning to Lucy, she jabbed in her direction with a red-tipped talon. "What the hell do you think you're doing here?"

"Just visiting," said Lucy, all innocence. "I have a message from my daughter for Fiona."

"You can leave it with the receptionist, on your way out."

Lucy suspected security was on the way. "O-kay."

"Now."

"Right," said Lucy. "Nice talking to you, Pablo."

She was leaving when she saw Camilla point at the display of cosmetics Pablo was photographing. "Not like this," she said, frowning and waggling her fingers.

Pablo stepped forward, attempting to preserve the carefully designed arrangement, but Camilla stopped him with a glance. Then, with a sweep of her arm she knocked over the open tubes of lipstick and mascara and eyeliner, sending them rolling every which way and spilling the open bottles of nail lacquer. "Smash them. Break them," she ordered, prying the little cakes of eye color out of their compacts with her nails and tossing them on the table. "Smear them all around. Show the colors. The colors!" She brought her fist down again and again until all that was left was a Jackson Pollock scramble of lurid hues.

Chapter Seventeen

FABULOUS FUN FURS FOR EVERY BUDGET!

Wow, thought Lucy, as she rode the elevator down to the lobby, that was one image she wasn't going to forget anytime soon. If she'd had any doubt that Camilla was crazy, really crazy, the sight of her smashing the cosmetics had convinced her that the editor was no more master of her emotions as an eminently successful fashion journalist than she was when she attempted suicide in college. Worst of all had been her voice, an eerie scream with which she spewed insult after insult at poor Pablo.

The elevator landed with a thud and Lucy exited the building, gratefully inhaling the cold, crisp air. Even loaded with pollutants, it seemed much fresher than the overheated atmosphere in the *Jolie* offices.

Lucy decided that walking the ten or twelve blocks to the hospital would do her good. She'd get some exercise and get rid of some of the tension she'd been building up; plus, she did her best thinking when she was in motion.

And she had plenty to think about, given the rivalries and jealousies she'd discovered at the magazine. Pablo, though he made no attempt to hide his dislike of Nadine, she dismissed as a suspect. It was his sense of humor, which indicated a certain sense of detachment, that argued against him being the killer. He didn't seem to take Nadine or Camilla all that seriously, viewing them as actors in an entertaining soap opera. His talent and standing as a photographer protected him; he could leave anytime he chose, which put him essentially above the fray.

She was also tempted to cross Phyllis off her list of suspects. In theory she had seemed a likely candidate since Nadine's death had meant a big promotion for her. But from what Lucy had seen of her, she didn't seem to be reveling in her new position. If anything, she seemed to approach her new, powerful job as a continuation of her old job. In truth, Nadine's death hadn't meant big changes in the beauty department because Phyllis had really done the lion's share of the work all along. So Phyllis went about her work as she always had, with no sense of self-importance or ego. She'd made a few minor changes, like sharing the samples, but Lucy hadn't sensed any hint of triumphant self-assertion, which she was sure would have been the case if Phyllis had harbored a festering resentment of Nadine and finally decided to take action.

She really couldn't cross off Arnold and Nancy until she knew more about their relationship, but from what Pablo told her it didn't seem as if that was a promising line of investigation. Arnold and Nadine had apparently worked out a relationship that suited them both: he got freedom to exercise his libido and she got money and status.

No, from what she'd learned so far, Camilla was by far the likeliest suspect, especially if what Pablo had told her about Arnold's plan to buy the magazine was true. From what she'd seen of Camilla, Lucy believed she had the most reasons to want Nadine out of her life, permanently, and was just crazy enough to do whatever it took to get rid of her.

Elise, she was sure, would have been happy to do whatever was required to help eliminate her rival for Camilla's friendship. Maybe she didn't cook up the anthrax herself, but she could have had connections who had access to the stuff: an old professor, a fellow student, or perhaps even a colleague. The very fact that she'd jumped to the conclusion that Lucy suspected her of producing the anthrax could indicate a guilty conscience.

Of course, the act of murder usually required a precipitating factor, and Lucy sensed that Arnold's proposed purchase of the magazine was probably the issue that pushed Camilla over the edge. If only she could find out if the sale was really in the works or just a rumor.

Lucy shoved her hands into her pockets and felt the business card Ed Riedel had given her when she visited him at the *Tattler*. Impulsively, she decided to give him a call.

"You probably don't remember me," she began.

"You're the dame from Maine."

Lucy was astonished. "How'd you know?"

"You talk funny."

After living for more than twenty years in Tinker's Cove, Lucy guessed she probably did have a bit of a Maine accent.

"Listen, I've turned up some interesting stuff in the anthrax death at *Jolie* magazine. . . ."

"Who did it?"

"I'm not sure but I've got some promising. . . ."

The editor cut her off. "Call me when you're sure."

Lucy wasn't about to brushed off so easily. "And I've got some scandalous inside stuff on Camilla Keith. . . ."

"Yeah, and the Pope's Catholic."

Lucy's spirits sank. "I thought I had a scoop."

"You and eight million other people. That woman has ripped into everybody at some point. The whole city's got scars—taxi drivers, florists, interior designers, dog walkers, they all wanna get their story in print."

"I didn't know."

"Keep on trying, kid," he said.

Disappointed at his reaction, Lucy replaced her phone in her purse. By this time she had worked her way over to

Lexington Avenue and found herself passing the Melrose, her home for three days, where Cathy was still in residence. As an industry insider, she might have the information about Arnold that Lucy was looking for. Impulsively, she ducked into the lobby where she was greeted warmly by the man at the desk.

"It's nice to see you, Mrs. Stone. How's your daughter doing?"

"Much better," said Lucy, surprised that he remembered her. "Thanks for asking."

"Are you coming back to stay with us?"

"No, I'm staying with a friend, uptown. I am hoping to catch Cathy Montgomery. Do you know if she's still staying here?"

"As far as I know," he said. "I'm not supposed to give out room numbers but you can call her on the house phone."

In a matter of minutes Lucy was connected and heard Cathy invite her up to her suite.

"I didn't really think I'd find you here," said Lucy, when Cathy opened the door. "I was sure you'd be out shopping, if you hadn't already left for Texas."

"Too early for me," said Cathy, waving her hand at the room service table set up by the window. "I like to take my time in the morning. Would you like a cup of coffee? There's plenty and it's hot."

"I would, thanks," said Lucy, seating herself in a comfortable sofa. Cathy's suite was a far cry from the cramped little room she'd shared with Elizabeth; the suite had a spacious living room as well as a large bedroom she could glimpse through an open door. She could hear a shower running, probably Tiffany, getting ready for another day of shopping.

From the large number of boxes and bags scattered around the room it seemed there had been plenty of shopping. Lucy wondered if they'd left anything in the stores for other shoppers to buy. Not that most people would be competing for the same goods—they'd been shopping at places like Prada, Armani, and Ralph Lauren.

"You girls have been busy," said Lucy, accepting a cup of coffee.

"Cream? Sugar?"

"Just black."

"It's appalling, isn't it?" said Cathy, crossing her legs and clipping on a pair of pearl and gold earrings. She was dressed for the day in a cream-colored silk blouse and a beautifully tailored pair of mocha slacks. "All I can say in my own defense is that it's mostly stuff for Tiffany. Her mother died quite a few years ago and there hasn't been anyone to help her with clothes and hair and things like that."

"She's lucky. You're more like a fairy godmother than an evil stepmother," said Lucy.

"Don't get me wrong—there are quite a few goodies for me, too." She took a sip of coffee. "You sure can't find stuff like this in Dallas—there's no place like New York for serious shopping. Except maybe Paris. London's good, too."

"It must be nice," said Lucy, who had never been out of the country and longed to visit places she'd read about. As soon as she'd said it, she wished she hadn't. She hoped there hadn't been any hint of jealousy in her tone.

"Believe me, honey, it is nice and I appreciate every cent I spend. I grew up poor, you know, and I don't intend to set my foot in a Wal-Mart ever again, not if I can help it."

"I don't blame you," said Lucy, completely disarmed by Cathy's frankness.

"I tell you, my first trip to Paris was a real eye-opener: there was no pink polyester anywhere! You can be sure I reported on that fact for the folks at home. And I also told them nobody wore those enormous white athletic shoes you see everywhere here."

"So you traveled for your job?"

"I sure did. I was like a yo-yo, back and forth across the Atlantic, so the folks in Dallas would know what was in fashion." She paused. "Not that I'm complaining. It was great fun, but now that I'm a wife and stepmom my traveling days are pretty much over. We have a full social calendar, and my husband needs me to entertain and to accompany him to events. I'll be running my feet off when I get home—Tiffany's coming out this spring, you know, at the Yellow Rose of Texas Ball and I want her to be the Texas Belle of the Year."

"How lovely," said Lucy, realizing that Cathy's privileged life was work in its way, too. "You know, I was wondering about a few things and I thought you might have the answers."

"Maybe, maybe not," she said with a shrug. "Fire away."

"Well, I heard a rumor that Arnold was planning to buy *Jolie* magazine and make Nadine editor. Do you know anything about that?"

"That rag is for sale, I can tell you that, and I'd bet my six-carat engagement ring that Camilla isn't happy about it because the first thing any buyer is going to do is take a long hard look at the job she's been doing. But I never heard Arnold named as a possible buyer." She studied the ring, which sparkled in the sunlight coming through the window. "If he was thinking of buying it he certainly wouldn't have put Nadine in charge—he's too smart a businessman for that. Nadine would just drive it into the ground. Believe me, I know about men like Arnold. He wants to make money, that's what he's all about, and there's no way he would throw his capital into a sinkhole like *Jolie* magazine."

"Not even as a payoff to Nadine for putting up with his affairs?"

Cathy snorted. "He didn't need to pay her off. If she

didn't like it, she could leave, right? And there was no sign she was planning to do that. Besides, from what I've heard, his money's all tied up in his real estate projects. I don't think he could afford *Jolie*."

"I thought he was enormously rich," said Lucy.

"Oh, honey, there's rich and then there's *rich*. These real estate guys are all the same. They've got lots of buildings and stuff, but cash flow is always a problem, which means they've got to borrow and put off payments, stuff like that." Her eyes gleamed wickedly. "But now that Nadine's gone, I imagine his position has improved."

"What do you mean?"

"Insurance, sweetie. I bet he'll pick up a million or two, which should relieve his cash flow problems for a while, anyway."

"At least," said Lucy, mentally kicking herself. Insurance. Why hadn't she thought of that? Rich people had life insurance, too. They could afford lots of it. Arnold suddenly went from the bottom of her list of suspects to the top. You could never ignore the basics, and the husband was always the prime suspect. If only she could talk to Arnold one on one, but how was she going to do that? Considering the way he'd kicked her out of the funeral it was hardly likely that he'd agree to see her.

"I'm ready, let's go." Tiffany was standing in the doorway, dressed in the teen uniform of tight jeans, tiny T, and shrunken blazer.

"Mrs. Stone is here, Tiffany." Cathy's voice was gentle, almost a whisper.

"Oh, I'm sorry." The girl was blushing. "I didn't mean to be rude. Hi, Mrs. Stone. Good morning. Can I get you some coffee?"

"I've got some. Actually, I should be going. I'm on my way to the hospital."

"How is Elizabeth? Say hi to her for me, okay?"

"I will." Lucy stood up and picked her coat off the back of the chair. "She's doing fine. I think we'll be able to go home soon."

"Wait for me, we can all go down together," said Cathy, shoving her foot into a sleek ankle boot and zipping it up. "Get the coats, please, Tiffany."

Tiffany opened a coat closet next to the front door, a feature that Lucy hadn't imagined existed in hotels, and pulled out a white parka for herself and a tawny full-length fur for Cathy. Lucy's jaw dropped at the sight; she'd never seen anything so fabulous. Whatever it was, lynx maybe, it was a lot more glamorous than mink. She had to bite her tongue to keep from asking to try it on. Cathy, however, treated it just like any coat, shrugging into it as they left the suite and patting the pockets to check for her gloves.

While they waited for the elevator Lucy broached her second question. "The other thing I was wondering about has to do with Elise."

"Ah, Elise," said Cathy, raising her eyebrows.

"What do you mean?" asked Lucy.

"That woman is living proof that it's who you know and not what you know that matters," said Cathy. "Camilla pulled her out from nowhere about two years ago and named her fashion editor. It was weird, even for Camilla. I mean, that's the sort of job people usually work into over many years. A good fashion editor knows the designers personally, she has relationships with them. She knows their histories, their muses, their influences."

The elevator came and they all got on.

"Do you know what she did before she joined the magazine?" asked Lucy.

"It wasn't fashion, that's for sure." Cathy snorted. "I don't think Elise could tell a Jean-Paul Gaultier creation from a Calvin Klein."

The elevator doors opened and Cathy sailed into the

lobby, turning every head. The bellhops and desk staff all smiled and greeted her, and the doorman stepped smartly to open the door for her. Lucy and Tiffany followed in her wake as, smiling and waving at everyone, she swept through the door onto the sidewalk, where she suddenly stopped.

Lucy watched, horrified, as a motorcycle with two helmeted riders dressed in gleaming black suits suddenly jumped the curb and came directly toward Cathy. She attempted to dodge the machine, and the doorman rushed to help her, but it was too late. She couldn't avoid the bucket of red paint that drenched her beautiful fur coat.

The driver wheeled the motorcycle around, attempting to escape, but the doorman heroically threw himself at the passenger. Lucy caught a glimpse of the driver's shiny imitation leather suit, embellished with numerous zippers, as the motorbike roared off. She rushed to Cathy's side and saw a uniformed cop pounding down the sidewalk to assist the doorman, who was struggling with the attacker he'd dragged off the motorcycle. The cop fumbled, attempting to handcuff the culprit, who took the opportunity to slip out of his grasp and dashed nimbly down the sidewalk and around the corner, leaving the two men bushed and breathing heavily.

"Are you all right?" she asked Cathy, who was standing in the dripping coat, apparently in shock. Next to her, Tiffany was in tears.

"I'm fine," said Cathy. "Just a little stunned."

"Your poor coat," wailed Tiffany.

"I'm afraid it's ruined," said Lucy, who felt like weeping at the loss.

"This old thing? I've had it for years. But why would anyone do something like this?"

"Animal rights," said the doorman, dusting himself off. "They don't approve of wearing fur so they do stuff like this. They even picketed the *Nutcracker* performances this year. My granddaughter was in tears, all upset about the little bunnies that were killed to make fur coats."

"Well, they made a big mistake, then," said Cathy, dropping her coat on the sidewalk. "Because now I'm just going to buy a new coat, and they'll have to kill a whole lot of furry little critters—and they won't be bunnies, I can tell you that."

"What a shame," said Lucy, shaking her head over the coat.

"If you don't mind, I'll need a statement," said the officer, panting as he reached for his notebook.

"Not at all," said Cathy. She turned to go inside, pausing first to say good-bye to Lucy.

Alone on the sidewalk, Lucy started walking in the direction of the hospital. But as she walked, she kept replaying the attack in her mind, like a video: the roar of the motorbike, the riders in their Darth Vader helmets, the arc of thrown paint, and then the splatters that fell like blood. Her steps quickened and she was quite out of breath herself by the time she reached the hospital.

Chapter Eighteen

THE NEW ETIQUETTE:
WHEN IT'S OK TO E-MAIL

The lunch trays had been delivered when Lucy arrived at the hospital but Elizabeth wasn't much interested.

"What exactly is Salisbury steak?" she asked, poking at a lump of mystery meat. It was covered with thick brown gravy and accompanied by an ice cream scoop of mashed potatoes with a puddle of bright orange margarine congealing on top.

"Are you going to eat it?" asked Lucy, who had eaten nothing all day except a bowl of cereal and too much coffee.

"No way. It's disgusting."

"You don't mind if I eat it, then?"

"It's your party," said Elizabeth, grimacing as Lucy took the tray and set it on her lap.

"When are they going to let me out of here?" asked Elizabeth. She was pressing the bed controls and suddenly shot from a reclining position to one that was bolt upright.

"I've been wondering the same thing," said Lucy, her mouth full of potato. "I keep hoping to run into the doctor but he's never here when I am."

"I'm not sick anymore. I feel fine," said Elizabeth, who was now lying on her back and raising her feet.

"Did you tell that to the doctor?"

"Sure. He just says that these things take time and I

should be a patient patient." Elizabeth snorted. "It's his version of a joke."

"I wonder if it's something to do with the investigation. Maybe the FBI wants to keep you safe or under observation." Lucy had finished the main course and had moved on to the rubbery rice pudding. "Maybe one of the nurses can tell me something."

"They'll just tell you to talk to the doctor," said Elizabeth, who was now alternately raising her head and her feet.

Finally satisfied, Lucy sat back and took a sip of brown liquid that could have been either coffee or tea. She looked around the room, bright with sunshine and fragrant with flowers. A small flowering bonsai tree in a jade pot caught her eye. "Who gave you that pretty plant?" she asked.

"Brad and Samantha. They were here this morning."

"That was nice of them," said Lucy, giving the plant a closer look. "Did you read the card?"

"I didn't notice it," said Elizabeth. "But I did thank them. Really."

Lucy couldn't help smiling. If there was one thing she'd pounded into her kids' heads it was the importance of saying thank you and writing thank you notes. That, and not opening someone else's mail. She passed the little envelope to Elizabeth, who opened it and pulled out a white card.

"There's no message. It's just his business card."

"Maybe the florist has a lot of corporate clients," said Lucy, tapping her chin thoughtfully with her finger. It had worked for the Trojans, she thought, why not her? Besides, what was the worst that could happen? She'd get thrown out on her ear. It was a risk she was willing to take, if there was even a slight possibility of talking to Arnold. "You don't need me, do you?" she asked.

Elizabeth's eyebrows shot up. "What do you mean? Where are you going?"

"I have to make a delivery," she said, grabbing her coat and shooting out the door.

It wasn't until Lucy was standing in the lobby of Nelco's famous Millennium Building, holding an overpriced philodendron from a fancy florist in her hand, that she realized her plan needed work. She hadn't realized that most New York office buildings had instituted strict security measures after 9/11 and the Millennium Building was no exception. Access to the elevators was blocked by a security checkpoint complete with a metal detector and several uniformed officers who checked bags. Lucy watched the procedure for a few minutes and was about to turn away when she made a startling realization: they were looking for guns and explosives, but they weren't checking identities. And since she didn't have any guns or explosives, they would let her through.

She soon discovered, however, that the situation was quite different when she reached the top-floor offices of Nelco. There the elevator opened onto a once luxurious lobby that had been converted into something resembling the Berlin Wall's Checkpoint Charlie. The formerly welcoming and spacious reception area had been awkwardly divided with a seemingly impregnable metal and glass wall that limited access to a pair of sturdy sliding metal doors that were activated only after one had cleared a metal scanner. The entire area was under observation from numerous video cameras, and at least twenty armed and uniformed private security guards were on duty; Lucy had never seen anything like it, not even at the airport. She was immediately assigned to one of the two lines of people awaiting entry. The process was slow as each person was questioned and checked against a list before being allowed to pass through the space-age doors.

Lucy quickly decided that a quiet retreat was her best course of action. "Oops," she said while turning to go back to the elevator, "wrong floor."

Her way was immediately blocked by two of the largest

men she had ever seen, both clad in matching blue and brown uniforms, with shaved heads and bulging biceps.

"I made a mistake," she said, appalled to discover her voice had become little more than a squeak.

"Just come this way," said one of the guards.

"But I already told you, I made a mistake. This is the wrong floor."

"We have a few questions."

Before she could utter another word, she was hustled across the lobby and through a cleverly disguised doorway she hadn't noticed before. She found herself in a small, bare room where she was immediately divested of her purse, coat, and plant and was thoroughly patted down by one of the guards while the other drew his gun and leveled it at her.

"What do you think you're doing?" she shrieked.

"Routine," said the guard with the gun.

"She's clean," said the other, who had worked his way down to her feet and removed her boots for examination, revealing a tattered pair of knee-highs.

"Give me those back!" she demanded.

Grinning, he handed the boots to her. "What is your business here?"

"I told you," she stammered. "I got off the elevator on the wrong floor."

His eyes were blank, his expression neutral. "What floor did you want?"

"Eighty-four."

"Why?"

"To deliver this plant."

"Who's it for?"

"Andrea Devine," said Lucy, feeling rather clever for coming up with a name so quickly.

"This Andrea Devine is with what firm?"

"Sparkman, Blute, and Blowfish."

As soon as she'd said it Lucy realized she'd made a mistake. She whirled and lunged for the door, and was actually through it, when she ran straight into another guard. He was shoving her back through the door when the elevator binged and the doors slid open revealing Arnold Nelson himself.

"What's going on?" he demanded.

"This woman attempted to gain unauthorized entry," said the guard, who was gripping her firmly by her upper arms.

"Let me go!" shrieked Lucy.

"You again," said Arnold, his eyes narrowing. "What do you want?"

"I want to talk to you about your wife and my daughter and why they both got anthrax," said Lucy. She spoke right up and was gratified to see that the people standing in line and waiting to be admitted were taking notice of the scene and looking on with interest.

"Come with me," said Arnold. His voice was quiet and authoritative.

The guard let go of her arms and Lucy practically fell to the floor in amazement. Catching herself, she trotted after Arnold, like a little page carrying the king's train. Everyone stepped back to let him pass, heads nodded, and people practically bowed and scraped. They eventually reached his office where his secretary's eyes widened in surprise as Lucy was allowed to enter Arnold's inner sanctum.

Arnold lowered himself heavily into a leather chair behind his desk and indicated with a nod that Lucy should seat herself, too. "You're that Stone woman."

"Lucy Stone. My daughter Elizabeth is still in the hospital with anthrax."

Arnold's voice was serious. "Is she getting better?"

"Yes," said Lucy, surprised at his concern.

"So what's the problem?"

"I want to know who did it. Who poisoned your wife and my daughter."

"How would I know?"

Lucy's eyes met his.

Arnold didn't get to be a multimillionaire because he was dumb. He got the point immediately. "You think I did it."

"Uh, of course not," stammered Lucy.

He looked straight at her. "I give you my word. I had nothing to do with it."

Arnold wasn't a handsome man. He was short and fat and flabby. His eyes were too small and his nose was too big, but Lucy understood why he'd been so astonishingly successful. When he looked you in the eye and gave his word, you believed him.

She sat for a minute, looking at the swirling design in the very expensive carpet. Raising her head she looked past Arnold, through the wall of glass behind his desk at the city stretched out far below. The view was magnificent, over the rooftops with their wooden water towers all the way down to the Wall Street skyscrapers and the Narrows beyond. An architect's drawing of the City Gate project was affixed to the window. It was rendered in scale on some clear surface, allowing a viewer in the office to see what the towers would look like if they were built on Governors Island. Other framed drawings of projects were displayed around the office: a shopping mall in New Jersey, apartments in Westchester, dorms for Manhattan College and a lab for New York University. The stylized architect's letters identified it as The Marcus Widmann Institute for the Study of Infectious Diseases. The image reminded her of something Geoff had said at the AIDS gala, that the lab project was in jeopardy.

"You've had threats and you're taking them seriously," said Lucy, turning away from the image of the lab and meeting his eyes. "That's why you have all this security."

Arnold shrugged. "It's part of the business."

"No, this is not your average security setup. There are dozens of guards out there, and that barrier looks pretty serious to me. I bet it's designed to resist sizeable explosions and the whole area can be sealed off in seconds in case of a poison gas attack."

Arnold didn't say a word.

Having gotten this far, Lucy wasn't about to give up. "It's about the lab you're building, right?"

Arnold's eyes widened slightly, but he remained impassive, giving no other clue to his thoughts. "Like I said, I get threats all the time. I don't pay attention. There's no point, because once I've signed a contract, the project is going forward. If I say I'm going to build something, it's going to get built."

"Do you know who's behind these threats?" From somewhere deep in the back of her mind Lucy dredged up a tiny bit of information. "There's even been sabotage, right?"

He shrugged. "Construction is a tough business, and when you're successful you make a few enemies. Competitors, unions, even neighborhood groups. That's how it is."

Lucy couldn't understand his attitude. Why wasn't he angry? Unable to get to him, thanks to his impenetrable security, these saboteurs had sent anthrax to his wife. Why didn't he want to get them? What was she missing here? "Don't you want revenge?" she asked. "Don't you want to make them pay for what they did?" She thought of Elizabeth, lying unconscious in the emergency room after collapsing at the photo shoot. "I know I do."

Arnold's head was down. He was intently studying his desk's burl-wood pattern. "I have confidence in the FBI," he said. "They have their job and I have mine." He glanced at his watch. "Now, I'm afraid I'm late for a meeting."

"The FBI?" Lucy couldn't believe it. "They still haven't

solved the 2001 anthrax attack. Why do you think they're going to do any better this time?"

Behind her, the door opened and one of the guards entered. The message was clear: the meeting was over and one way or another, voluntarily or not, she was going to leave. Lucy got to her feet. "Thanks for your time," she said. "And I'm truly very sorry about your wife."

"Me, too," he said. Much to her surprise, Lucy believed him. He may have been a philanderer, but there was no doubt in her mind that on some level he truly loved Nadine.

One of the security guards was waiting for Lucy in the reception area outside Arnold's office. He helped her on with her coat, then presented her with her purse and the foolish plant, which she refused, before escorting her to the elevator. He accompanied her for the ride downstairs and walked her to the door, where he stood watching to make sure she left the building.

Outside, the cold air was like a slap in the face. Lucy took a deep, invigorating breath. She felt as if she were waking up from a dream. She could remember bits and pieces but she couldn't put it all together so it made sense. It was exactly the same feeling, she thought as she walked along, that she'd had so often upon waking. She would be afraid or confused and would lie in bed trying to remember the dream so she could discover its meaning. The most she could ever do, however, was to recapture a series of disjointed images. Yet always, there was the feeling that there was something more, if she could only remember it.

Heading back to the hospital, she kept thinking about Arnold. What was he really like? There was the obnoxious womanizer she'd encountered at the ball, and then there was the angry Arnold at the funeral who had kicked her out. Today, she'd met the rich and powerful Arnold, secure in in his skyscraper fortress high above Manhattan. None of these men seemed to bear any resemblance to Nancy Glass's version of Arnold, the bereft widower in need of her tender loving care, or the suave salesman Arnold she'd seen on the *Norah!* show.

Okay, Lucy admitted to herself, most people were a mix of contradictions, herself included. She loved her family; she loved getting away from them. Nobody was entirely consistent one hundred percent of the time, but Arnold certainly seemed to be an extreme example. Maybe, she thought, he had some mental problem. Split personalities? Schizophrenia? Or maybe he was just a chameleon who adapted to different situations with different responses.

She didn't know the answer, she concluded as she turned the corner by the hospital, but she now suspected that the anthrax attack was designed to send a message to Arnold and he'd gotten it. There had to be a reason for all that security. But who was trying to stop the lab? And were they the same group that was running around town tossing red paint and tomatoes?

When Lucy returned to Elizabeth's room she found Lance sprawled in the chair and clicking through the TV channels with the remote. He seemed quite at home, as if he'd been spending a lot of time there.

"Hi, Lance," she said, setting a couple of chocolate bars she'd picked up in the gift shop downstairs on the bedside table. "It's nice of you to visit Elizabeth but I hope you're not neglecting your studies."

"Nope," he said, turning off the TV. "Classes are over for the day; I studied for a quiz and I've started researching a paper that's due next week. Everything's under control."

"Isn't he amazing?" Elizabeth was beaming at him. "Did you know he's got a 3.9 grade average?"

"Good for you, Lance," said Lucy, watching as Elizabeth picked up one of the bars and began unwrapping it. Lance also had his gaze fixed on Elizabeth, but he wasn't watching to make sure she actually took a bite of chocolate. He looked positively lovesick; it was almost as if he were worshipping at a shrine or something, thought Lucy, feeling like a third wheel.

"I guess I ought to get going," she said, standing.

Elizabeth took another bite of chocolate. "You know, I almost forgot. Brad called. He was looking for you."

"Brad?"

"Yeah. He said he was going out to some island and he thought you might like to go along. Get away from the hospital for a while." She sighed dramatically and rolled her eyes. "Like you're actually here that much, taking care of your poor, sick daughter."

Lucy paid no attention to the sarcasm. "Governors Island?"

"Maybe. He said you'd like it."

"Yeah, it's cool out there," said Lance, his eyes still fixed on Elizabeth.

"Have you been there?" Lucy was surprised; she thought the island was restricted.

"All the time. I've been helping Geoff with a research project. It's real interesting. Because they've cleaned up the water so much, these marine worms have made a big comeback. Problem is, they eat wood, like piers and bulkheads and all that stuff. So Geoff is trying to find a way to protect the wood without hurting the worms."

"Eeew," said Elizabeth. "Do you have to touch them?"

"Actually, no. Geoff handles that stuff. I mostly collect water samples and go exploring." He paused. "There's interesting stuff out there. It's an old military base, you know."

Suddenly, Lucy was convinced she'd found the missing part of her dream, the piece that had been floating around just outside her consciousness. Somehow, she was certain, Governors Island was the key.

"Did they ever do germ warfare research out there?" she asked.

"I don't know. They might have. It makes sense, if you think about it. I mean, if you're going to play around with deadly microorganisms, it's better to do it on an island than in the middle of a big city."

"Isn't it dangerous, poking around a place like that?" asked Elizabeth. "What if some of the stuff is still around?"

"If anything's left, and I very much doubt there is, it would be harmless. That's the big problem with infectious agents. It's hard to sustain viability over the long term. . . ." He slapped his forehead with his hand. "Except for anthrax. Boy am I dumb! That's could be where it came from! It can be viable for forty or fifty years, that's one of its advantages." Lance had pulled a laptop computer out of his book bag and was opening it up.

"Do you think they actually did anthrax research over there?" asked Lucy.

"I know how we can find out," said Lance, clicking away on the keyboard.

"From the computer?" asked Lucy. "That research would probably be classified, and it was all done long before computers, wasn't it?"

"I'm not doing research," he said. "I'm e-mailing Geoff. He says he'll meet us at the marina at three o'clock and take us over there."

Lucy was puzzled. Somehow it had never occurred to her that such a thing as a marina existed on the island of Manhattan. "Geoff has a boat here in the city?"

"Sure. A twenty-two footer. How else could he do the research for the project?"

"Of course." Lucy was still trying to get used to the idea. Somehow New York Harbor, with its ferries and water taxis and tugboats towing barges and container ships and enormous oil tankers, didn't seem like a good place for a little twenty-two-foot boat. Not even for the short crossing to Governors Island. "Is it safe?"

"Sure. We do it all the time."

That was reassuring, kind of, but she didn't think that the makeover outfit she was wearing—a light wool-blend pantsuit with a silk blouse and high-heel boots—would keep her very warm on a small boat in winter. "I'll need to change into some warm clothes. Maybe Sam has some stuff I can borrow."

"Good idea," agreed Lance, reluctantly dragging his eyes away from Elizabeth. "We're also going to need some protective gear like gloves and masks if we're going to be looking for biological toxins. Better safe than sorry."

Lucy couldn't agree more. "And where are we going to get those?"

"This is a hospital, right?" Lance had a naughty gleam in his eye.

"Oh no," cautioned Lucy.

"Don't worry. I know where there's a supply closet." He was out the door before Lucy could protest.

"I better stop him before he gets in trouble," she told Elizabeth, as she shot out the door after him, teetering on her high heels.

Lance was already at the end of the corridor, and Lucy was afraid she'd lose him. She was hampered by those darned boots and she didn't dare run for fear of attracting attention. Lance, on the other hand, was wearing athletic shoes, had awfully long legs, and knew his way around the hospital. She could see him at the end of the hall, rounding a corner, but when she got there found he had vanished into thin air. Lucy's feet hurt and she was out of breath; she was deciding that she might as well go back to Elizabeth's room when she felt a tap on her shoulder. She whirled around and saw an arm extending from behind a door; she quickly stepped inside the supply closet.

"This is stealing. It's not a good idea," she told Lance, who was scanning the shelves of neatly stacked boxes of supplies.

"They'll never miss a few masks and gloves," he said. "Put your weight against that door."

"Oh, great, now I'm an accessory," said Lucy, bracing herself with her feet

"Why are they hiding this stuff?" muttered Lance, peering into box after box.

"Probably because of people like you," said Lucy. She was about to make a joke about the high cost of health insurance when she felt pressure from the opposite side of the door. "Help!" she hissed, throwing her weight against the door. "Somebody's trying to get in."

"Push harder."

"I'm trying," gasped Lucy, pressing with all her might. It was barely enough; she was terrified the door would give.

Lance had joined her and was also pressing against the door. His eyes were round with panic. "What are we going to do?" he whispered.

"Pray," said Lucy, as the pressure on the door continued. She was horrified at the thought of being discovered in the closet. Stealing was bad enough, but even worse was the fact that Lance was a very attractive young man. She couldn't imagine anything more embarrassing than being discovered in a closet with him.

"This door is not supposed to be locked," declared a stern female voice. The knob rattled. "Darn!" They heard footsteps, clicking down the hall, away from the closet.

"That was close," said Lucy, breathing out a huge sigh of relief. She stuck her head out in the hall to make sure the coast was clear while Lance frantically searched the boxes. She was about to abort the mission when he finally found some masks and a second later got the gloves.

"We're out of here," he said, stuffing them in his pockets. But as they strolled ever so casually down the hallway Lucy couldn't help wishing Lance had been a little less impulsive. They were lucky this time, but she was afraid their close escape didn't bode well for the expedition to Governors Island.

Chapter Nineteen

LOOKS THAT GO FROM DAY TO NIGHT!

After trying three times to reach Sam by phone, Lucy finally acknowledged the gruesome truth that she would not only have to stick close to Lance in order to keep an eye on him but also have to borrow his clothing. There was no way she could venture out on the water in her makeover black pantsuit and sleek, black leather city boots. Why oh why had she been so quick to give up her duck boots for these pointy-toed numbers with a three-inch heel? Her feet were killing her, too. How did these women do it?

"Don't worry, I've got plenty of clothes," Lance assured her as they exited the subway a few blocks from his dorm.

"Slow down," she gasped, out of breath from trying to keep up with him. "You're twenty and have long legs. I'm five-two and, well, never you mind how old I am but I am old enough to be your mother."

"Oh, sorry." He looked genuinely abashed. "I didn't think."

"No problem. You don't usually hang out with old fogies like me."

"You're hardly an old fogey, Mrs. Stone. You're actually pretty good looking for somebody your age."

Lucy wasn't sure which was worse: being too old to

keep up with his young legs or his condescension. Pretty good looking for her age—ouch!

"My room's on the third floor," he said, full of concern. "Do you think you can make it?" he continued, adding insult to injury. "It's no problem if you can't because there's an elevator, but you're only supposed to use it if you're handicapped."

"I don't think it will be a problem as long as there's oxygen available," she said.

He looked at her oddly. "Oxygen?"

"Just a joke." Lucy was dismayed. What was the matter with kids today? They had no sense of humor and apparently, if Lance was typical, absolutely no ability to focus. While Lucy pointedly checked her lobster watch and tapped her foot, Lance paused in the dorm lobby to check his mail and chat with a friend. Then, when they'd reached the second-floor landing he dashed off, leaving Lucy standing in the stairwell, getting madder by the minute.

"Where did you go?" she demanded when he returned.

"I got these for you." He held out a sturdy pair of well-worn winter boots. "They belong to my friend Julie. Do you think they'll fit?"

"They'll do," said Lucy. Maybe he wasn't such a doofus after all. "Thanks."

They were starting down the hall to his room when Lucy asked where the bathroom was.

"Just around the corner," he said, pointing.

Lucy had a frightening thought. "It's not coed, is it?"

"Nope. The guys' room is on the other side."

What a relief. "I'll meet you in your room."

"Okay." He started down the hall.

"Uh, Lance," she said.

He turned. "Yeah?"

"Your room number?"

"Uh, sorry. It's 306," he said.

But when Lucy emerged, Lance was still in the hallway,

leaning against the wall and deep in conversation with another student. "You can borrow my notes, man, no problem, but they won't do you any good 'cause all Philbrick cares about is dates. If you get the years right that's a B, throw in the months and you'll get a B plus and if you get the days you're guaranteed an A."

"Shit. I suck at memorization," moaned the kid, who had shaved his head and was wearing an earring, nose ring, and eyebrow ring. "Uh, sorry," he muttered as Lucy approached. "I didn't know your mom was here."

"She's not my mom."

The kid's eyes widened. "Whoa, cool. Like Ashton Kutcher, huh?"

"Not like that," said Lance, opening the door to his room for Lucy.

"Who is this Ashton Kutcher?" she asked.

"Never mind," he said, showing her in with a flourish. "Welcome to my humble abode."

Lucy knew all about messy rooms and had fought a running battle with her oldest son Toby for years over his habit of dropping clothing on the floor, but she'd never seen anything to compare with Lance's room. It not only smelled like a laundry hamper, it looked like one. In fact, Lucy felt as if she was actually inside one.

"Just take what you want," he said, gesturing generously.

"Aren't there any clean clothes?"

"I don't think so." He opened the closet door so she could see. It was empty except for a lone blue blazer hanging crookedly on a wire hanger.

"Waiting for the laundry fairy?"

He laughed feebly. "If only."

"That's why they invented washing machines." As soon as she said it Lucy realized she was talking like a mother, but she wasn't his mother. He was helping her investigate the anthrax poisoning that had killed Nadine and sickened

Elizabeth, and she had no business talking to him like that. Fortunately, he didn't seem to notice.

"This sweatshirt isn't too bad," he said, holding out a thick, hooded number. "And I've got lots of sweatpants and sweaters. I think we better wear dark colors. There's watchmen on the island. . . ."

"Point taken," said Lucy, unbuttoning her jacket.

He pulled a CD out of a wire rack. "Uh, well, you'll probably want some privacy, and I promised to lend this to the girl next door."

"Don't be long," said Lucy. "We've got to meet Geoff in half an hour."

"We've got plenty of time," he told her. "It only takes about ten minutes to get there by subway."

"Right." She didn't believe him for a minute, but she was tired of sounding like a nag.

When he returned ten minutes later Lucy was ready to go, although she felt like the Michelin tire guy in two pairs of sweatpants, a turtleneck, sweatshirt, and sweater topped with a windproof jacket. Everything was much too large, of course, but the boots were only a size or two too big thanks to two pairs of extremely fragrant gym socks, and she had her own gloves and hat. It was a good thing the editors at *Jolie* couldn't see her now, she thought as she clumped down the hall. Or smell her.

Once they were outside the smell didn't matter; the air was filled with noxious gray smoke.

"Is it often like this?" she asked, assuming it was air pollution.

"No," said Lance. "There must be a fire."

As they approached Broadway they saw the street was filled with fire trucks, and hoses were snaking down the steps to the subway station. Cops were busy setting up a barricade and blocking people from the stairs, which were filled with exiting passengers. Some were able to make their own way out; others were carried on stretchers to waiting ambulances with flashing red lights.

"We'll have to go to the next station," said Lance.

"That'll be a waste of time. Trust me. Something like this will shut down the whole line, maybe the whole system," said Lucy. "We better grab a cab."

A lot of other people had the same idea, so they started walking down Broadway in hopes of finding a taxi where it wasn't so crowded. Lucy checked her watch and it was already five minutes before three. They'd never make it in five minutes.

"There's a gypsy, come on." Lance grabbed her hand and pulled her into the street, darting in front of a slow-moving bus and directly into the path of a big black Mercedes, which didn't actually hit them although the driver expressed his deep disappointment at the missed opportunity. Lucy found herself clambering into a beat-up white sedan with a light on top but no official medallion. The driver took off before she'd even closed the door.

"We're going to be late," said Lucy.

"Maybe not," said Lance. "This guy is flying."

It was true. The driver was speeding down Broadway, weaving his way between slower moving vehicles and running all the yellow and some red lights. Lucy held on to the door handle and prayed as an oncoming taxi swerved to avoid them at Seventy-second Street.

"How far do we have to go?"

"South Ferry."

"Lord have mercy."

Lucy wasn't exactly sure how far that actually was, but she knew South Ferry was at the very bottom of the island of Manhattan. They had miles to go, through a maze of city streets crowded with vehicles of every description, all with the potential of causing dreadful bodily harm. The driver careened past taxis, darted in front of delivery trucks, tailgated limousines, braked once for a cement mixer, and cut off bicycle messengers who shook their fists and swore. When they reached West Street, in sight of Battery Park, the driver took the turn too wide and clipped another taxi that was waiting for the light. He would have sped away but was stopped by two other officially licensed cabbies who quickly moved their cars to block the gypsy cab's way.

Lucy put her head in her hands, fearing it was all over. As passengers they were witnesses, maybe even liable in some way. There would be questions to answer, forms to fill out; they'd never make it to the marina before dark.

"Come on." Lance was pulling her out of the cab.

"We can't leave!"

"Oh yes we can." Lance tilted his head toward the cabbies, who were shouting and raising their fists. A crowd was gathering, and it looked like a full-fledged brawl would soon erupt. The only sensible option was to get away as fast as they could.

"How far to the marina?" asked Lucy, as they ran down the street.

"Eight or nine blocks. Can you make it?"

Lucy didn't know, but she was sure going to try. She pounded along the sidewalk, attracting stares, as she followed Lance's lead. It was a little too late to realize it, but she should never have given up jogging. Now she was out of breath and had a stitch in her side and she'd only gone two blocks. One thing Lucy did remember from her jogging days was that if you didn't give up, eventually your body cooperated and it got easier. So instead of collapsing and throwing herself on the ground to catch her breath, she concentrated on making it to the marina without losing sight of Lance. She followed as he pounded past the ferry terminal and made his way along the waterfront, where chain-link fencing and corrugated metal walls barred access to the piers that extended like fingers into the East River.

He finally stopped at a gate with a forbidding AUTHORIZED PERSONNEL ONLY sign. Geoff was waiting on the other side.

"I was just about to give up on you guys," he said, opening the gate for them. Dressed in his yellow Grunden fishing pants, he looked just as he had at home in Tinker's Cove where he operated a lobster boat every summer. He led them through a grubby parking area filled with official New York City vehicles to the dock, and Lucy was amazed to see an assortment of small boats bobbing in the water right in the shadow of the big skyscrapers.

"What is this place?" she asked between raspy breaths. Her heart was pounding and she felt as if it was ninety degrees instead of thirty-five.

"It's one of those odd bits that belongs to the city," explained Geoff, leading the way to a rather dilapidated dock. "I got permission to use it because my project is partly funded by the parks department."

The three hopped aboard Geoff's boat, *Downeast Girl.* Lucy was dismayed to discover the cabin was really only a cramped cubby, equipped with a basic toilet and two small bunks filled with an amazing clutter of buckets, rope, books, and cases she assumed contained scientific instruments. They would be making the crossing to Governors Island in what was essentially an open boat.

Geoff quickly got the engine going while Lance untied the lines, but it was already starting to get dark by the time they pulled away from the dock. Lucy sat on the molded fiberglass bench, wrapping her arms around herself and trying not to shiver too violently, lest she upset the boat. It would be bitterly cold out on the water; a sharp breeze was already cutting right through her layers of clothing, now topped by a life jacket. Not that it would be much help if she was unlucky enough to tumble into the water. She'd be dead of hypothermia long before anyone could rescue her.

"Geoff," she began. "Maybe this isn't such a good idea."

"What do you mean?"

"This is too risky."

"There's risks, and then there's risks," he said with a shrug, neatly steering the boat around the end of the dock and heading for open water. "Nadine's dead, Elizabeth had a close call, and now they're threatening Norah."

"Yeah, I heard about the tomatoes."

"Well, it's a lot more serious than throwing a few tomatoes. Sidra got a phone call demanding time on the show for this bunch called OTM. If they don't get it they said Norah would be sorry, just like her friend Nadine."

"You think this group sent the anthrax?"

"I don't know. Maybe they're just making a threat, but I'm inclined to take them at their word. We've to get to the bottom of it or it won't stop. Who'll be next? Sidra? You? Me?" Geoff was gazing ahead, looking out over the water. "If there's even a slim chance they got the anthrax on the island, it's worth checking it out."

Lucy shivered. "There's an awful lot of traffic on this water."

"We've got lights," said Lance, ever the optimist.

"Lot of good they'll do," muttered Geoff, slowing the boat and waiting for a huge oil tanker to pass. "From the bridge of that thing we're just a little speck. Nope, we've got to watch out for them because chances are they can't see us."

"Ferry's approaching starboard," said Lance, alerting Geoff who was keeping an eye on a tug pushing a barge off the port side.

"Thanks," he said, shifting the rudder and gunning the engine. The boat shot forward and dodged around a sleek, white harbor cruise boat.

"Maybe we ought to turn back," said Lucy. She was beginning to feel very queasy.

"We're halfway there; might as well go on as turn around." Geoff's voice was tight and he was straining to make out the shapes of approaching ships in the fog as he tried to navigate by the sounds of foghorns and the clang of a buoy.

The tension was horrible: at any moment they could be annihilated by one of the huge freighters headed for the docks on the Brooklyn shore.

"What's in those ships?" asked Lucy. "I don't want to die for bananas."

"You name it, they're bringing it in. Cars, computers, air conditioners, clothing . . . have you heard about the trade deficit?" Geoff's voice was more relaxed. "We're out of the shipping lane now; it should be clear sailing from here."

Now they were alone on the inky water, a large rounded shape looming over them.

"What's that?" asked Lucy.

"Ventilator for the Brooklyn-Battery Tunnel."

"Ohmigosh," said Lucy, who was beginning to picture the waterfront as an illustration in one of the Batman comics Toby used to love so much when he was a kid, filled with massive, threatening structures that seemed to mock the insignificant human inhabitants of the city. Bad thought, bad thought, she chided herself, switching instead to a bright Richard Scarry illustration, where cute animals rode the colorful boats and planes that filled the friendly harbor.

Downeast Girl was suddenly rocked by the wake of a passing tugboat, its powerful engine propelling it swiftly through the water without anything in tow, and Lucy held on to the gunwales for dear life. Coming out here was a really bad idea, she decided. Where was Batman when you needed him?

Chapter Twenty

ACTIVEWEAR THAT FLATTERS
WHILE YOU GET FIT!

It was growing dark when they approached the dock, and Lucy braced herself as Geoff slowed the motor and Lance grabbed hold of a ladder and climbed up to make *Downeast Girl* fast. When he'd securely tied the boat to the dock, Lucy hauled herself up the ladder, followed by Geoff. As they stood there on the exposed pier, in the dark and whipped by the wind, the island suddenly seemed very big.

"Where do we begin?" asked Lucy.

"At the old infirmary," said Lance. "Follow me."

There were very few lights on the island, in contrast to the illuminated skyscrapers standing side by side on the much larger island of Manhattan across the water. There was no concern for the price of electricity there, thought Lucy, gazing at the amazing nightly spectacle of the skyline. Even the Brooklyn Bridge and the Williamsburg Bridge were outlined in lights, which were reflected in the black water below. Looking in the other direction she could see the glittering and seemingly endless expanse of the Verrazzano Bridge, stretching across the Narrows between Brooklyn and Staten Island. She knew the Statue of Liberty would also be alight, but it was blocked from view by the many buildings on the island.

She was grateful for the darkness as they made their

way along winding paths, staying in the shadows and trying to be as quiet as possible to avoid detection by the night watchmen. She felt a little surge of adrenaline; it was exciting to be taking part in a covert nighttime mission.

The island was much larger than it appeared to Lucy from the ferry, and she wished they had some other way of getting around besides their feet. Hers were cold, and the borrowed boots felt heavy and clumsy as she trotted along, doing her best to keep up with the two tall men. Wherever they were going was very far from where they'd docked the boat, and Lucy was beginning to wonder why they couldn't have tied up closer. She was also beginning to think the whole mission was foolish; there were dozens of buildings on the island and they could never search them all. This was worse than searching for a needle in a haystack: how would they know anthrax if they found it? She was tired and out of breath and about to suggest they give up when she realized Geoff and Lance had stopped abruptly at the corner of a building.

She joined them and peeked around the corner where she saw a circle of light.

"Watchman," whispered Geoff, holding his finger to his lips.

"We can't go around, we have to go through," said Lance, anticipating her question.

"Too risky," said Lucy, shaking her head. "Let's go back."

"I'm gonna take a look," said Lance. Before she could stop him he was gone. She and Geoff watched as he crept up to a window and slowly raised his head to peer in. A minute later he was back.

"Coast is clear. Nobody's there."

"If they're not here, they're out on patrol," said Geoff. "We've got to be very careful."

Lucy found herself crouching as she followed the others, although she wasn't quite sure what good it would do.

Covert operatives always crouched in the movies and she supposed it was helpful in some way; she hoped it was worth it because it was murder on her back.

They had reached an enormous round fort, towering over them like some sort of ancient Colosseum, when they heard the sound of a car engine.

"Down!" hissed Geoff.

There was no handy bush to hide behind so Lucy dropped flat on her stomach on the grass; it was prickly and stiff with frost and she liked how it felt cool on her chin. She was sweating underneath all the layers of clothing she was wearing; she should have opened her collar and taken off her hat.

They watched as the car proceeded slowly along the road at a steady crawl; occasionally the driver stopped and used a spotlight. The wait was nerve-wracking. There was nothing they could do but hope that the light didn't come their way because they would surely be discovered if it did.

It didn't, but they couldn't move until the car was out of sight, and Lucy was frozen stiff by the time it was safe to get up. She was no longer overheated; the cold had penetrated her to the core and she was shivering. Geoff pulled her into the shelter of the fort's tunnel-like entrance. It was dark and dank but at least they were out of the wind.

"Is this it?" she asked, praying that they wouldn't have to go any farther.

"No. There's nothing here."

"Nothing?"

"Just old blankets and stuff." Lance was already moving out. Geoff took her by the elbow and propelled her out of the shelter and back into the cold wind.

"How much farther?" she asked, trying not to whine.

"Your guess is as good as mine," whispered Geoff. "Lance is the one who explored the island. I just poked around the edges, looking for worms."

This side of the island was more crowded and the buildings were closer together with lots of leafless trees and evergreen landscape shrubs; they appeared to be in the section once devoted to housing the military personnel stationed on the island. Lucy could imagine the days when it was a bustling suburban neighborhood with kids riding bikes and skateboards after school. Now the families were all gone and it was eerily quiet, a ghost town.

"This is it," hissed Lance, pointing to a low, square building with a flat roof. A square metal sign with a red cross hung from a bracket above the door, creaking as it swung in the wind.

Geoff tried the door. "It's locked."

Lance snorted. "What did you expect? We'll have to break in."

Lucy was uncomfortably aware that if they were discovered, the charges would be breaking and entering instead of merely trespassing—quite another kettle of fish. On the other hand, there didn't seem to be any other way to get the evidence they needed.

"Are you game?" asked Geoff.

"Sure." Lucy shrugged. "Anything to get warm."

They stood in the shadow of a holly bush, stamping their feet and rubbing their arms, while Lance worked his way around the building. Their ears were pricked for the least sound, but all they heard was the howling wind and the regular moan of a foghorn. Except for the glittering skyline they could have been back in Tinker's Cove.

"We're in." Lance's whisper startled Lucy and she gave a little jump.

"Man, you sure are quiet," said Geoff.

"I jimmied a window."

Great, thought Lucy. Even though the building was low, the windows were a good five feet up from the ground. She'd need a hoist for sure. This was going to be clumsy and potentially noisy, increasing their chances of discovery.

When Lance stopped at the window Lucy knew she was right. It was even higher than she thought; a small awning window opening outward.

"I can't get up there!"

"Sure you can!" She found herself grabbed around the hips and hoisted upward in one smooth motion. It happened so quickly, however, that she neglected to grab onto the sill and slid back down.

"You were supposed to . . ." gasped Geoff.

"I know. I know. Let's try again."

Geoff was giving her a leg up when the silence was broken by a siren and the dark night was suddenly filled with light. Lucy and Geoff ducked down behind a bush and watched as two police cars screeched to a halt in front of the infirmary and four uniformed watchmen with flashlights ran up to the front door.

"Wha . . ." whispered Lucy, but Geoff firmly placed one hand over her mouth and signaled her to be as still as possible. She crouched lower, heart pounding, as two of the watchmen pounded past their hiding place and made for the back door. Lance was trapped, unless he could find a hiding place.

They waited for what seemed an eternity, listening to the voices of the watchmen as they worked their way through the building. Then came the cry, "Got him!" and it was all over. Lance was hustled out of the building, in handcuffs, and shoved into the back of one of the cars, which immediately took off. The other two watchmen began working their way around the outside of the building, and Geoff signaled to Lucy that they should split up and move away from the open window. Lucy crawled along on hands and knees, her shoulder against the side of the building, until she heard footsteps approaching. Then she froze, afraid to even breathe.

"Must've got in here," said a voice. The bright beam from a powerful flashlight danced around the open window and one of the men shut it. "That'll have to do for now," he said. "Maintenance can reset the alarm in the morning."

"Yeah, let's get back," said the other. "It's colder than a witch's tit out here."

"You can say that again."

Shivering, Lucy agreed with them. She was crouched on the ground, trying to make herself as small as possible, and trying to think warm thoughts so her teeth wouldn't chatter noisily. Feeling a hand on her shoulder she jumped a mile.

"Shh, it's only me," said Geoff.

"What do we do now?"

"Try to think up some story that'll convince them to let Lance go."

"Like what?" asked Lucy, scrambling to keep up with him as he started walking back to the watchman's post.

"I don't know. A fraternity prank?"

"We're kind of old for that, and I'm a girl. What about your science research?"

"I don't think that'll explain breaking and entering."

"How's this?" said Lucy. "We were doing research this afternoon but the boat wouldn't start and it got dark and we were stuck on the island and Lance was looking for shelter for the night?"

"It might work, if they're not too bright," said Geoff. "Maybe we should just tell the truth."

"That's probably best," said Lucy.

They walked along in glum silence. The hulking shadow of the old round fort covered them, wrapping them in darkness. Lucy felt especially low. This whole expedition had been a dumb idea. Lance was in trouble and they would soon join him. She was about to apologize to Geoff for dragging him into this mess when he suddenly stopped and put his gloved finger over her lips. She strained to listen and heard an odd, whirring sound. They dropped to the ground and waited, listening. The sound, although faint, came closer until two dark figures on bicycles whipped past them.

Geoff leaped to his feet and started after them, springing silently across the frosty grass. Lucy followed, doing her best to keep up, relying on instinct rather than sight or sound, and was startled when Geoff stepped out from behind a large tree.

"They went in that building," he said, pointing toward a large brick rectangle punctuated with rows of dark windows. "I'm going to follow them."

"Bad idea. We should tell the watchmen."

"Not yet. We need more information. They'll think we're sending them on a wild goose chase."

He had a point. Nobody would believe they'd seen bicyclists on the island in the middle of the night, in December.

"I'm coming," said Lucy.

"Okay. But let me go first."

Lucy nodded and followed when Geoff opened the door and stepped into the pitch black interior of the building. She couldn't see a thing, and then she saw stars.

Lucy's head hurt and everything was blurry when she opened her eyes. Unbelievably, the image that swam before her was of a gigantic woman with long hair swirling about her face and a bird perched on each shoulder. One arm was raised above her head, holding a flashing sword. Lucy blinked, realizing it was a poster.

"Boadicea?" she asked.

"Good guess, but you're wrong." said a voice. "That's Queen Medb."

Painfully, Lucy lifted her head and turned to see who had spoken. It was Helena Rubinstein. She squeezed her eyes shut and looked again. It wasn't actually Helena Rubinstein; it was Elise wearing oversized black-rimmed glasses and a white lab coat with her hair slicked back from her face. Lucy tried to sit up but couldn't. A thick strap had been fastened across her chest, holding her flat on her back. Her hands were also in some sort of restraint.

"Whuh?" Her voice was thick and hoarse; it was more of a grunt than a question, but Elise was eager to explain.

"She's the heroine of an ancient Celtic legend. A warrior-goddess."

"Ah," said Lucy, dropping her head back on the bed, gurney, whatever it was she was fastened to, and looking around. What she saw didn't encourage her. She guessed she was in some sort of laboratory; there were tables and shelves holding all sorts of beakers and jars and other scientific equipment. More ominously, she noticed, the walls were entirely covered with translucent plastic sheeting; even the door was sealed. She had no way of knowing whether she was ten stories high in the sky or in a sub-sub-basement; there were no windows. Even worse, she was at the mercy of Elise, who was apparently some sort of mad feminist scientist. There was no sign of Geoff.

"Queen Medb is our symbol." The voice was filtered through some sort of sound system and Lucy strained to see where it was coming from. She saw a figure in a white space suit, then realized it was a hazmat suit. Her heart skipped a beat, wondering why the suit was necessary, but she was reassured by the fact that Elise wasn't wearing any sort of protection. If this was some sort of evil scientist's lair, which is what it certainly seemed, she decided they must cook up the microbes in another room.

"Symbol of what?" asked Lucy, trying to make out the face behind the mask

"Operation Terra Mama. We're warriors in the fight to reclaim the earth and restore the proper order of nature. Procreation. Woman power. Matriarchy."

"Sounds good to me," said Lucy. "Can I join?"

"Very funny," scoffed Elise.

"I'm serious," said Lucy. "I believe in all that stuff. Save the planet. Love your Mother. I recycle bottles and newspapers. I even take those awful plastic bags back to the supermarket."

"What we're doing here is a bit more serious."

"I realize that," said Lucy. "But since you're holding me captive I think I deserve some sort of explanation. And where's Geoff?"

"He's fine, just like you," said the robot voice. It sounded eerily familiar and this time, when she peered at the mask, Lucy recognized Fiona.

"Fiona!" she exclaimed, feeling betrayed. "I thought you were Elizabeth's friend!"

"I am. Really I am. She wasn't supposed to get sick. That was a mistake. But she's going to be okay, right?"

"No thanks to you. She could have died, just like Nadine."

"That was unavoidable," said Elise. "We had to show Arnold that we meant what we said."

"He's building this big laboratory for NYU where they're going to do all sorts of tests on animals. We sent letters and faxes and . . ."

"Numerous warnings," interrupted Elise.

"All he had to do was stop the project, stop building the lab."

"Typical man," snorted Elise. "He wouldn't take us seriously."

"So we had to show him."

"And Nadine was hardly blameless herself," said Lucy. Their terrible logic was suddenly clear to her. "She wrote that article for *Jolie* saying how important animal testing is for developing new cosmetics."

"I couldn't believe that!" squeaked Fiona in her robot voice. "That was too much! Rabbits don't want to wear mascara or lipstick, they don't want to be squirted with perfume. It's cruel and unnecessary. Why not use people to test these products? After all, they're the ones who are going to use them. She even wore fur—she gave no thought at all to those poor little creatures who died so she could flaunt her wealth. How many for one coat? Dozens! She deserved to die."

"Cosmetics are a form of submission to male domination," said Elise, her voice oddly flat, as if she was repeating an argument she'd made many times. "Nadine subjected herself to male domination and she encouraged others to do the same thing." Her tone changed, becoming waspish. "Like that Cathy Montgomery, turning herself into a walking advertisement for her husband's wealth with her furs and jewels."

"You certainly showed her," said Lucy, remembering the incident outside the hotel. She was now convinced Fiona was one of the attackers, but who was the other? It certainly wasn't Elise. "I bet she'll think twice before she wears fur again."

"That was a warning," said Elise. "Next time it won't be paint, it will be blood. Her blood."

Lucy shivered, suddenly cold. Until now she'd thought they were mad as hatters, suffering some bizarre obsession or shared mania, but now she realized it was worse than that. They were evil, utterly evil, and would have no pity for anyone who posed a threat to their plans. She had to figure out a way to save herself and Geoff, but all she could think of at the moment was to keep them talking as long as she could. Maybe she could even convince them she was sympathetic to their cause, that she was on their team. Or perhaps convince Fiona to switch sides and help her. "This is quite a setup you've got here. Are we still on the island?"

"It's an old bomb shelter. Elise is so clever, she found it," said Fiona.

Even through the suit Lucy could hear the admiration in her voice. She was one of the faithful, and the job at the magazine was only a cover for her real work: terrorism. She'd do whatever Elise told her to do. And she was very good at it, Lucy realized. Lucy had never guessed. She'd even supplied Sidra's phone number, which Fiona had promptly used to make terrifying threats. If they weren't stopped, Norah would be next. And who else? Sidra? The other workers on the show? The audience? Lucy was convinced they'd stop at nothing. And it looked like she was nothing more than an inconvenient impediment they wouldn't hesitate to remove. Determined not to reveal her fear, she struggled to make it sound as if she were impressed with their ingenuity. "Really! How did you ever find it?" she asked, hoping that Elise's weak spot was flattery.

"I was over here a couple of times with Arnold and Nadine; he was giving tours to investors, that sort of thing. Then I came back in the summer, when they have the ferry and let people visit the island." Elise chuckled; it was a horrible sound. "It wasn't difficult to slip away on my own. If you're a woman of a certain age and you dress in comfortable, practical clothes, you're practically invisible."

Lucy had heard this sentiment before, although it was usually a complaint. She fleetingly wondered about Elise's sexuality and her relationship with Camilla. Had part of her motive for killing Nadine been to eliminate a rival for Camilla's attention, if not her affection? "You really outsmarted them. And you found the anthrax here, too?"

"Anthrax here on the island?"

"I thought the government might have experimented. . . ."

"No! There were never any anthrax experiments here, not that I know of, anyway."

"So where did you get it?"

Elise's eyes were cold. "You can get anything you want if you know the right people and you're willing to pay."

The plastic sheeting rustled and another figure in a shiny white hazmat suit entered the room and announced

"Everything's ready" in that spooky electronic voice. Lucy didn't like the sound of this at all. Whatever was ready, she had a feeling wasn't going to be good for her.

"Good," said Elise. "Let's go."

Instinctively, Lucy strained against her bonds, but it was useless. They didn't give an inch, not even a millimeter. Her heart raced as the hooded robot figures came forward, one on either side of the gurney, and began wheeling her through the plastic curtains that shrouded the door and out of the room. As she was rolled along Lucy struggled to identify the second figure, who she guessed must have been the other motorcycle attacker. The light was poor and she couldn't make out the face until she was pushed through more plastic curtains into a brightly lit space where Geoff, still unconscious, was arranged on a similar gurney.

"Agent Christine!" exclaimed Lucy, remembering the supposed FBI agent's dated Goodwill clothes, her plastic wallet, and her confusion about felonies and misdemeanors. "I knew there was something fishy about you."

"Tape her mouth." It was Elise's voice, coming over some sort of intercom system. She hadn't entered this area, and Lucy suspected it was because she wasn't wearing a hazmat suit. There was apparently a greater chance that this area was contaminated. Belatedly, she wished she'd re-membered to fill that Cipro prescription Dr. Marchetti gave her at the hospital. It was still in her purse, where she'd tucked it away and promptly forgotten it.

Her thoughts were interrupted when a piece of thick tape was slapped across her face, and she watched mutely as Geoff was wheeled up to a structure that looked like a small garden shed completely covered and sealed with plastic. A flexible metallic tube, like the duct from her clothes dryer, extended from the roof to a glass window through which Elsie could be seen moving about. The shed appeared to be some sort of isolation chamber, and Lucy watched in horror as Elise gave a signal, the door was opened, and he was wheeled inside. It was an experiment of some sort and Geoff was a human guinea pig. Angrily, furiously, Lucy wanted to protest their twisted logic. They wouldn't experiment on some stupid mouse—and living in the country, she knew all about mice—but they were willing to sacrifice a human being, a committed teacher, and a loving husband to their crazy plan.

Lucy wanted to give these conscienceless maniacs a piece of her mind, but she couldn't, thanks to the tape. She twisted and thrashed as hard as she could; she couldn't say words but she could produce moans and groans. She tried to make as much noise as she could. She might be at their mercy but she wasn't going to go down without a fight. This was horrible. They were monsters and she knew she was next. Tears came to her eyes as she thought of the kids, of Bill, even the dog. She drew in a big breath through her nose and produced a high-pitched squeal. She made it as loud and as long as she could, again and again, until, to her amazement, the room was suddenly filled with black-clad SWAT team members in gas masks and armed with assault rifles.

One bent over her, peeling off the tape. "Boy, am I glad . . ." began Lucy, only to find herself once again mute as a protective gas mask was placed over her face.

Chapter Twenty-one

THIS NEW YEAR, RESOLVE TO BE YOUR BEST SELF!

Hours later, after a frantic trip by ambulance and ferry to the hospital where she was thoroughly examined by a masked and robed medical team and intensely questioned by a couple of very serious and utterly genuine government agents, Lucy was finally released. She staggered out of the hospital, clutching a vial of Cipro that this time she was determined to remember to take, and hailed a taxi. Sam and Brad greeted her with hugs when she arrived early in the morning at their apartment.

"Boy, did you give us a scare!" exclaimed Sam. "Where were you?"

Too tired to talk, Lucy gave Brad the papers she'd been given and collapsed on her bed in the guest room. When she finally woke up, around one P.M. on New Year's Eve, she was surprised to find Elizabeth sitting at Sam's kitchen table.

"I've got a clean bill of health. They let me go early this morning."

"It was more like they kicked her out," said Sam. "They must have needed the bed for someone else. I got a phone call to come and pick her up."

'You should have gotten me up," said Lucy. After years of motherhood she wore guilt like an old sweater. "I should have gone."

"It was a pleasure," said Sam. "It's great to see our girl looking so healthy."

It was true. Elizabeth did look good. She'd gained a pound or two in the hospital, and her cheeks were round and rosy.

"It's sure good to be out of there," said Elizabeth. "It makes you appreciate everyday things." She took a long swallow of coffee. "This coffee is so good. And your apartment is so pretty and colorful, after all that hospital beige."

"Is there more coffee?" Lucy asked. "I could sure use some."

Sam was pouring when Brad returned. Lucy looked at him uneasily. "Am I going to jail?" she asked. "And what about Geoff and Lance?"

"Amazingly enough, you're all heroes," said Brad, joining them at the kitchen table. "It seems that the FBI has been watching Elise and company for some time but were never able to find the lab. It was thanks to you that they got the break they needed."

Lucy took a long swallow of coffee. "The FBI was there all the time?"

"Yeah. They'd been concerned about Operation Terra Mama for some time. It's an international feminist ecoterror group. They've been mainly active in England—apparently quite effectively. They managed to indefinitely halt construction of a lab at Oxford University by threatening the contractor and anybody else connected with it. It got so bad that truck drivers wouldn't make deliveries, and taxis wouldn't even go there for fear of retaliation."

"So Fiona brought their tactics over here?"

"Fiona!" Elizabeth's jaw dropped. "She was part of this?"

Lucy nodded and gave her daughter a hug.

"You bet. She's wanted in England on a number of charges, including arson and murder."

"She seemed like such a nice girl," said Sam, who was standing at the counter, making sandwiches.

"It was the accent," said Lucy. "It'll fool you every time."

"Elise was definitely the leader here," continued Brad. "She first got acquainted with OTM when she was doing graduate work at Oxford. She laid low when she returned to the U.S., however, working quietly on building a network of contacts in the science community. She was very patient, getting herself hired at *Jolie* by her old friends and biding her time until an opportunity for action presented itself. Arnold actually took her out to Governors Island several times; he couldn't have been more helpful."

"Where did she get the anthrax in the first place?" asked Sam, setting a platter of sandwiches on the table.

"That's the one thing she won't talk about. She's apparently determined to protect whoever it was. They're checking out all her former colleagues, anyone she might have come into contact with as a scientist. Apparently there's some similarity with the 2001 attack." Brad looked thoughtful. "Maybe this will help them solve that, too. Anyway, at some point she decided to set up her own lab. That's when Fiona—she has a doctorate in microbiology, you know—came over to help."

Lucy and Elizabeth's eyes met over the sandwiches.

"Fiona had a doctorate? I thought she went to beauty school," said Elizabeth. "She sure had me fooled."

Lucy took a bite of tuna salad on whole wheat and chewed thoughtfully. "How did they get back and forth to the island? We had an awful time in that boat."

"They didn't use a boat. This was really clever. They got official transit authority uniforms and used the Brooklyn-Battery Tunnel. Apparently there's some sort of escape hatch in that ventilation tower on the island. They even used an official MTA van, and they had bicycles hidden on the island."

"And the lab?" asked Lucy, talking with her mouth full. "Where exactly was that?"

"It was an old bomb shelter, left over from the cold war. They think Elise must have heard about it somehow and searched until she found it. She made regular weekend trips to the island all last summer on the public ferry."

"This is so weird," said Elizabeth. "Here everybody's worried about Islamic militants but these Terra Mama people were homegrown. I mean, Elise is American and Fiona's British. We're supposed to be allies in the fight against terrorism."

"They were driven by ideology, though," said Sam, "just as much as the Islamists are. They didn't hesitate to kill Nadine."

Lucy shook her head. "I'm not so sure it was all ideology, at least on Elise's part. A lot of it seemed like a grudge against men and women who liked men. I think Fiona was the idealogue. She said she felt badly about Elizabeth getting sick, but it didn't stop her. She thought it was perfectly okay to use me and Geoff as human guinea pigs. It's twisted. Like animals are worth more than people."

"Well, animals are innocent," said Brad. "Only humans cause harm deliberately. It's like those signs in the zoo that identify the most dangerous species in the world."

"Tigers?" guessed Elizabeth.

"Nope. People like us, you and me. The sign has a mirror instead of a picture."

"That's why we have forgiveness," said Sam. "Like the Bible says, faith and hope are important, but charity, love, forgiveness—whatever you call it, it's all the same thing— is the most important. Without love, we have nothing."

They sat silently, pondering this important truth, when Lucy's cell phone began to ring. She expected to hear Bill's voice but instead heard Ed Reidel's gruff New York accent. The *New York Tattler* editor had a proposition for her.

"The FBI's announcing a big arrest in this anthrax case," he said. "You wouldn't know anything about it, would you?"

Lucy perked right up. "Boy, have I got a story for you. I was held captive in an underground anthrax lab by a mad feminist scientist."

She figured he'd laugh it off. After all, she'd lived through it and she still could hardly believe it. But Ed didn't bat an eyelash.

"Cool," he said. "Can you write a first-person account?"

"Sure," said Lucy. "What will you pay?"

There was a pause. Finally, he said, "One hundred."

Lucy's heart sank. So much for the six figures she'd been promised. "This story is worth a lot more than a hundred. Why, even back home I can get at least two from my editor."

"A hundred fifty," he said, with a big sigh. "One hundred fifty thousand, but not a penny more. And it better be worth it."

Lucy's jaw dropped and she swallowed hard. "It will be," she finally said. "I'll get right to work."

She put the phone down and, after taking a few deep breaths, asked Sam if she could use her computer. "The *Tattler* is going to give me one hundred fifty thousand dollars for my story, but I've got to do it right now. He wants it yesterday."

All of a sudden everyone was jumping up and down and hugging her, and Elizabeth was actually crying. "This means I can go back to school, right?"

"Absolutely," said Lucy. "And Sara and Zoe, too. And maybe even Toby, if he wants to try again."

"What about you?" asked Sam. "Don't you want anything for yourself?"

Lucy smiled, considering the possibilities. "Maybe I'll finally get to take that trip to Europe."

"You should."

"We'll see," said Lucy. "First things first. There's no sense counting my chickens until they're hatched. I've got to write the darn thing and see if Ed likes it before I start spending the money."

Elizabeth and Brad exchanged a nervous glance.

"Right now?" asked Sam. "It's New Year's Eve and you're in New York. Don't you want to see the ball drop for real?"

"Yeah, Mom," added Elizabeth. "This might be the only chance I get."

"Well, that's not until midnight. I've got hours, right?"

"People start gathering early, to get the best spots," said Sam. "We usually leave around now."

"You go. I'll work on my story and watch it on TV. Maybe I'll see you."

"No, that's all right," said Sam. "We'll wait for you."

When they left the apartment around ten o'clock by the lobster watch, Lucy still wasn't convinced the expedition was a good idea, given Elizabeth's recent illness. Furthermore, she was worried because she hadn't been able to reach Bill on her cell phone, although she'd called home several times. There was no answer, just the machine, which puzzled her. Where could they all be? Why weren't they home, getting ready to greet the new year?

The subway wasn't very crowded but when they emerged at Times Square they immediately found themselves part of an enormous, boisterous crowd. Everyone was in good spirits, and the weather was perfect: a lovely, clear night with the temperature hovering at a mild forty degrees.

"Where shall we stand? We want a clear view of the ball."

"Let's go over by the TKTS booth up at Forty-seventh Street," suggested Brad, winking at Sam. "That's our favorite spot."

He pointed it out and they began making their way through the throng that packed the entire area, which on an ordinary day would be filled with cars and trucks and taxis. The amazing neon display of colorful lights blinked all around them; enormous billboards advertising everything from underwear to the NASDAQ exchange to perennial Broadway shows like *The Phantom of the Opera* and *A Christmas Carol.*

"That's MTV," said Elizabeth, pointing to an upper-story window where a curvaceous girl in a low-cut tank top and a wisp of a skirt was interviewing a rap group of four young men covered head to foot in oversized clothing. The crowd gathered beneath the window was watching raptly, and young girls were screaming in rapture at seeing their idols up close.

"They're broadcasting right now?"

"Yeah."

"Wow. We're really here in the center of things. Everybody, all over the country, is watching and we're right here." Lucy felt as if a veil was being lifted; she just hadn't made the connection. "Wow, this is really cool."

Elizabeth managed not to roll her eyes. "Right, Mom."

It took them a long time to make their way through the crowd to the little island where the TKTS booth stood, and Lucy couldn't quite figure out why it was so important to get to the statue of George M. Cohan, which Brad insisted was their destination. You could clearly see the Times building, with the huge, illuminated ball poised to fall, from anywhere in the entire square. Lucy felt it was a bit rude to keep pushing through the crowd, but people didn't seem to mind. Many were wearing party hats and paper leis, some were holding signs for the TV cameras, and just about everyone had some sort of noisemaker. They laughed and held their breath and joked about resolving to lose weight as their group squeezed past.

Finally, with moments to spare, Lucy felt a strong hand

grab her arm and haul her over the curb and onto the TKTS island. She turned to thank the man who'd assisted her and saw Bill's beaming, bearded face. The whole family was ranged around him: Sara, Zoe, Toby, and Molly, too. And Lance. She couldn't believe her eyes. "What are you all doing here?" she stammered.

"We came for New Year's."

"Norah bought us all plane tickets and Lance met us at the airport."

"To surprise you!"

"To make sure you start the year off right." She found herself engulfed in Bill's arms as he bent to kiss her. The crowd roared as the ball began its descent.

"Happy New Year," she whispered. "I have a feeling it's going to be very prosperous."